LORENCE

Book 1 in the Lore Trilogy

Jessica Harden

Ordering Information:

For details, contact jessgowrite226@gmail.com

ISBN: 978-0-578-98826-9

Printed in the United States of America on SFI Certified paper.

First Edition

To Mom,

For giving me the gift of stories.

CHAPTER ONE

Florence paused; the stillness of the woods may seem quiet to an untrained ear, but not to her. She could hear all the usual sounds: the birds chirped to one another, telling each other off for stealing the best perches. Squirrels chasing and chattering about their day. Everything in these woods made a sound. Even the fall of the lightest leaf seemed to whisper, only adding to the chaos. To Florence, there was something peaceful about the noise.

Taking one more moment to catch her breath, Florence took off again, jumping over fallen branches, her steps sure. This was her favorite place in the world, and after spending most of her nineteen years here, she knew this forest well. Making a shuddering turn caused her entire body to come to an angle with the sudden change in direction. She crouched down and hid behind a tree panting slightly. She waited, feeling her breath slow but not her heartbeat. That continued to pound, not from the effort of running but in anticipation. She waited, perfectly still with only her eyes moving, scanning the woods in front of her.

"You're going to have to try harder than that if you want to hide from me, Flor!"

Florence turned around, laughing. "Well, I guess you have found me again, Rasful. I thought for sure I could lose you this time!"

A grinning childlike face was hanging upside down from the lowest branch of the very tree Florence was hiding behind. Rasful was about the size of a toddler, with pudgy arms and legs. He was short, only about three feet tall, and was dressed in a variety of bright green leaves that clashed with his vibrant blue skin and hair.

"It's hard to hide from a fairy in these woods," he said, puffing out his small chest. "Especially one as clever as me!"

Florence laughed again, making a grab for him, which he avoided by disappearing behind the tree. "There's nothing bashful about you, Rasful," she said, peeking around the tree to its other side.

"I don't know what you mean, silly human," he said, reappearing on another branch and looking as if he had been there the whole time. "Fairies don't know the meaning of that word."

"Well, you certainly don't," Florence said, laughing again. Rasful had been her friend for almost as long as she could remember. He always made her laugh and forget her troubles. Not that she had that many worries, but her parents had been acting odd lately. It wasn't something she could put her finger on, but something was off. It was almost like the time a rat died in one of the walls of the house. Everything seemed fine at first, but then the smell started. She would catch a small whiff every time she walked by a certain wall. Then it grew to fill the whole room, and more, until eventually it took over the entire bottom half of the house.

"You alright, Flor?"

Florence shook herself back to the present. "I'm fine, Rasful. Just got a little lost in thought," she said, smiling up at his concerned face.

Perhaps she was overthinking things and letting her imagination get away from her. It was an easy thing to do when you lived on a farm in the middle of nowhere.

"You've been getting lost in thought a lot more recently," he said, his face serious.

"Now look at you being all concerned! I hardly ever see you serious, Rasful; it's a weird look for you," Florence teased.

Rasful didn't laugh like she thought he would. Instead, he continued to look at her with his concerned dark eyes.

A bell sounded, making Florence jump. Her mother always rang the bell when it was time for supper, something she had done for as long as Florence could remember. "Looks like that's my cue to leave. Same time tomorrow?"

"Well, see, the problem is, Flor," said Rasful, looking nervous. "I am going to meet with my… well… he's kind of like my boss."

"Your boss? You have a boss?" Florence asked, her eyebrows knitted together. He nodded nervously.

"I didn't know you had a job. What is your job? Are there a lot more fairies like you?"

"There are more fairies like me," he said, carefully avoiding the other question. "I don't see them much because I'm too busy playing with you!" He leaped into the next tree, heading back towards their special meeting place.

"Wait! Rasful!" cried Florence, running to catch up. "I have more questions!"

"You'll have to catch me if you want those questions answered!" came Rasful's mischievous voice from several trees ahead.

She followed the sound of his voice running over the soft leaf floor, not making a sound. Finally with a stitch in her side, she caught up to him.

Every afternoon, she and Rasful would meet at a special tree. It was the biggest tree in the forest, so tall you couldn't see the top. Florence had been climbing this tree for years and no matter how high she climbed, she never seemed to make any progress. She was convinced it was a magical tree, one that somehow connected her to another world. At least that's what she'd thought as a child. Especially when a strange blue-skinned creature came climbing down from it one afternoon.

"Too slow Flor! I win again!" he said, dancing around the ground, jumping about and doing little bows.

"Oh sure, only because you were swinging from the trees like a monkey! I bet you couldn't beat me if you stayed on the ground!"

He stuck out a very red tongue at her and continued his victory dance. She laughed at him and then grew serious, remembering what he said before they raced.

"Rasful," she said, sitting down and leaning up against the tree. "Who is your boss? And what is it you do for him?"

Rasful stopped dancing and sighed. "I'm afraid I can't tell you that Flor. It's top-secret information for a tip-top fairy," he said, puffing out his blue chest.

Florence laughed again at his silly antics. She looked up at the sky and saw how dark it was getting. She jumped up, heart in her throat. "Oh no! Mother called me home ages ago. They must be worried. I have to go Rasful! When will I see you again?"

"Soon, Flor, very soon."

She looked over at his serious face one more time. "Soon then," she said, taking his small hand in hers for a moment before running off towards the farm.

"How could I have lost track of so much time?" she asked herself as she ran. It was almost twilight and getting darker by the second. She knew she was going to be in terrible trouble when she got home. Her parents didn't like her being out after dark. There were lots of dangers in the woods, even on a quiet farm like theirs. She wasn't sure what they were, but sometimes at night she would hear strange noises. Animalistic growls and sniffing. Just thinking about that now was enough to make her run even faster. She could almost imagine those noises behind her, like something was following her in hot pursuit.

She burst out of the forest just as the last sun rays went behind the horizon, blanketing everything in shadow. She ran the last twenty yards to the front door at a sprint and took the three small steps to the patio in one leap.

"I'm so sorry I'm late! I was in the forest and—" her apology died on her lips as entered the house and almost hit her father with the door. She looked down; he was sitting on the floor, almost perfectly still, staring straight at the door and sniffing the air frantically. "Father?" Florence asked tentatively as she edged past him and all the way inside.

Their house was really more of a cottage, small but cozy. The downstairs area consisted of the living room and the kitchen. The living room had a fireplace that took up half the back wall. There wasn't much furniture in the room, just a couch and two small chairs that were pushed awkwardly together to face the open window. The walls were a sort of brownish color which wasn't identified as being natural or because it needed a good scrubbing. There were no decorations, which suited all of them just fine.

Florence carefully took off her shoes on the opposite side of the doorway from where her parents left their shoes. Her father looked alert and his body was taut as a bowstring.

"Father?" she asked again, crouching down closer to get a better look at him.

"He's coming," he said, his voice so soft it was almost a whisper, as he continued to stare at the door. He was nearly motionless.

"Who's coming?" she asked, trying to prompt him into telling her more.

"Florence!" her mother barked, coming into the room. Florence flinched, standing and lowering her gaze. "Where have you been?! I rang the dinner bell ages ago!"

"I'm sorry Mother," she said, in a submissive voice. "I was in the forest and—"

"I can smell that," her mother said, wrinkling her nose. "I don't know what you do out there but it's time to grow up. Learn what's important and stop playing around in the forest."

"Yes Mother," she answered obediently but she didn't believe it. What was so wrong with spending time in the forest?

"Go get cleaned up. Quickly, dinner will be ready soon."

Florence nodded and escaped up the stairs, taking them three at a time to get to her bedroom. She had the entire top floor to herself. It sounded like a lot, but it was really only a bathroom and her room on a small landing. She loved her space and treasured it almost as much as her horse, Beatrix.

Gathering her clothes, she washed as quickly as possible. In no time at all, she skipped back downstairs. But any joy she was feeling was taken from her when she reached the last step.

Her mother and father were sitting in the living room, but they weren't alone.

"Florence," said her father with a cheerful smile caked on his face. "Won't you come and greet our guest?"

Florence took a few tentative steps forward. The man was someone she had never seen before. He was middle aged with black hair flecked with gray, and even to Florence's untrained eye, his clothes looked very expensive. He held himself with an important air, one that demanded attention. But there was something about his eyes that Florence found unsettling. She couldn't put her finger on it, but something just felt off.

She curtsied and said, "I'm pleased to make your acquaintance, my lord."

"Hmm," was all he replied with, never taking his eyes off her.

"Come and sit down, Florence," said her mother, gesturing to a seat across from their guest. "Baron Loch was just telling us the most fascinating story."

Florence sat down cautiously. Who was this man and why was he in their house? Her parents never mentioned someone coming over today. And what was with the staring?

"Oh yes, I believe I was talking about the time I hunted a wild stag the size of my horse," his voice was deep and carried around the room.

He continued his boring hunting story while her parents asked all the polite questions, seeming genuinely interested. Florence couldn't pay attention. Why was this man here? Why hadn't her parents told her about this meeting? A feeling of dread began to grow in the pit of her stomach. Something bad was going to happen, she was sure of it. But she didn't know what.

"Excuse me," she said, finally breaking, unable to take it anymore. She stood quickly before saying, "I need to use the facilities."

Her mother glared at her, indicating that she had done something horribly wrong. Which maybe she had. But she couldn't stand sitting there a moment longer.

"Hurry back," was all her mother said, but her eyes let Florence know they would discuss it later.

She walked as quickly as she dared back to the hallway. As soon as she rounded the corner, she felt something in her chest loosen and it was like she could breathe properly again. She made her way upstairs to her room and sat heavily on the bed. Now that she was out from under his stare, she knew why she had felt so uncomfortable. It was not just a look of curiosity he was giving her. No, it was something different altogether. He was looking at her with a look of possession, like he owned her.

This can't end well, she thought bitterly.

Dinner was not much of an improvement. Florence wore her plainest, ugliest dress to try and dissuade Baron Loch's interest, but to no avail. He would not stop staring with those dark, brooding eyes. It was making Florence jumpy.

Her mother and father prattled on, asking the Baron questions about his land and how his crops were doing. Apparently, he had one hundred acres to his name, given to him as a gift from a fine lady, one that he still served to this day, for his service in the war. Which war? Florence didn't know, or care for that matter. There was always some kind of war happening at any given time.

"Florence, you've hardly touched your supper," her mother said, her voice disapproving.

"I apologize mother, I just find myself not feeling hungry tonight," Florence said stiffly, trying to make her anger at being kept in the dark known.

"Oh, now Florence, there's no need for that," said her father, laughing. "She's not usually this stiff," he told the Baron. "She's just upset we didn't tell her about this meeting."

She glared at her father, embarrassed by what he had said. Of course, it was true, but that didn't mean he had to announce it to the world.

"That's good to hear," said the Baron, interrupting her thoughts. "I prefer a little more fire than this."

She felt her face flush with anger and embarrassment, lowering her gaze to her plate.

She kept her mouth shut for the remainder of dinner and was relieved when she was finally excused to go to bed.

She kissed her father and mother goodnight and after just a moment's hesitation, curtsied to the Baron and muttered a goodnight, trying not to be rude. She turned about to head down the hallway when she heard, "Good night, Florence. I will see you tomorrow."

Her skin crawled at the sound of his voice. She nodded, trying not to bolt, and calmly walked out of the room before taking the steps two at a time and rushing into her bedroom.

Florence closed the door and threw herself down on her bed, utterly exhausted. The Baron's voice was still echoing in her head. What was going on? What were her parents hiding from her? Is this why they had been acting weird? What was she going to do? She sat up suddenly, a prickly feeling rising on the back of her neck. Crossing the room to her door, she pulled a key from her special hiding place and locked it from the inside. You could never be too careful, and with this so-called Baron, she wasn't taking any chances.

CHAPTER TWO

Florence woke up smiling. She had just had the most wonderful dream and was trying to hold on to the last images before totally waking up. She had been in a beautiful meadow surrounded by flowers and sunshine. She was running and laughing, being chased by someone and enjoying the feeling of being pursued.

She was jerked out of this daydream by a loud knocking on her door. "Florence? Why is your door locked?" her mother's worried voice came from the other side of the door.

Florence got up leaving her nice warm bed and went to the door. "Were you still sleeping? Oh, Florence there's so much to do! I need your help to get breakfast ready for your father and the Baron. Hurry up now and come downstairs."

Florence felt like all of her good feelings from that dream were being sucked out of her like a water pump. How could she have forgotten about last night so easily?

"Mother, why is the Baron here? And why didn't you tell me he was coming?" she asked, in a sickly-sweet voice.

Her mother sighed and said exasperated, "Florence, I don't have time to talk to you about this now because I have breakfast to prepare. Now hurry up and come down to help me." With that she turned and walked back down the stairs before Florence could so much as protest.

She got ready as slowly as possible, the one bit of rebellion she dared before making her way down to help. Breakfast passed much the same as the previous evening, with her parents entertaining the Baron while she tried to make herself as unnoticeable as possible. Finally, it was over, and her father took the Baron out to show him the lands.

As soon as they were alone, she turned to her mother. "Mother, what is going on? You owe me an explanation."

Her mother sighed and began handing Florence dishes to wash. "Florence, he is here on business."

"What sort of business? I'm not sure anything on our humble farm is going to tempt him."

"Well, there is one thing," her mother said, not meeting her eyes. Florence froze with a dish in her hands, cold dread filling her.

"Mother," she said, softly. "Please don't tell me he wants what I think he wants."

"Florence, your father and I are poor. We have had a bad season and there is no money left. We are in an enormous amount of debt which the Baron has kindly agreed to settle for us. This is what's best for everyone."

"No," Florence said, with a false calm. "No, I don't believe this is what's best for everyone."

"You are an ungrateful child!" her mother raised her voice. "After all we have done for you. We raised you! All we are asking in return is your marriage to the Baron. This is what happens to farming girls. Did you think you could just run around in the forest for the rest of your life? This is what we brought you up for!"

Anger filled Florence at the injustice of it all. She took the plate in her hands and slammed it on the ground, shattering it. Then she ran straight out of the house. She knew she probably shouldn't have broken the plate. But how could her family do this to her? Did she not even get a say in any of this? Deep down she had known this was why the Baron was here, but she had hoped that her parents had cared about her more than that. Why was it her job to get the family out of debt? She hadn't had any say in how the money for the farm was managed. Why was it her job to dig everyone out when she hadn't been a part of it?

She stopped running, realizing where she was. It was her and Rasful's tree. She called for him only then remembering what he said about meeting his boss. Tears sprang to her eyes, and she didn't fight them. The loneliness bloomed in her chest like a flower.

She had no intention of going back to the house so instead she walked to her second favorite place on the farm: the stables. She had a beautiful tan mare named Beatrix that she had raised from a filly, and they shared a bond like no other.

Beatrix whickered when Florence came into the stables. Beatrix always seemed to pick up on her moods and it was something Florence took great comfort in. She entered the stall and spoke quietly to her, petting her nose. Beatrix began to search her for a treat, which made Florence laugh. She handed her the carrot she had picked right before coming in, which Beatrix wasted no time in eating.

"Ah, here you are, Florence."

Florence jumped and whirled around. There stood the Baron, leaning on the frame of the stall door. Florence's heart began to pound.

"It's not good to sneak up on people like that, Your Grace, especially when they are tending to horses. I would hate for there to be an accident."

"And what kind of accident do you mean?" he asked in a pleasant voice.

"Horses are frightened easily, and they are big animals. Sometimes they tend to lash out if they feel threatened."

"Oh, is that so?" he asked, coming off the frame. "And what about girls? Do they lash out when they feel threatened?"

He moved towards her in the enclosed space. Beatrix stamped her hoof nervously, sensing Florence's distress.

"Who can say?" Florence said as she ducked under Beatrix's neck, trying to get out of the stall and away from the Baron. He was expecting this, however, and managed to corner her just outside of the stall. He stood in front of her and blocked her path out of the stables. "Excuse me, my Lord," she said, trying to get around him.

"No, I don't think I will excuse you," he said, taking a step closer and forcing her to retreat. "You see I have some things I would like to discuss, and since I don't think you are particularly interested in being alone with me, I am going to make the most of this opportunity we have now."

He took another step forward and she took another back. Now she was in trouble. Of course, he would corner her here, there was no other exit. She was trapped. "Now I want you to tell me something. Why are you so resistant to the idea of marrying me?"

"What gave you that idea?" she asked sweetly, eyes darting, looking for any way around him.

He chuckled at this. "Nice try, but you aren't very good at hiding your emotions, Florence." He continued to walk forward at a slow pace, and she matched him step-for-step, walking back. She was hoping she could back up against one of the walls and make it back around to the front of the barn without turning her back to him. All she had to do was keep him talking.

"Oh really? And here I was thinking I was a splendid actor."

He smiled again at this. "Careful my pet, sarcasm will only get you so far with me."

"I thought you preferred a little more fire," she said, quoting his comment at dinner.

"Oh, I do," he said, continuing his slow walk forward. "Do you perhaps know why that is, little one?"

"I haven't the slightest idea," she said, continuing to look for an exit.

He took three quick steps forward then, taking her by surprise. She stumbled backwards and felt the stable wall dig into her back. He was uncomfortably close now; she could smell his breath which was minty, like he had just chewed on some basil. It turned her stomach. She was definitely panicking now.

He put both arms on the side of her head blocking her in. She looked into his eyes and felt her whole-body freeze. She had seen how a snake would freeze its victims before going in for the kill and this was how its prey must feel.

"Allow me to enlighten you, my dear. I live on a very large amount of land. I use this land to train and sell horses. When my hired hands bring in a new shipment, I always go out to check the new stock. When they unload them, I watch and always pick out the wildest one. This is the one I will personally train. Oh yes," he said, noticing the surprise in her eyes. "I still train. I don't leave all the fun to my hired hands. Now you may be wondering, why do I pick the wildest one?"

At this he leaned in even closer. She could feel his body warmth as he leaned into whispering into her ear. "Those are the most satisfying to break."

He leaned back and chuckled again, proud of the fear he knew he had inflicted on her.

That moment of broken eye contact was enough to break the spell. *I must not show fear*, she thought and hardened her gaze. "Sir," she spoke calmly, without a tremble in her voice. "This is highly inappropriate. We are not married and so I must ask you to step back."

"No, we are not married. Yet," he said, softly smiling the whole time. He took a step back, lowering his arms to his sides. "I greatly look forward to more stimulating conversations with you, my pet." He gave a slight nod of his head and looked at her one more time with that horrible possessive stare. He didn't even try to be subtle about it and she felt the heat rise to her face. He smiled again and, with a turn of his heel, he walked away.

She waited until he was completely out of the stable before sinking to the floor. She was shaking all over and felt the need to vomit. A feeling of helplessness washed over her, and she pressed her cold clammy hands to her face trying to calm down.

What was she going to do?

The next week passed in a blur. Florence decided that since the Baron wanted fire, she would cool herself off to a glacier. She refused to speak at all, even when spoken to. She would not let him win.

Her iciness did not stop the looks from him, however. Anytime they were in the same room together he would fix her with that possessive stare. She refused to acknowledge him, but that didn't seem to dissuade him. She always felt his eyes on her.

Her parents chose to ignore her unhappiness by acting like everything was normal. When she refused to answer their questions, they stopped asking them. They prattled on and on to the Baron, talking about the economy and politics. Both of which she knew nothing about. They could have been speaking another language for all she understood.

Florence was starting to lose it. She didn't feel safe wandering around alone anymore. Not just because of the Baron cornering her, but strange things had begun to happen. Every night when she went to bed, she would hear these strange animalistic noises. She had heard them before, but they had only seemed to happen once a month.

When she was young and first heard the noises, she had tried to talk to her parents about them. They had brushed it off as being wild animals, which was why they always warned her to come home before it got dark. Now she heard them every night, strange sniffing and rustling sounds. She had never actually seen one of these animals until, one night, she crept to her window in the hope of catching a glimpse of them.

She was not disappointed. As soon as she heard the weird noises she crept out of bed and peeked out her window. What she saw caused her blood to run cold. The animal was huge, bigger than a grown man. She could only see its silhouette, but it had huge ears that stood up and came to a point. It was covered in patches of fur, which was strange, almost like it had been through a fight. It was sniffing around the ground, perhaps looking for food, when another one showed up. This one was smaller than the first, but still large. The first creature looked over at the second and then began to stand up on its hind legs. It grew even taller, at least seven feet tall, and its arms hung down at its sides, reaching towards its knees. She couldn't see much besides the claws that extended out of its hands, each one the size of a large kitchen knife. She shrank back from the window, not wanting to bring any attention to herself. Heart pounding, she crawled back into bed, waiting for morning to come.

She had not been sleeping well to say the least. These noises had been happening every night and she was losing more and more sleep over them. Between the sleep loss and the staring, she was one inch away from snapping. She didn't know how much more of this she could take.

After being excused from dinner one night, she decided to do something that could get her into loads of trouble. But to her, the risk was worth it if she could glean just a little information about the Baron's plans.

She crept back downstairs, not making a sound in her socked feet. It was pitch black, but she had gone up and down these stairs enough times to know which steps squeaked, so she avoided them easily. This didn't stop her heart from pounding at the anticipation of getting caught.

Once she made it down, she edged towards the living room where she could hear their muffled voices.

"How much longer do we wait, Master?" came a voice that sounded like her father's, but it was different somehow, almost throatier.

"Just two more days. When the moon is at its fullest, then I will show you the strength of my growing power," came the Baron's voice in reply.

There was a shuffling of feet as something moved closer to the sound of the Baron's voice. "Then we will be triumphant! You will be the strongest yet, Master!" A third voice spoke, sounding a bit like her mother's but, again, something was off about it.

"Fool!" came the Baron's voice. "It will take longer than that. How many times do I have to tell you? Are those brains of yours growing smaller?"

More shuffling, this time like bodies going down to the floor. "Please Master, have patience with us! We are but poor humble servants to your wondrous power!"

"I know you are, my pets." The Baron's voice had softened. "One full moon will not be enough to sustain me, you should know this. What we are waiting for is the blood red moon in a few months' time. This is when the human's blood will run; this is our victory."

"And what about the girl?" asked the voice like her father's. "What will become of her?"

"What do you think you've been raising her for? Have I not explained this enough?" came the Baron's angry voice. "I have entrusted you to raise her to be my wife. Don't you remember eighteen years ago when I brought you and her to this place? She will serve me in every way I desire."

Florence's blood ran cold. This was too much to process all at once.

"Now, my pets, go fill your bellies. The time grows near."

She heard the sounds of feet walking toward the front door, and she took the opportunity to go silently back up the stairs to the safety of her bedroom.

She sat down heavily on her bed, head spinning. What did all of this mean? What sort of powers did the Baron possess? Why was she stuck in the middle of this?

The Baron's words echoed in her head. *Don't you remember when I brought you and the girl here to raise her?* A horrible thought struck her almost like a blow. Were the people that had raised her not really her parents? What did it mean that he brought her here?

She heard footsteps coming up the stairs. Her bedroom was the only room upstairs. Heart pounding, she threw herself down on her bed and covered herself in her blanket.

Her door opened quietly, spilling candlelight into the room, and she chided herself for not thinking to lock the door.

"I see that you are sleeping," came the quiet voice of the Baron. Florence held her breath, willing herself not to make a sound. "I thought I had heard the slightest noise a few moments ago. No matter. All this will be made clear soon enough." He edged the door open a little further and said almost as if to himself, "Soon we will be married, and you will be mine forever." The door closed with a small snap. Her heart pounding in her ears, Florence released the breath she had been holding.

She sat up and made her decision. Since her parents weren't really her parents, she didn't owe them anything. In two days, the Baron's powers were going to grow, whatever that meant, and she didn't want to be anywhere near him when that happened. She wasn't going to sit helpless any longer. She would run away tonight.

CHAPTER THREE

She began packing a bag of necessities. Extra clothes and things she thought she might need, a hunting knife, her sturdiest boots and a travel cloak. No use in getting sentimental. Nothing from her parents mattered anymore.

She was just taking one last look around the room when she noticed a face at her window. She barely stopped herself from screaming. It was Rasful!

She threw the window open, letting him in. "Rasful! I'm so glad to see you!" she whispered, wrapping him in a tight hug.

He squirmed out of her arms back to the window, closing it firmly. Turning back to face her, he said, "Flor! I have a lot to tell you and not a lot of time. We need to leave and—" he broke off, looking at her travel cloak and bag. "Wait, were you already leaving?"

"Yes, Rasful it's been horrible!" she felt tears begin to prick at her eyes. "I don't know what to believe anymore, everything is so confusing. But I can't stay here. There's this Baron and—"

"Yes, yes that's why I'm here," Rasful interrupted, waving his hand impatiently. "To help you. Now come on! There's not a moment to lose!"

Taking her hand in his small blue one, he led her out of the room. His footsteps didn't make a sound and his hand felt strange in hers. It was warm, almost buzzing with a sort of electricity that left her hand tingling.

The door opened noiselessly without him even seeming to touch it. He seemed to know where the squeaky steps were as well, and he avoided them easily. When they got to the bottom of the stairs, he took a sharp right. "Rasful," Florence breathed, trying to tell him that there was just a wall there.

He turned and brought a finger to his lips, then gave her a wink before continuing to lead her forward. If you had asked Florence just a moment before where all the doors in the house were, she would have told you without a doubt that there was only one that went through the kitchen. However, now she wasn't so sure. Rasful led her down the hallway into what had only moments before been a solid wall but now was a very small door, one that had a strangely familiar shape on it. She realized, with a start, that it looked just like her and Rasful's tree. Had that always been there? He grinned at her surprised face and led her through the door.

Once they were out in the cool night air, Rasful peeked around the side of the house checking to see if the coast was clear. He gestured to her to get low and took her hand again. She half crawled; half ran across the field. Instinctually, she started to head towards the stables, but Rasful held her back.

"Rasful," she panted. "What about Beatrix?"

He paused for a moment, looking thoughtful. "I'm not sure it would be wise to bring her, Flor."

"Rasful, she's my horse! I can't just leave her here!"

He looked around, silencing her with a gesture. His eyes never stopped moving. "Flor, she belongs to the Baron. If we bring her, he will have a much easier time tracking us. She will be safe here. Please, we have to keep moving."

This time tears did begin to fall, blinding her. Everything in her life, up until this point, had changed in such a short time. She knew she had to be strong, though; now was not the time to fall apart.

Holding tight to Rasful's hand, she let him lead her farther away from the house and into the forest. It was a nerve-racking few minutes, with every noise making them freeze for fear of discovery. After what felt like ages, they made it to the cover of trees, but this time there was something wrong.

As they ran through the familiar trees, something felt off. Florence couldn't put her finger on it for a moment, but then she realized with a start what it was. The forest was silent. There were no animals or bugs, nothing at all made a sound except for her and Rasful's footfalls, which seemed to echo around them. Then a horrible, animalistic howl shattered the deafening silence around them.

"Hurry, Flor! They've discovered you're missing!" said Rasful, pulling her hand harder and dragging her to go faster.

She ran and ran feeling more exhausted as time went on. Her legs felt like they were led, and her breath was coming out in gasps. The only thing that was keeping her going was Rasful's hand in hers. "Just a little farther Flor!" Rasful did not sound winded at all.

She heard the howls again, this time much closer, sounding like they were just a few yards behind them. Florence stumbled over a large tree root, losing her balance and almost falling to the ground. She would have fallen if not for Rasful's surprising strength keeping her on her feet. However, it was just enough time for the animal behind her to gain the advantage.

Florence felt hot breath on the back of her neck, and she suddenly felt something grab on to her cloak to drag her backwards. She gasped, choking as the cloak dug into her neck. Then she felt something hit her back and at the sudden change of direction she lost her grip on Rasful's hand as she went down. The wind was knocked right out of her.

She turned, trying to get away, and as she did so she got a good look at the creature. The thing on top of her was even bigger than it looked out her window. It must have been at least seven feet tall, and it smelled horrible, like rotting meat. Its skin was gray and it had patches of fur all over its long lean body. It had razor-sharp claws on either side of her body, trapping her beneath it. Its ears stood straight up and came to a point, but it was its eyes that looked somehow familiar to Florence, though she was too scared to give it too much thought. It had the mouth like a dog and was growling, exposing its long, sharp teeth. Florence was gasping, trying to get air back into her lungs. The creature seemed to grin at her, leaning back to let out another hideous howl, when it flew off of her.

She tried to sit up to see what had caused this when she felt Rasful's hand on her shoulder. "Stay still a moment, Flor," he said, pushing her back down gently. "Better not to get in the way."

She heard the sound of a skirmish, with growling and whimpering coming from the creature. Yet, she didn't hear any other noises. It was almost like the beast was fighting itself. With one more loud whimper it scurried away. At Rasful's nod, Florence slowly sat up, looking around.

There, where the sounds of the fight had come from, stood the most beautiful creature Florence had ever seen. It was a huge white stag with antlers that seemed to reach up to the heavens. He had big, kind brown eyes and when she looked into them, she felt herself relax for the first time in days. Never had she seen something so majestic and beautiful. She let out a huge breath and stood up; a feeling of total peace surrounded her like a blanket.

"May I present the king of the forest, Ziv," Rasful said, taking a bow.

Florence felt the need to show this majestic animal some respect as well, so she dropped into a curtsy. "Thank you for saving me, Ziv."

The stag pawed at the ground, almost seeming to understand her thanks and brushing it off. Rasful came up beside her and took her hand again. She looked down at him and smiled. "Thank you, Rasful, you've helped me so much tonight."

"Well, I'm afraid I can't go on with you now. I had strict orders from my boss to get you to Ziv. I have other things I need to get done. I've spent too much time here already."

A huge weight of sadness and panic washed over Florence. "You mean you're not coming with me? Where am I supposed to go? What if that thing comes back?"

"Flor, I'm not leaving you to defend yourself alone! I've brought you to Ziv! Trust me, he will keep you far safer than I can."

She looked back over at the stag, feeling that peace slowly wash over her again. After all, Ziv had been the one to save her from the beast. She was in capable hands. Or antlers.

"One more thing before I go, Ziv and I have orders to get you as far away from here as we can. There will be a point where you may have to walk on foot, but don't worry. You won't ever be completely alone, there are lots of us watching out for you. Take this," he handed her a bag containing a change of clothes that looked like they were for a man. "Even though we will be watching out for you, it's not safe for you to go walking around like this. Someone could recognize you and tell the Baron. For now, disguise yourself as a boy looking for work. That should help throw him off a little."

Rasful escorted her to Ziv's side; the stag leaned down so she could climb up.

"Rasful, what do I do? How long do I need to disguise myself?"

"I wish there was time to explain, but I can't right now. Hopefully we will meet again, and I can explain it then. For now, go with Ziv. He'll take you somewhere safe."

"When will I see you again?" asked Florence, trying to be brave but still distressed about everything that had happened so far.

"Soon. Hopefully, soon. Now go!"

Florence felt the muscles under her tense as Ziv broke out into a run. She took one more look behind her as they flew across the forest, but Rasful was gone. She held on to Ziv's neck and let the tears she had been holding back all-night fall silently for all she had lost.

They ran for what felt like hours. Ziv's hooves didn't make a sound. He was the quietest stag Florence had ever come across. Most animals made some kind of sound when they ran but Ziv was different. His movements were gentle, they didn't jostle her around as he ran. Even though he was leaping over fallen tree trunks the ride felt smooth. It was almost as if he never even touched the ground.

Her tears long dried, Florence kept her eyes wide open. They had reached part of the forest that was unfamiliar to her. She had never gone this far from home, but she wasn't sad to be leaving. Although, she wasn't feeling much of anything at the moment. Too many changes happening too quickly left her feeling nothing but numb.

The sky began to lighten as they ran. She had never stayed up all night before, so she was becoming very tired. Just when she thought she couldn't keep her eyes open any longer, Ziv reached a clearing where he slowed and came to a stop. She got off his back, stumbling only a little, and looked around.

The clearing wasn't very big, probably the size of her room back home. There were a few flowers scattered about it and a group of four or five trees that grew in a perfect circle.

Inside the cluster of trees was what could only be called a bed. It was completely shaded by the canopy overhead and there was a pile of leaves that was the perfect size for a person. Florence looked back and saw that Ziv had settled down to watch her, as if to say, Go on! She thanked him and walked into the small circle of trees.

The leaves were surprisingly comfortable for someone who had never slept outside before. The shade kept the area cool but not cold, and Florence wrapped herself up in her cloak and immediately fell asleep.

She was awoken a few hours later by something tickling her. She opened her heavy eyes to see a tiny hairy thing run across the leaves. She gasped and sat up, worried at what had been crawling on her while she slept. It was a tiny, pure white mouse. He was very cute and didn't seem to be afraid of her. Her head felt strange and, as she reached back, she realized it was because her hair had been brushed and braided.

"Did… Did you?" she asked, trailing off. Surely one single mouse couldn't do that. At least, she didn't think so.

She looked back down at the mouse who continued to look at her with patient eyes as if he was waiting for something. "Well, if you did do this, thank you."

The mouse seemed to accept that, and he scurried off out of sight. Deciding this was probably the most cover she would get, she went ahead and changed into the clothes Rasful had given her. There was a pair of pants, a shirt and vest, a hat, sturdy boots, and a new cloak. Her cloak had been ruined by the creature from the night before, so she left it on the leaf bed. The rest of her clothes she packed into the bag, then stepped out of the trees.

Ziv was in the same spot almost as if he hadn't moved in the few hours she had slept. He stood when she came near and shook himself, then he bent forward to let her climb back up on his back. As soon as she was seated, they were off once more, bounding through the trees just as fast as they had the night before.

They continued for a few hours and came to a line of trees just as it was starting to get dark. The forest was thinning out and Florence could see lights up ahead, almost like those from a town. Ziv slowed to a walk and, at the edge of the trees, he stopped and bent down to let Florence off. Florence should have been stiff from the hours of hard riding, but she wasn't sore at all.

She looked up at Ziv and he pointed with his hoof through the trees. "Is this where you've taken me?" Florence said, peering through the trees. There was a tiny inn up ahead, not too much bigger than a regular house, but it could have been larger in the back.

"I assume you can't come with me?" Ziv stamped his foot in an answer. "I thought so," sighed Florence. She squared her shoulders and then said, "Thank you Ziv, for everything."

As his big brown eyes bore into hers, it was almost like he was speaking to her. "Will I ever see you again?" she asked, trying to keep the fear out of voice.

He touched his nose very softly to her forehead, and after one last look he turned and bounded back into the forest. Florence turned to the town and, not knowing what to expect, she stepped out of the trees.

CHAPTER FOUR

Florence stepped out of the trees and found herself right next to the inn. The trees made it difficult to see but the town itself was a pretty decent size. Houses lined the main street to the center of town. There were different shops all around a fountain visible just down the street from where she stood. She had been to shops a few times with her mother, but only when they had a rough season. The farm had provided everything they needed so there hadn't been much reason to go to the market. Florence had always looked forward to going, even if the trips were always tinged with stress, mostly from her parents.

Her parents. Who may not be her parents from what the Baron had said. Oh, she wished things had turned out differently. But wishing for things didn't help anything. She squared her shoulders and made her way to the doors of the inn before she could lose her nerve.

She walked in and immediately thought she had made a grave mistake. The room was dark and there were a few people scattered about the room. None of these things made her think she was over her head, however. The thing was, she didn't know what to do in an inn. Who did she talk to? How was she supposed to go about this?

The longer she waited debating all this, the more she began to panic. Why did she think she could do this? She had never been anywhere without her parents, what was she supposed to do?

"Hello there!" came a friendly voice. Florence snapped her head around to see a smiling man behind the bar waving her over. She sighed a breath of relief and started over to him.

The closer she got to him; she saw that he couldn't have been too much older than herself. Maybe in his early twenties, just a couple years older than her. His hair was a reddish-brown color, and he had an open happy face like he had no problems in the world.

"New in town?" he asked when she was across from him. He had a slight accent, but she couldn't quite put her finger on it.

"What makes you say that?" she asked, trying not to panic.

He smiled. "Well, I know everyone in town, you see, and just between you and me," he leaned in close to her and he said this in almost a whisper, "We are in an inn, which is a place where people who are new in town, typically stay at."

"Right. Well then yes, you could say that," she answered, fidgeting with a loose seam on her pants leg.

He leaned away from her smiling. "So, what brings you to our humble little inn? And what's your name?"

"Um," she said, searching her brain for anything that might help her make up a story. "I'm traveling and I'm looking for work."

"For work?" he repeated, looking at her strangely.

"Yes, isn't that what I said?" she snapped. "Sorry."

"Aye that's alright!" he smiled. "You seem to have been through something recently. Just a hunch I'm getting."

"Right. So, about work…"

"About work. We could always use help in the kitchens, that's for sure. Our cook isn't the best. Can you cook and clean?"

"Yes of course. I can do laundry as well. And you wouldn't have to pay me. I just need a place to sleep and some food probably."

"Probably. Yes, I reckon' food'll be important. Now what did you say your name was?"

"F-I mean Lorence."

"Hm interesting name. I had a cousin named that. How do you spell it?"

"I'm sorry?"

"The spelling. See I'm interested in how things are spelled. It's a weird quirk of mine."

Was he messing with her? "L-O-R-E-N-C-E," she spelled out.

"Interesting. Never seen it spelled that way before. Most people spell it L-A-W-R-E-N-C-E."

"Well, I guess I just spell it differently," she said in what she hoped was a nonchalant voice.

He looked at her long and hard. No smile on his face, not frowning, just a serious look that made her feel like he could see through her disguise.

"So, about a room?" she prompted, hoping to dissuade any thoughts he was getting.

"Right you are. Here, let me show you where you'll be staying." He walked out from behind the counter and led the way up a staircase in the far corner of the restaurant.

"And how long did you say you will be staying?" He asked pleasantly.

"I didn't. I'm not sure to tell you the truth." She wasn't sure. She wasn't even sure if Rasful would meet her here.

"Well, that's alright. As long as you're earning your keep, we should be fine. Here we are!"

He opened a door at the farthest end of the hallway. The room was a comfortable size with a medium sized bed. There was a nightstand and a dresser that was pushed into the corner. The most surprising thing about the room was that it had its own washroom. Her room at the farm didn't even have that.

"Thank you. I truly am grateful for the kindness you have shown me," she said, turning back to face him.

He wasn't inside the room, just leaning with a lazy smile against the doorframe. "Ah that's alright. Don't mention it. Now I should probably tell you how things are run around here. We serve breakfast and dinner in the restaurant. Breakfast is at 7 so we need to be cooking no later than 5. I know it's early, but we'll give you breaks. We serve breakfast until 10, then we clean up and take a morning break until 12 when we start getting rooms cleaned after the guests have left. That usually takes a couple of hours. After that we take another break until 4, and then we get ready for dinner. After dinner we clean up and then are done for the night. You got all that?"

Florence nodded at him. It was all pretty straightforward. She didn't think she'd have too much trouble remembering everything.

"Good. Well, I'll introduce you to everyone tomorrow. I'll let you settle in for tonight."

He turned to go but Florence said, "Hold on a minute!" He turned back towards her with an easy smile on his face. "You made such a big deal about my name, but you never told me yours."

He slapped his hand to his forehead in exaggerated surprise. "I guess you are right! I beg your pardon, that was rather rude of me. The name's Robert. And before you ask, it's spelled in the regular way." He smiled at her, his eyes lighting up mischievous way.

"Well, if you won't be needing anything else, I'll be going to bed myself. Good night, Lor-ance," he said, putting emphasis on the Lor.

He turned and walked back down the hall. Florence went into her room and closed the door firmly. She took in her new surroundings. This was her new home now. She hoped Rasful would come soon.

Florence woke up with a start. It was still dark outside, but the sun was beginning to rise. She rubbed her face, trying to remember what had woken her up. Then she remembered. Her parents, the Baron, and the strange creatures she had run from. Now here she was in a small inn, passing off as a young boy named Lorence because she couldn't think of any other name under pressure. She had to be down in the kitchens at five, so she may as well get up and get ready. She had only had the one change of clothes that Rasful had given her, so she had washed them in her small bathtub and hung them to dry overnight. While this couldn't go on forever and she would have to get a new set of clothes soon, this system would work out for the time being.

She brushed her tangled golden hair and braided it. She looked at the hunting knife she had unpacked last night; she hadn't known what to do with it, so she'd left it on the table next to her bed just in case someone tried to sneak into her room. As she looked at it, a thought began to form in her mind. If she really wanted to pass as a boy, she was going to need to look like one. She took the knife and carefully cut her braid. It pulled horribly but eventually she was able to cut her hair to her shoulders. She tied her hair back at the nape of her neck with a leather thong she kept with her just for situations like this.

She surveyed her handiwork in the mirror. It was passable, perhaps a little uneven in places but she didn't have time to worry about that now.

She walked out of her room and ran straight into someone. She looked up, mumbling an apology, and saw the person she had run into was none other than Robert.

"Well now look at this! Here I thought I was going to have to wake you up yet here you are bright eyed, and bushy tailed ready for the day!"

Florence took a large step back. The last thing she wanted was for him to find out she was a girl by bumping into her.

"I can get up by myself thanks," she said trying to keep the offence out of her voice. Why did it seem like he was patronizing her?

"I can see that. Good, well then let's be off! I'll show you where the kitchens are."

He led her to a stairway down the farthest end of the hallway, which she completely would have missed had he not showed it to her, for it seemed to be a broom closet. He opened the door and she was surprised to see a set of winding stairs.

"This is the servants' stairway. This house was built a couple hundred years ago when we still had those kinds of servants," he said as he led the way downstairs. "Watch your step."

"Robert, why is it so dark down here?" Florence asked, gripping the wall. There was also no railing, she noticed too late.

"Can't keep any lights on down these stairs. I don't know what the issue is but no matter what we do, no lights. This is the fastest way to the kitchens though so that's why I'm showing them to you."

They continued down the steps with Florence mostly concentrating on not falling. As she went, she began to see a small sliver of light up ahead. They stopped at the foot of the stairs, and she realized how close she and Robert were to each other. They were standing with their shoulders and arms touching. Florence couldn't get away from him and was starting to feel slightly claustrophobic as well as something else, something she was not ready to start thinking about.

Finally, he opened the door and stepped through. She blinked in the sudden light, trying to get her eyes to adjust. The kitchen wasn't huge, but it was decently sized. It had a counter in the middle of everything to hold food being prepared and had both a stove and a furnace for cooking.

It smelled amazing, like freshly baked bread, which made perfect sense considering the other person in the kitchen was pulling out a loaf of bread from the oven. The chef was a middle-aged man, with salt-and-pepper hair. He was huge, not just in height but also in girth. He seemed to take up the entire kitchen with just the sheer size of him.

"Good morning, William," said Robert pleasantly as soon as Florence had stepped into the kitchen.

William didn't say anything, he just began to take the piping hot bread to the counter.

"This is Lorence," continued Robert as if William's silence was normal. "He's going to be working with us for a while."

William grunted in reply to this, still setting his bread carefully and slowly on the counter.

Robert looked at him thoughtfully, then leaning over to Florence said, "You know he actually goes by Will. In fact, if you really wanted to make him happy you could call him Billy."

At this William looked up, anger flashed in his eyes. "You know perfectly well that would not make me happy."

"Ah he speaks! And here poor Lorence thought you were mute."

"Don't pull me into this!" Florence exclaimed. The last thing she wanted was to make this huge man upset.

"Ah well you see Lorence, you were pulled into this as soon as you agreed to work here," he said, giving her a wink. "Now look here William, now that you are speaking to us, what is the problem?" he asked, coming around the counter to face him.

William gave Robert a look that would have had Florence shaking in her boots had it been turned on her.

"The problem is you didn't give me any notice that I'd be having someone in my kitchen until this morning," he growled.

"Lorence walked in late last night! What was I supposed to do? Wake you up? Last time I did that it didn't end well for me!"

William continued to glare at him and, pulling out a large knife, began to slowly cut the fresh bread, not taking his eyes off of Robert.

Robert leaned forward on the counter, something Florence would have thought twice about, especially considering William was armed. "See here, don't you hate gathering water? Haven't I heard you complain endlessly about doing dishes? What about all the prep work that takes you forever to do?" Robert gave a grand gesture in Florence's direction.

William continued to slice the bread not saying anything, but his look had grown less severe. Robert threw up his hands in surrender. "Fine, be brooding and silent for all I care. Just make sure Lorence has something to do. We can't let him stay here for free now can we."

He turned back to Florence and said, "Don't let him bully you, Lorence. He's all bark and no bite. Now if both of you don't mind, I'm going to the dining room to get things ready for breakfast." With that he left the room, a spring in his step.

Florence wasn't entirely sure where to stand or what to do. William continued to slice the loaf of bread at a snail's pace not looking at her. Finally, after what felt like an agonizing few minutes, although it was probably only a few seconds, William said, "There is a bucket by the back door and a water pump outside in the back. We need at least five buckets of water to make it through breakfast."

"Right," Florence said and headed to the place he indicated.

As she walked past him, he looked up and stared at her. "What did you say your name was again?"

"Lorence," she said, her heart began to pound. Did he recognize her somehow?

He raised an eyebrow and continued to stare for a moment longer. Then he grunted and went back to his bread. Florence grabbed the bucket and went out the back door, trying not to rush. When she got outside, she leaned against the wall and attempted to slow her pounding heart. This was going to be interesting. How long could she keep this up before someone discovered her secret? How long would it take Rasful to come and get her?

As these questions swirled in her mind, she felt a light tugging on the laces on her boot. She looked down and saw a small rabbit. He was pure white with long floppy ears. He had her shoelace in his mouth and was tugging on it. Florence had never seen an animal act this way before, especially one that was usually prey. She took a tentative step in the direction it was pulling her. It let go of her shoe and bounded away from her for a few feet and then turned to look at her. She continued to follow, with it running farther ahead and then waiting for her to catch up.

It led her to the edge of the forest just past the first set of trees. There, leaning up against a tree, was a bag. As she got closer, she saw that it looked almost identical to the one that she had upstairs in her room. She curiously bent down and opened it. Inside were several changes of boy's clothes and on top was a note. She unfolded it and read:

Dear Flor,

I hope this letter and bag find their way to you. Inside are clothes for you to keep up your disguise. I'm sorry I couldn't come myself, but I am on important business for my boss. Just know all my work is trying to keep you safe. Stay where you are at the inn for the moment; you are safe there. Ziv has graciously asked some of his friends to keep an eye on you. If you ever see an animal of pure white with brown eyes, it is a messenger from us. I will send another message when I have more to tell you. Stay safe, Flor, and we'll talk again soon.

The note wasn't signed but Florence had a pretty good idea who it was from. She looked down at the rabbit at her feet.

"Thank you," she said. She gathered up the bag and note and made her way back to the inn. She didn't know what was going to happen next, but knowing that Rasful was on the case made her feel a little better. Hopefully, she would hear more soon.

CHAPTER FIVE

The morning passed in a bit of a blur. The amount of food and water that was used during those few short hours was astonishing. Florence had never been to a restaurant before, much less worked in one. It was amazing how two people, now three, could get so much done. Robert took the orders and brought them to William, who put the food on the plates, and then Robert took them out to the customers. It was like a well-oiled machine the way they almost seemed to read each other's minds. Florence was impressed by their efficiency, to say the least. Her job mostly was to stir things and make sure nothing burned as well as washing many dishes. Being the first time she had worked in this kind of setting, Florence was exhausted by the end of breakfast.

She had just finished the last dish when Robert came in to announce that the last guest had left, and breakfast was over. "Great work today everyone! And now for breakfast ourselves!"

He made a grab for some bread but was stopped by a huge ladle William smacked across his path. "Are we animals? I will serve the food. You and you," he said pointing to Florence, "Go sit and set the table."

Robert grinned and began gathering silverware and cups. He handed some of these to Florence and directed her to a table off to the side. Robert directed her to place the items just so, in order to make sure everything would fit on the table.

"This is good for you to learn anyway; we might be needing some help out here at some point so it's good for you to know this."

"Oh, please, no! I don't want to work in the dining room!" Florence said in a panic. She couldn't work out here with all those people! What if someone recognized her somehow, or found out that she was a girl?

Robert paused, one cup midair as he stared at her. "Well now, what would be the reason for that, I wonder?"

Florence looked anywhere but at him, trying to think of a response. "Well you see, I'm incredibly... shy," she finished lamely.

"Shy," he repeated looking at her.

"Yes. I am shy. Spelled S-H-Y."

"I know how to spell it," he rolled his eyes.

"You said you liked spelling," she said, boldly. "Also, I don't think I'd make a good server."

"You didn't seem to have too much of a problem talking to me," he said thoughtfully as he began to set the table again.

"That was different because..." she trailed off, not wanting to give her desperation away.

"Because..." he prompted her to finish.

"Because," she said, struggling for words. "I needed a job. If I didn't talk to you, I wouldn't have been able to get this job and well I desperately needed it."

"See that is the thing I'm not sure I totally understand," he said putting his finger on his chin thoughtfully. "Why were you so desperate? Why is a young boy coming and looking for work without any sort of belongings or ways to distinguish himself? If you ask me," he said, looking straight at her. "It sounds like that young boy might be in some trouble. Running away from something, you might say."

He let the weight of his words settle around them. Florence was unsure of what to do. Should she try and make a break for it? She would but Rasful had told her she should stay here for her own safety. She hoped this man wouldn't turn her out in the streets. That would be the last thing she needed.

"Please," she said, this time not trying to hide the desperation in her voice. "Please let me stay here."

He looked at her for a moment, just seeming to take her in. "I'm not going to make you leave. However, at some point I'm going to ask for the truth. Don't look so frightened," he said, holding up his hand and smiling at the look of sheer panic on her face. "I understand that the truth needs to be earned through trust. All I'm asking is for the chance to earn your trust. Do we have a deal?" he asked, holding out his hand.

She looked at his hand and then into the kind eyes of this stranger before her. "Deal," she said as she placed her hand in his. His hand completely covered her own and was warm as well as callused. He had long fingers and she felt the strength in them as he pumped her hand up and down twice. They stared at each other for a moment. Him trying to figure her out and she is praying he wouldn't.

"You got that table set up yet?"

They both jumped at William's voice and Robert pulled his hand back. "Yes, it's ready," he said, running his hand through his hair, the lazy grin back in place.

Florence let her own hand drop to her side, feeling the spell break. It was a different kind of spell than the one she had encountered with the Baron. This one was mutual somehow and full of freedom. She could have looked away if she wanted to, but she somehow didn't. She peeked up at him while he wasn't looking.

He really was handsome. While she had noticed before, she hadn't given it much thought. He had a few inches on her so he must have been close to six feet. He had reddish brown hair that was kept relatively short, although it still had some length. It wasn't long enough to tie it back but only by a little bit. He had a strong chin and jawline, broad shoulders and well-muscled arms. He was lean, slender but not skinny. It was his eyes she kept coming back to. They were emerald green, dark around the edges with flecks of gold in the middle. She had never met someone with green eyes before and she couldn't get them out of her head.

Just then Robert looked over at her. She jumped but refused to look away. He grinned, knowing he had caught her staring, and said, "Let's eat!"

Florence looked around at the table which was now laden with food. There was bacon and eggs all mixed in a big pot with roasted potatoes. There was porridge and freshly baked bread with a big slab of butter on the side. Florence felt her mouth begin to water and her stomach give an uncomfortable growl. When was the last time she had eaten? She wasn't sure she cared at this point; she was just ready to dig in. They all filled their plates and as Florence took the first bite, she couldn't help but let out a little moan of pleasure. The food was amazing, just the right amount of flavor, and it was hearty and filling which she now decided was her favorite kind of breakfast. Finally, after three full helpings her hunger subsided, and she leaned back in her chair perfectly satisfied with the world.

"Well, you certainly can put food away, can't you," Robert's voice pulled her out of her contented daze.

She shot him a look. "I was hungry."

"Clearly," he said, smiling at her.

She rolled her eyes and looked over at William who was watching this exchange without saying a word.

"Thank you for the food, William," Florence tried tentatively. She wanted to show her appreciation for him as well. "I've never had anything like it before. It was amazing."

He gave her a nod and then stood up and began clearing the table. She stood up to help and picked up a plate, but Robert said, "I think you've worked enough for one morning. Why don't you go up to your room and rest for a while?"

He took the plate from her and she let him. Now that she was full of delicious food, her body had begun to feel like lead.

She nodded at him and went back into the kitchen which was the fastest route to her room. As she passed by the back door, she remembered the note and bag Rasful had left for her. She looked around to make sure no one was in the kitchen yet. The coast being clear, she opened the back door and quickly grabbed her bag where she had left it behind an extra bucket for water. She shut the door and ran up the stairs to her room. The stairs were as pitch black as they had been that morning, so she took them two at a time to get through them as fast as she could.

Finally back in her room, she unpacked the bag and hid the extra bag inside the one she originally brought with her. She'd figure out what to do with the second bag later, but right now all she wanted was to sleep.

As she shut her eyes, the only thing she saw was emerald green eyes, darker around the edges with flecks of gold in the middle.

Florence woke after a couple of hours feeling well rested. She decided it was time to see what was next on the day's agenda. She left her room and was surrounded by an amazing smell. Following her nose, it led her to the kitchen. She walked in and saw Robert leaning against the center island while William was stirring something in a pot on the stove. They looked so comfortable together and somehow complemented each other. William was so stoic while Robert was a bit of a goofball. They seemed to understand each other and still managed to get things done in their own way despite their differences. Robert had just thrown his head back, laughing at something William said, when he looked over and saw her.

"Well look who decided to join us! Hello sleeping beauty! Did you have a good nap?"

She shot him a look, which was quickly becoming a habit. "Yes, I did, but wait. How did you know I was sleeping?"

"Your hair gave it away! It's sticking straight up," he said with a laugh.

Her hand flew to her hair. It certainly felt messy. She left her room without even thinking about it, also her short hair was having a bit of a mind of its own. Without having the weight of long hair, her new short hair had decided to stand up on end. Remembering she was supposed to be a boy who didn't care about such things, she dropped her hand and shrugged.

Robert laughed again, which she chose to ignore and walked fully into the kitchen. William looked over at her and said, "Hungry?"

Right on cue her stomach rumbled. How she was hungry again, she had no idea yet here she was feeling like she could eat a huge meal.

William's eyes softened, and he gave her a rare, closed lip smile and put a bowl of steaming stew with more fresh bread.

Florence had grown up on food that was very different from this. They had eaten the same thing three meals a day. Most of the food her parents had liked were bland ground meat with maybe some kind of veggie and bread. However, this magical concoction was nothing like what she grew up on. The broth had almost turned into a gravy with the thickness of it. The meat was so tender you almost didn't have to chew it and the potatoes were soft without being mushy. The flavor was something else entirely. She could taste the beef in the broth but there was something else. Something she just couldn't quite put her finger on. A sound of pure pleasure escaped her lips.

"Whoa William! Looks like you've got a fan!"

She glared at Robert again although he didn't seem particularly bothered. "William, this is wonderful."

William shrugged off her compliment though, as he turned around, he clearly looked pleased. She finished her lunch quickly, not to get it over with but because it really was that good.

"Well now that you're finished, let's get back to work. I'll show you how to clean up after the guests," said Robert, taking her plate to the sink.

She stood feeling unsure again. For the first time in her life, she was new at something. She had been new at things before, of course, but this time it was different. She had someone relying on her to do her job and to do it well. She had cleaned and cooked before but not on a large scale like this. She just hoped she could do the job well.

He led her to the counter in the restaurant where they had first met and showed her a book.

"This is where we keep track of all of our guests. This is how we know which rooms are available and what rooms are full. We write down the guest's name and how long they will be staying. Pretty simple if you think about it." He gave her an easy smile.

He led her upstairs and showed her how each room had a number on the outside of it and that was how they kept track of what guest was in what room. Usually people were just passing through, so those rooms needed to be cleaned for the next guest coming in. This was all new to Florence but when they actually got into cleaning she felt more in her element.

"So, is it just you and William that run this inn?" she asked nonchalantly as they worked together to put a clean sheet on one of the beds.

He paused for a moment, getting a thoughtful look. "I'll tell you what, you're curious about me and frankly I'm dying to know about you. How about we make another deal?"

She looked at him warily. "What kind of deal?"

"How about a simple exchange. A question for a question. You can ask me a question and then I'll ask you one."

"And what happens if I'm not comfortable answering those questions?" she asked, her stomach dropping at his words.

He shrugged. "Then I won't answer your question. No harm done."

She thought it over. It didn't seem like there was anything he could trick her into doing or saying. And she was curious about him.

"Fine. What do you want to know?" she asked, lowering her eyes back to her work.

"How old are you?"

"Nineteen."

"You look pretty young for a nineteen-year-old boy," he said. Her eyes flashed back up to him.

"Well maybe I just look young for my age." How could she have been so stupid? Of course, she didn't look nineteen as a boy! She should have said fifteen or something that would have been more believable. She was going to have to think of an answer before just blurting one out.

"Now I've answered your question. It's your turn to answer mine."

He grinned at that. "Yes, it's just William and me working here."

"Would you care to elaborate?" she asked, feeling like he didn't give her much of an answer.

"Would you?" he countered a playful look on his face.

"This is not going to get us any closer to understanding each other."

"Look, Lorence, I want to understand you. I truly do. I'm not just being nosey into your personal life, but I can't give you more information about me until I know more about you. What if you are a mass murderer or crazy magician and you just want information from me to end up killing me, or worse, taking over the inn?"

"Murderer? Me, really?"

"You get the idea," he said, throwing up his hands. "Do I think you are a murderer or someone who is after my business? No, I do not, but I just don't know anything about you, Lorence." He looked straight at her; those green eyes boring into her.

"I understand," she said looking back down at the sheet in her hands.

She heard him heave a huge sigh and she looked up to see him run a hand through his hair. "I'm not upset with you, Lorence. And I do think I can trust you. I just need some more information from you first."

"I'm just not sure how much information I can give you."

He nodded. "Well, it seems we have come to an impasse. For now, let's just finish making this bed, shall we?"

She nodded and they finished in relative silence. Florence wasn't sure how she was feeling. She did want to tell Robert everything, she just wasn't sure what all was possible. The last thing she wanted was to put him or William in any danger, and she was worried that the more information she gave him the more at risk they would both be.

The rest of the day was uneventful. Florence did all the tasks that William asked of her during dinner. Maybe she was just imagining things, but Robert seemed to keep his distance a little. She wasn't sure if it was because of the impasse they had reached or if the dinner rush really was that busy.

Tonight, for dinner William had made a spectacular roast beef with mashed potatoes and roasted carrots. By the time she started working, her stomach was already grumbling. She had never been this hungry back at home. Maybe it was because of all the physical work she was now performing, or maybe it was just that William was an amazing cook. She was finding that mealtimes were her favorite time of day.

Dinner passed by quickly, but not quickly enough for Florence. She was getting tired, even with multiple naps throughout the day; she had never had to work like this before. Her days back home had been spent doing some chores, but most of the day was for her to do as she pleased. Having a set schedule and all the work was starting to drain her a bit.

After the last guest had been fed, she and William began to prepare for their dinner. She set up the table in the same spot they had lunch. Luckily, William had planned enough food for the dinner rush that there was plenty left over for the three of them as well. Florence was grateful for this. She had been smelling this amazing meal for a few hours and instead of growing tired of it, she had actually become hungrier and hungrier.

Dinner between the three of them was a quiet affair. It took Florence a while to notice, because she was very involved with her meal. Once she had had her first serving and was working on her second, did she notice no one was talking.

"Is something wrong?" she asked both William and Robert.

They both stopped eating and looked at her. "What do you mean?" Robert asked.

"No one is talking. Is there something I'm missing?"

Robert and William looked at each other and then back at her. "You think something is wrong because we aren't talking?" Robert genuinely seemed confused.

"Yes?" Florence said, only now second guessing everything she had just said.

"We didn't notice we weren't talking, honestly," Robert answered, looking over at William who nodded his head in agreement.

"That silence wasn't awkward for either of you?" Florence asked, getting more and more confused as this conversation continued.

Robert and William looked at each other and then back at her. "No, not really," Robert said gently. "When you've known someone as long as William and I have, you are comfortable just being around them, you don't have to be talking the whole time."

"Huh," Florence said, thinking over this new concept. She was starting to worry she was giving herself away, but it just seemed so weird.

"Don't you have someone in your life you can just sit with? Someone you don't have to be talking to constantly. Maybe like your parents?"

Florence thought about it. Growing up it always seemed like there was some kind of noise happening at any given time. Her parents were always chatting with each other or chatting with her. If there wasn't any noise happening it usually meant something was horribly wrong. They never had just sat and enjoyed each other's company, it always seemed like they had to be doing something or saying something. She never really thought of it as a problem or something to be concerned or even aware of.

"My family was always talking, I've never just sat in silence before," she finally answered.

"Did you have a lot of siblings or something?" Robert prodded, though he tried to pretend he wasn't.

"No, I'm an only child. At least I think I am," Florence added, feeling unsure.

Robert's eyebrows rose in surprise. "That's interesting," he said finally, after some time had passed.

"I know it seems weird, but I didn't know it was weird until just now. You know what, forget it," Florence said in frustration, standing up. "I'm going to bed. William, is there anything else you need from me?" She didn't want to leave him with all the work of cleaning up.

He shook his head but kept his dark eyes on her in a questioning stare.

"Good, then I will see you in the morning." With that she turned on her heel and stomped out of the room. She knew she was probably being ridiculous, but she had been under too much pressure the last couple of days. When she made it to her room, she threw herself down on her bed.

Too much in her life had changed too quickly and she was having a hard time keeping up with it. She didn't know how long she would be here. She didn't even know if her parents had been her real parents. The Baron's words echoed in her head, "I have entrusted you to raise her to be my wife. Don't you remember eighteen years ago when I brought you and her to this place? She will serve me in every way I desire."

She shivered involuntarily. What did that all mean? There had been something off about the ways her parents had treated her. They never forced her to do anything other than learn how to run a household. As she was growing up, she had wondered why they wanted her to know all these things, but now the horrible truth was sinking in. Their sole purpose in raising her had been to marry the Baron. Did they even love her? If they weren't her parents, then who were? Where had she come from? Why had the Baron picked her of all people?

All these questions swirled in her head, making her dizzy. How was she supposed to cope with all of this?

A knock on her door jerked her out of her grim thoughts. She stood and slowly opened the door. Robert was there with an enormous piece of chocolate cake.

"Look, I didn't mean to upset you. I was just surprised by what you said. I understand your need for secrecy, and I promise not to be pushy about it. I've brought this as a peace offering," he said, holding it out to her. "The only thing I ask is please don't get any chocolate on the sheets. This is William's special recipe and it can tend to leave a mess."

"Thank you," she said, taking the plate. "I'm sorry for rushing out. It has just been a bit of a rough couple of days."

"That's alright," he said, brightening. "No trouble at all. We'll see you bright and early."

"Thank you," she said again as he turned to go. "Good night."

"Good night," he repeated, giving her a warm smile. Then he turned and walked back down the hallway.

She took her cake into her room and tried not to cry again. The gesture was so sweet from these two men who had shown her so much kindness. She took a bite and momentarily forgot all of her worries. Needless to say, the cake was amazing. Never before had she had anything that was so decadent and rich. One thing was for sure, she could get used to someone bringing her chocolate cake.

CHAPTER SIX

The next few days passed in a blur. She would start her morning in the kitchen doing lots of walking with heavy water buckets and tons of dishes. William still didn't speak very much, but he did give her a small smile if she ever did something he approved of. She wanted to learn how to cook from him so badly, but she wasn't quite sure how to ask. He was so serious and stoic, and all she wanted was to please him and get that small, rare smile of his. Perhaps one day she would get brave enough to ask him, but she didn't see that happening any time soon.

Robert, on the other hand, seemed to be an open book. He said exactly what was on his mind at any given time. It almost seemed like he was too blunt about his opinions on things.

"William, you're stirring that wrong," Florence heard Robert say one morning as she was coming into the kitchen for the breakfast rush.

"What do you mean?" William growled dangerously.

"You don't need to scrape the spoon all the way to the bottom of the pan. It's bad for the pans! And then we'll have to get new ones."

"The food will burn if I don't stir it like this," William said dangerously. "More food will be more expensive in the long run than another pan. Also, you will have to deal with the unhappy customers, not me."

Florence was always surprised at how Robert could stand under the pure anger that William directed his way. She was sure she would have cowered under his stare had she been the one to cause William's anger.

"Ah, good morning Lorence!" Robert called cheerfully. "Come settle this debate for us."

"I will not be pulled into this," Florence said, grabbing the bucket by the back door. "Unlike you, Robert, some of us have work to do."

While she would never have normally talked to anyone in this manner, Robert was the exception. He was annoying yet somehow charming. His laughter followed her out the back door. She knew she could get away with sassing him and frankly he deserved what he got.

As she went to the well, she kept her eyes peeled, looking for pure white animals. She hadn't heard anything from Rasful since his last note. She wasn't panicking yet, but she had hoped to hear from him by now. It was not that she wasn't enjoying her time here, but she certainly didn't want to put anyone in danger by staying in one place for too long. Especially her new friends.

Friends. This was a new concept to Florence. The only real friend she had before this had been Rasful, and now she wasn't sure what their relationship was. She was comfortable with Rasful and he had saved her from the Baron, she just wasn't sure what their relationship entailed. Had he been sent to protect her, or were they truly friends? Maybe it was a silly question but so much of what she thought she knew had been turned upside down. Rasful was a mystery, and she wasn't sure she wanted to know everything about him. At this point she almost felt like she didn't want to know any more about Rasful or Ziv. At least with the information she had, she could pretend they were friends and nothing else was interfering with that. Still, every day she looked for a white creature.

When she finally came back into the kitchen, Robert was gone, and breakfast orders were rolling in. She got to work. She had gotten used to her role in the kitchen. William did all the cooking while she mostly stuck to cleaning. Cleaning was something she was relatively good at. While it wasn't something she felt like she could do for a living, she was pretty good at keeping things clean. Although now that she thought about it, she guessed she was doing it for a living.

Her job in the kitchen mostly consisted of cleaning pots and pans, keeping the counters clean of crumbs and spills, and making sure the food got out to Robert.

She liked working with William. He was quiet but he would talk when things needed to get done. He was nothing like Robert who seemed to talk constantly.

"So Lorence, what's your favorite color?" he asked when she brought him some food for the customers.

"Aren't all colors kind of the same?" she asked him.

"Some colors might be similar, but each color is unique and should give you a different feeling. Your favorite color should make you feel warm and happy inside."

The question gave her pause. She had never thought about it before. "I'm not sure," she said, trying not to feel panicked as the time it took her to answer stretched longer.

"Think about it and let me know later, how about that?" he said with a wink. He grabbed the plates from her hands and rushed off to deliver them to the customers.

She didn't know why stupid things like him asking about her favorite color gave her so much to think about. Why had she never thought about this before? Why had no one asked her?

She thought about it all morning and finally when they were sitting down to their own breakfast, she had an answer for him.

"Green, green is my favorite color."

"Well now that's interesting. How would you figure that my eyes are green?" he smiled.

She tried not to blush. Of course, that's why green was her favorite. Not a smart answer on her part. But she had answered truthfully and that had to count for something.

"You know you can tell a lot about someone by their favorite color," he continued.

"And what can you tell about me?" she countered.

"Well, green has to do with growth. Most things that are green are alive so the fact you like green means you're alive and on your own path to grow. Now don't look at me like that," he said at her skeptical look. "It may not be perfect, but I think everyone is attracted to a different color for a reason."

"Well then what's your favorite color?"

"Mine? Oh, that's easy, it's red. An orange red if I'm being specific."

"What does red say about you?"

"Well now that is for me to know and for you to find out," he said with a mischievous grin.

She rolled her eyes but she was curious. Could people's favorite colors really say that much about them? She wasn't sure, but then again, she wasn't sure about a lot these days.

"Take William for example," Robert said, interrupting her thoughts. "His favorite color is brown. The most boring color in the world if you ask me."

"We didn't ask you," William said, through gritted teeth.

"What does this color choice say about our dear William? Well, although it is an extremely boring, dingy color, our William loves it. The reason is because it reminds him of freshly baked bread or the wooden spoons he uses to create his masterpieces. It really tells a lot about him."

"Fascinating," she said, resting her chin on her hand. "Now if only you would bring your infinite wisdom to tell me why your favorite color is red."

"Well, you see I—" he looked at her and grinned. "Oh, look at this! You almost got me! Flattery will get you many places, my dear, but I'm afraid I'm too clever for that."

"According to whom?" she asked, innocently.

He laughed a big belly laugh at this. "We need to watch out for this one, William."

She smiled, glad to have been involved with these two. For maybe the first time in her life she was feeling comfortable. She was able to truly be herself. This was something she hadn't even realized she hadn't been. It was fun to make Robert laugh and to get those rare smiles from William. She had to remind herself that they couldn't get too close. She was starting to worry that she was getting too comfortable with them and something might slip. She would just have to be careful and make sure that did not happen.

"William," Florence asked in a tentative voice.

He turned to face her, and she almost lost all of her courage she had been trying to build up for this occasion.

"You are an amazing cook. I would love to learn from you if you wouldn't mind... That is if you would be willing to teach me," she said, stumbling over her words.

William looked at her hard for a few moments. "I'm afraid I can't."

"It's alright," she said, trying to hide her disappointment. "I knew it was a bit of a long shot anyway—" she broke off at the hand he held up.

"You didn't let me finish," he said in his soft way of speaking. "I can't teach you to cook until you have mastered the basics. You've done well with everything I've asked you to do, so I know that I can trust you to listen to what I tell you. But you still have a long way to go. First the basics."

This was the most she had ever heard him speak and her excitement was over the top. "Oh, thank you William!" she said as she rushed over and hugged him. He seemed surprised by this but please. Florence knew she probably shouldn't have done that, but she was just so excited. "When can I start?"

"Soon,' William promised, giving her that signature small smile. "Very soon."

A few days later William had made good on his promise, and she was working in the kitchen. It was the dinner rush and things were getting a little crazy. It wasn't anything they couldn't handle, of course, but Florence did feel her stress level rise with each new order Robert put in.

Florence was standing at the counter, happily chopping up ingredients. William looked over her work and grunted his approval. It took her awhile at first to chop up everything the correct way. Apparently, she had been chopping wrong for years and she had no idea. He took the vegetables she had just chopped up and handed her a few potatoes.

She gripped the potato with her fingers curled under themselves just like William had shown her and began to bring the knife down when something went wrong. Somehow the knife slipped off the potato instead of slicing through it like it was supposed to. The knife slipped from her fingers and began to fall towards the floor. Her heart leaped in her chest, not only for the fear of losing a toe but also how William might react to this mishap. She watched as the knife flipped over itself and then, right when it was about to hit the ground, it froze. She watched in disbelief as the knife rotated, end over end, in opposition to how it had fallen. It defied gravity almost like a strange wind had caught it, until it fit right back into her hand like nothing had happened. She stared at the knife, wondering if she had imagined the whole thing.

"You doing alright there, Lorence?"

Her head snapped up and she found herself looking directly at Robert's expectant face.

"Did you see that?"

"See what?" he asked, confused.

"The knife it seemed to…" she saw she had lost him. Besides, if he had seen it, knowing him he would have said something. "Never mind."

"Alright then," he said, taking the plates of food that were set out for the customers. "You know if you stare at the knife long enough, it may start chopping vegetables on its own."

She gave him a piercing look. Had he seen anything after all? He laughed and walked out of the room. Robert wasn't one to be subtle. Maybe he hadn't seen anything after all.

She looked back at the knife. Had she just imagined it? Maybe it was just the hunger that was gnawing at her. How had she gotten so hungry again?

She gave herself a little shake, trying to get her head back to earth again, and went back chopping. This time she was being very careful.

She couldn't shake the weird feeling she had gotten from the knife incident throughout dinner or even after dinner. Maybe the heat from the oven had just been getting to her. After all, she reasoned, things like that didn't just happen. At least, she didn't think they did.

"Robert, what was your childhood like?"

"Well now, look who's decided to stop giving me the cold shoulder!"

Florence put down the sheet she was working on stretching across the bed. "I have not been giving you the cold shoulder! At least I don't think I have… What does it mean to give someone the cold shoulder?" she asked, having the vision of someone's shoulder on ice being handed to someone.

"A cold shoulder is when someone doesn't talk to someone because they are being stubborn," Robert answered. That was one thing Florence loved about Robert. She could ask him anything and he would answer it without making her feel small. That had not been the case with her parents.

"But I talk to you every day," she said, confused.

"You didn't let me finish explaining," he said, holding up his hand. "The reason I said you were giving me the cold shoulder is because we have been working together for weeks and the only time you talk to me is when there is a counter or a table in between us. All these weeks we've been working together. You have not talked to me while we were cleaning rooms. Now I have to wonder, why is that Lorence?" He stopped his work as well and looked straight at her.

His stare was starting to make her uncomfortable. "I don't know," she said, looking away from him and trying to think of a better answer.

"I don't know, isn't a proper answer, Lorence," he said calmly.

"I know it isn't," she snapped, looking at him. "I am thinking and am going to continue. Hold on."

He made a gesture that said carry on. They both went back to their work in silence.

After some time had passed, she said, "I think it's because the last time we talked up here, we both got upset. I didn't want that to happen again, so I just kept quiet," she finished. It wasn't the best answer she had ever come up with, but it was the truth.

"You didn't talk to me because you were afraid of upsetting me?" Robert's voice was soft and soothing.

She nodded, keeping her head down. It sounded so foolish when he said it like that. She wasn't sure if he was just messing with her, but she really didn't know how else to react.

"Lorence, look at me."

His voice was gentle, not demanding, yet she found herself looking up all the same into those dark green eyes. "You won't upset me. Nothing you can do will upset me. Alright?"

"Alright," she said, not seeming to be able to take a full breath. His eyes were locked onto hers again. It felt like they were the only two people in the world.

"Well, there is one thing you can do that would upset me greatly," he said in a serious voice.

"What's that?"

"Not talk to me like you had been up until this point," he said with a grin.

"Ha-ha," she said, sarcastically. "I won't anymore I promise."

"I'll hold you to that promise," he said, in the same serious voice but there was a light in his eyes.

"Now what was it you asked me? What was my childhood like?"

"Oh, yes," she said, remembering what started all of this. "I was just wondering if you had any siblings, is all."

"Yes, sure do! I have three brothers and a sister."

Florence gasped. "That's so many!"

"That's nothing! We had some neighbors that lived a few miles away from us and they had thirteen children! We had a blast getting together with them, let me tell you."

Florence was trying to keep her head from spinning. She couldn't imagine that many people growing up in the same space. She had a hard enough time imagining four other siblings, much less twelve.

"I guess I had a pretty normal childhood. I have two parents that love me, we lived on a farm and had an all-around good time together."

"Where is your family now?"

Robert grew sober at that. "I think that's enough questions for now. We really should finish up before William starts to worry."

Florence nodded, understanding his reluctance but burning with curiosity. They worked in silence for a few minutes longer.

"How do you feel about nicknames?" he asked, breaking the uncomfortable few minutes they had spent in silence.

"I don't know that I've even had a real opinion about them before," she said, continuing her work. "I like them I guess."

"I don't mean to brag, but I'm pretty good at making up nicknames," he said with a playful grin.

"Oh really? Because as I recall, William did not like any you made up for him."

"Oh, but William is prim and proper," he said, pretending to drink tea out of an invisible teacup. "But I've got a great one for you."

She groaned. "I don't know about this, Robert."

"Hear me out!" he said, holding out his hands and sounding excited. "Here is your new nickname: Lor."

She pretended to think it over. "That's not incredibly inventive but it's alright."

"Then how about this one: Rent. This one has a double meaning because you owe me rent."

"I do not!" she said indignantly. "I am working right now, aren't I?"

"That you are, however, as I recall, I let you sleep the first night free. That being said, you are technically one night's behind on rent and frankly I'm not sure you'll ever catch up."

"Well then, why don't I sleep outside?" she countered. "That way I can be caught up on my rent that I apparently owe you."

"Whoa now, there's no need for that! Plus, I kind of like you indebted to me. It makes me feel powerful," he said, puffing out his chest in an exaggerated manner.

"I'll be sleeping outside thanks," said Florence, gathering up the basket for washing and walking out of the room. Robert's laughter followed her into the hallway.

The next day was clear and cool. Fall was finally arriving. Florence was enjoying the new crisp air outside in the back of the building. All she was doing was staring off into space, enjoying the air, when a small movement caught her eye. There was a pure white bird with brown eyes sitting on the fence next to her. She smiled, knowing it was a messenger of Ziv.

"Hello," she said, smiling at the tiny thing. When she spoke, it cocked its head to the side in the most adorable way. She laughed with pure pleasure, enjoying the way the sweet little bird moved. "Do you have something for me?"

The little bird began to hop slowly away from her, leading her to the forest. She eagerly followed as she was ready to hear from Rasful. He led her to the same tree as before and she saw there was a note. No bag this time but she was still good on clothes, so she wasn't expecting any. Really, she just wanted to hear from Rasful.

She opened the note that said:

Dear Flor, I'm glad to see you have been doing well! I'm not sure how much longer you should stay at this place. There is nothing wrong with the innkeepers, but I just worry about your cover getting blown. We can't afford to take any risks; I will come and get you personally when we find a new place for you. For now, stay put and wait to hear from me. I will write more when I have more information.

Florence read the note twice. How could a note give her so little information? She already knew all of this stuff. Why did he even waste the paper writing this note? It may seem sort of harsh for her to be thinking that, but she was frustrated. How long was Rasful going to leave her here? Where was the Baron and why did he want Florence so bad?

She walked back to the side of the house still reading the note, looking for any hidden meaning in the few short words Rasful had written.

"What's that?"

She nearly jumped out of her skin at the sound of Robert's voice. Hand flying to her chest to try and calm her pounding heart she said, "Don't sneak up on people like that!"

"I didn't sneak up on you, I made the normal amount of noise a person makes when coming out of a house. We are a little jumpy today, aren't we?"

He smiled at her, but Florence didn't smile back. She was feeling stressed, not just from Robert's sudden appearance but also what little information Rasful had given her. What was going on today?

He took a couple steps towards her. "Lor, are you alright?"

Sometimes when someone asks those few small words, it makes an avalanche of emotions cascade down. While this phrase is well meaning, sometimes it can be hard for the person being asked. She felt her eyes prick with tears, and she bit back a sob that was trying to escape. All of this was crazy. She wasn't sure who to trust anymore and she felt so trapped.

Robert looked at her for a moment then he said, "Come on, I want to show you something."

Florence followed him, trying to discreetly wipe the tears from her eyes as they walked. She hadn't meant to get so overcome but things were so stressful, and she wasn't sure where she stood on a lot of things. She wasn't even sure who she was as a person, which was a whole other can of worms she was not wanting to get into.

Robert led her into the forest. She realized she probably should have been more wary of him. After all, he was leading her somewhere there weren't any other people. But she couldn't. It was just Robert.

After walking what felt like a long time, they came into a small clearing. There were a couple of things that caught her eye. First of all, there was a small pond off to the right. It had lily pads and what sounded like a family of frogs. The water was that greenish gray color that still bodies of water usually are.

Right next to the pond was a little garden. Florence had never seen anything so small yet so beautiful. It had the brightest beautiful flowers she had ever seen, lilies, daisies, daffodils, sunflowers and yet there were so many more that she couldn't name. It didn't look like there were any vegetables in there at all. It was almost like this little garden was here solely for the pleasure it brought to those who came across it. It was a bit chaotic with each plant flowing into the one next to it, yet there was somehow beauty in that chaos.

The last thing she saw were several targets set at different lengths in the space. She had no idea what those were for, so she only gave them a passing glance. Really, she was way more interested in the pond and garden.

"Robert, this is beautiful," she said, turning in a circle to get a full look at everything. "Did you make this?"

He ran a hand through his hair, looking slightly uncomfortable. "Sort of. A lot of it was already here, I've just been taking care of it."

"It's wonderful, you should be proud of the work you've done here," she said, meaning every word.

He shrugged, his ears going slightly pink at her compliment. "Anyway, the real reason I brought you over here was for this."

He led her to the far end of the clearing where she had seen the targets set up. "This is target practice. Sometimes I come out here when I need to let off some steam."

"You need to let off steam?" she asked, her surprise coming out in her voice.

"Of course, I do! Everyone gets overwhelmed sometimes. Life can throw you for a loop if you let it. That's why I firmly believe you should throw things at life before it can throw things at you."

"Throw things? What sort of things?"

"Well, let me show you," he took her over to a small chest she hadn't yet seen, leaning up against a tree. Inside were an assortment of weapons. There were throwing knives, bows with arrows and two swords made out of wood.

"You know when someone brings someone else into the woods and then shows them a chest full of weapons, one could get the wrong idea."

He laughed a big belly laugh at that. "Trust me, Lor, if I wanted to harm you I would have by now."

"Oh? Do you have such confidence in your skills then?" she asked in a playful tone.

His smile faded slightly. "Yes, I'm afraid I do."

She wasn't sure what to make of that. "No offence but you don't seem the type to know how to handle weapons."

"None taken," he said, easily. "However, I wouldn't be so quick to judge people by their appearances. There may be more to them than meets the eye." He looked at her for a long moment, waiting for her to reply.

"I guess you are right," she said in a slow, measured voice, trying not to give too much away. Was he still talking about himself, or did he know something he wasn't letting on?

"I am right, thank you for acknowledging that. Now to move on," he said as she rolled her eyes at him. "The basics. Have you ever shot a bow and arrow before?"

"No," she said, coming around to see what he was pulling out of the chest. It was what looked like a child's bow. It was very small, probably only the length of her arm. The arrows were only about the length of her forearm and they were thin. They almost looked like if she bent them, they would break.

"I'm going to start you out with this one. It's light and small. This will be easier for you to shoot than a full sized one. Plus, you aren't a particularly big g-person," he said, stumbling a bit. "So, this should be ideal for you. Go ahead and give it a try."

He handed her the bow and watched as she held it awkwardly. "No, like this," he said, fixing her grip on it.

They spent the next half hour just practicing how to hold the bow the proper way. There was a lot for Florence to keep up with. Not only was there a certain place her hand should go, even her finger had a particular place it needed to be. Robert was a good teacher, which was surprising, and he was very patient. Even though she managed to only pick it up and hold it the correct way by herself once, he never got mad. He was quick to reward her with praise for even the smallest thing she did right.

"I think that may be enough for today," he said, looking up into the sky. "It's starting to get dark."

Florence found herself disappointed. She was enjoying learning this from him, and she didn't want it to be over.

They put the gear away and began walking back to the inn. "Robert," she said, breaking the silence they had fallen under. "Thank you for showing me that place. And for teaching me so much today."

"You're mighty welcome, Lor," he said, smiling. "We can come back tomorrow and learn some more if you would like to."

"I would love that," she said, meaning it.

That night when Florence was getting ready for bed, she found the note that Rasful had left for her. She had forgotten about it already. She pulled it out and read it again. She still wished he had given her some more information, but her situation didn't feel as hopeless as it had before. Maybe, like Robert said, it was time to start throwing things at life instead of being the one life threw things at.

CHAPTER SEVEN

Florence was learning a lot these days. Between learning to cook with William and learning how to shoot with Robert, her days were pretty full. Every day after lunch, she and Robert would go to their place to train. She had finally worked her way up to shooting. She wasn't super good at it, but every day she could feel herself getting better and stronger. She was beginning to get muscles in her arms and back from the strain of drawing the bow. Her hands had become calloused as well, not only from cooking but also from holding her arrows. She hadn't moved up to a bigger bow and she wasn't sure she wanted to. She had become attached to her little bow and it was working just fine for her. Plus, she had to master the basics before she could move on to the more advanced things. At least, that's what Robert said anyway.

Now she was getting to the point where she could actually hit the targets. She still wasn't anywhere near a bullseye, but she was certainly getting close. She also found herself just wanting to sit in this space.

Fall had finally come. The leaves were all a glorious red and yellow and Florence just wanted to be in those beautiful leaves. She wanted to somehow be a part of all the glory of fall. She wasn't totally sure how to do that, but she knew she had to be outside. She went to the garden to just take some time for herself.

As she looked around the flowers, she saw something out of the corner of her eyes, flit in and out of the plants. She paused, not wanting to scare away whatever it was that she saw flit by. There was a flash of what looked like a wing. She assumed it was a large butterfly and wanted to see it. So, she sat very still and looked with intent where she had last seen the movement.

Something small and bright red zoomed past one of the sunflowers. It finally stopped at one of the daisies, so Florence was able to get a good look at it. The creature was something that could only be described as a pixie. It was tiny and human-like but not quite human. It had a torso like a human, but its arms and legs were longer and thinner. It was very pointy, for lack of a better phrase. It had a pointy face and ears, and its hair was slicked back into a point as well. It was a bright cherry red and had what looked like red leaves covering its body down to its knees and elbows. Its shoulders were bare, leaving room for its multicolored wings. They came out of its shoulder blades and went down almost to its feet.

It was looking in a droplet of leftover dew from that morning and seemed to be preening itself in front of it. The pixie was checking its hair and face as well as its outfit trying to make sure everything was in place.

Florence had never seen anything like this little creature. Maybe it was native to this part of the country. She wasn't sure but just then the little pixie turned and saw her.

They both froze, just staring at each other, but then the little pixie smiled and said in a high-pitched voice, "Hello, tall one!"

"H-h-h-ello," Florence stammered, flustered.

"Does a beetle have your tongue?" she asked, sticking out her cherry red one and winking one eye.

"No, you just surprised me. I didn't think you could talk."

"Of course, we can talk!" said the pixie, laughing. "Can't everybody?"

"I suppose so," said Florence, smiling. "What brings you here? Do you live in this area?"

"Oh no! I follow fall of course!" she said happily doing a twirl. "Fall is the best time of year don't you think? It's perfect for me! I get to bring all of the red leaves, that's my job," she said.

"Only the red leaves?"

"Yes, my siblings get the boring job of making the leaves other colors. But I think my job is the best!"

"There are more of you?"

"Oh yes, yes! I have tons of other family! They control the other seasons. Some bring snow and other flowers. As for me, I bring brightly colored leaves!"

"I had no idea you did that," said Florence a bit in awe.

"Yes of course! Us pixies work very hard to do our jobs well," she said, giving a little salute.

"So where do you go when it's not fall anymore?"

"We follow it all around the world. For me it's fall every day!" she said, doing a little dance. Then she froze, listening intently. "Someone is coming. We'll talk again later, I'm sure." And with that she took off on her wings, disappearing in a blink of an eye.

"Wait! When will I see you again?"

"Lor? What are you doing?"

She froze at the sound of Robert's voice. "Nothing, I was just looking at these flowers."

Robert came around the garden to get a better look at her. "Were you talking to someone just now?"

"Um, no, just sitting here," she answered, wishing she had come up with a better excuse.

"Alright," he said, still peering around the bush, looking for the mystery voice. "You know, sometimes I wonder if you can speak to animals."

"What do you mean?" Florence asked, heart pounding.

"I've just seen you talk to a couple of different animals is all. It's always strange when it happens. The animals have been pure white and after you talk to them you both disappear in the forest. Don't look at me like that," he said, laughing. "I know you can't talk to animals, no one can. I was just commenting is all."

She had no idea how to respond to that, so she didn't. She had thought no one had been around when Ziv's helpers had shown up. Maybe she would have to be more careful.

"Right well then, shall we?" he said, gesturing to the targets.

Florence nodded and stood up, walking over to him. This was becoming Florence's favorite part of the day. She liked being alone with Robert. She could almost forget her troubles when she was with him.

Except this practice was rough. She was getting so close to making a bullseye, but something was slightly off. She couldn't figure out what it was that was preventing her from reaching her goal. Robert was watching but not offering any advice. He was letting her figure it out for herself.

She was getting more and more frustrated. Finally, she took a breath and felt a tingling in her fingers right before she released the arrow. She watched holding her breath as the arrow shot straight and true right into the bullseye. She paused, surprised that it had worked.

Robert pushed off of the tree he had been leaning on and walked towards her. "Do that again."

She nocked an arrow, took a breath and, just like before, her fingers tingled when she released the arrow. Sure, enough it flew true and went straight into the red center of the target. Another bullseye.

Robert came up behind her and said, "Again."

When the same thing happened a third time Robert whistled. "Good job, Lor. I think you've got the hang of it now."

She smiled at his praise, happy to have done a good job. "Well, I had a pretty good teacher," she said, smiling up at him. They were close, almost touching and Florence was struck again at how handsome he was. Those green eyes seemed to see into her very soul.

They both stood still staring at each other for what felt like an eternity. Florence was the first to look away feeling awkward. She wanted to keep staring at him but her pretending to be a boy made it feel kind of weird. She was worried about getting too close to him, she didn't know how much longer she would be here.

"What's wrong, Lor?" came Robert's soft voice.

"Nothing," she said, smiling up at him. "I'm just feeling a little tired for some reason." This was true, even though it wasn't the reason she had looked away first. She was feeling tired. It felt like she had done a full day's work. She found herself yawning and feeling ready to drop right there.

"I think that's probably enough practice for today," Robert said, laughing. "We should head back anyway. Don't want to cause good old William to worry."

Florence was sore and tired, but she was smiling as they walked back to the inn together.

Florence was in the kitchen just like any other day. She was busy chopping up vegetables to put into a stew that William was making. Only William wasn't in the kitchen. For some reason, Florence was alone and chopping like her life depended on it. She continued to chop faster and faster, like something was forcing her to. She felt like her hand was glued to the knife.

She heard a familiar laugh and she looked over to her right. There was the Baron, leaning against the wall and smiling at her. "I love a woman who can cook," he said, laughing again. He looked at her with that possessive stare, smiling the whole time.

She tried to take the knife in her hand and throw it at him, but her hand wouldn't obey her. It kept chopping on its own accord.

Faster and faster it went, until it became a blur in her hand. Then the fire from the furnace started to go out of control. Flames started licking up the walls, engulfing the entire kitchen. Florence screamed and tried to run but her feet stayed planted where they were. The heat from the fire was overwhelming and the smoke was choking her. The Baron's laughter rang in her ears as the fire began to burn her.

A knock on her door woke her with a start. "Lor?" came Robert's voice. "It's time to get ready for dinner."

"I'll be right there," she croaked out. Her voice wasn't working for some reason. She coughed feeling like there was smoke in her lungs. She tried to get out of bed for a drink of water and cried out at the pain that shot up her foot. She looked down and saw the tips of all ten of her toes were burned.

Robert burst in at the sound of her cry. "Lor? What's wrong, what happened?"

He looked down at her feet which she was holding and knelt next to her. "How did this happen?"

She couldn't answer. She was sobbing with fear and pain. He got some water and bandages and worked on tending to her feet. She couldn't stop crying and was starting to hyperventilate now.

"Lor, breathe, you're alright," he said, taking her face in his hands. "Look at me." She didn't have much of a choice with him being so close, but she obeyed. "Lor, how did you get burned?"

Florence shook her head, unable to answer. "I don't know," she said, tears streaming down her face. "I just don't know."

Winter was coming to the inn. It wasn't quite here yet, but things were definitely cooling down even more than they had been. Most of the red and golden leaves had fallen off their trees, there were only a few left.

Florence was recovering from her foot injury well. She was able to walk and had started working in the kitchen again. She sat on a stool but stayed away from chopping.

She hadn't been sleeping much. After her nightmare she couldn't close her eyes for more than a few minutes at a time. Robert had noticed and as he came into the kitchen he asked, "Are those meals ready yet William?"

William grunted and handed him the food. Robert took it and then, turning to Florence, said, "Why aren't you sleeping, Lor?"

Florence sighed, tired of this question. "Why don't you get that food out to the customers, Robert?"

He smiled at her and said, "I will ask again. Over and over until you tell me." He gave a cheerful wave and was gone.

She sighed again, shifting in her seat rubbing the back of her neck. She was exhausted and was holding tension in her neck. She felt eyes on her and, looking over at him, saw William looking back at her.

"I'm fine, William," she said, trying not to sound exasperated. She wasn't used to people worrying about her. It hadn't been that way with her parents.

She remembered a time when she had climbed too high in a tree. She didn't know the branches near the top were rotted through. She put all of her weight on a branch that must have been ten feet up in the air. When she fell, the other branches had broken her fall before she hit the ground, so she hadn't broken anything. But she remembered the pain of all the cuts and bruises all over her body.

She had gone running home, crying and wanting comfort for the pain she was in. Her parents had been furious with her, asking how she could have been so foolish. Once they found out nothing was broken, they sent her on her way and treated her as if nothing had happened. Her body had ached for weeks after, but she made sure not to mention it. Her parents didn't really seem to care much about her recovery.

She jerked herself out of her gloomy thoughts. She didn't need to be feeling sorry for herself. What she needed was to keep working.

After the dinner rush they moved everything to a table in the dining room to eat their own dinner. As soon as they sat down, Robert said, "This looks great William! Lor, why aren't you sleeping?"

Florence had reached a breaking point. Too many days of not sleeping. "I can't sleep! The last time I did I dreamed the kitchen was on fire and when I woke up my feet were burned. It felt so real like I had actually been there. So now here I am terrified that when I do fall asleep the same thing will happen. Excuse me for not wanting to talk about it!" With that she took a huge bite of food and chewed furiously. She didn't miss the look that was exchanged between William and Robert but she didn't care. She was too exhausted and hungry to care.

"You dreamed about a fire and then woke up like this?" William asked, quietly.

Florence swallowed her food and snapped, "Yes William, isn't that what I just said?"

She knew she was being rude, but it was easy to be snappy when she hadn't slept in days.

"I knew someone that that very thing happened to," said William, in a thoughtful way. "Not with a fire specifically, but things that happened in her dreams began to have effects on her real life."

Florence put down her spoon. "I'm sorry for being rude William. Will you please tell me what happened to your friend? What did she do to… get rid of it?"

"Well, she went to a physician, and he gave her something to help with it. I don't remember what it was. Maybe I can go visit him and ask."

"Where does he live?"

"Oh, just one town over. Maybe a day's ride from here."

"If you would be willing to go, I would be incredibly grateful," said Florence with meaning.

"Yes, I will go to him; I was planning a trip down there tomorrow, as a matter of fact. Don't worry your head about it," said William, giving her a rare smile.

"Now let's eat! The food is getting cold!" Robert's voice lifted the mood, and they all had a lovely time in each other's company.

After dinner they cleaned up and all went their separate ways to get ready for bed. Florence felt much better knowing that she would only have a couple more sleepless nights. She was just about to settle in when she heard a quiet knock at her door. Wondering who it could be, she got up and answered it.

Robert was standing on the other side, holding a pillow and blanket. "Good evening, Lor. Mind if I come in?" he asked, cheerfully.

"What are you doing here, Robert?" she asked in a tired voice.

"Look, you're afraid to sleep, and I don't blame you at all. I would be terrified too if my nightmares were having an effect on me. So, I'm going to sleep in here and keep an eye on you."

"I don't know if that's such a good idea."

"Why not? It's not like you have anything to hide, do you?"

They stared at each other waiting for the other to crack first. If she kept fighting him on this, he would probably get suspicious. After all she was exhausted and having someone watch over her would help her feel better.

"This is only until William comes back," said Robert, seeing her waver. "I promise you can have your room back to yourself in a couple of days."

"Oh, alright," she said, stepping aside and letting him into the room.

She shut the door behind him and crawled back under the covers. He set up a pallet on the floor close to her bed. It was a little strange to have him in here, yet at the same time something about it felt natural. She would probably ponder over that later, but right now she was way too tired.

"Thank you, Robert," she said, feeling sleep begin to take her.

"You're welcome, lass," she thought she heard him respond, but she couldn't be sure. She drifted off into a much-needed sleep.

CHAPTER EIGHT

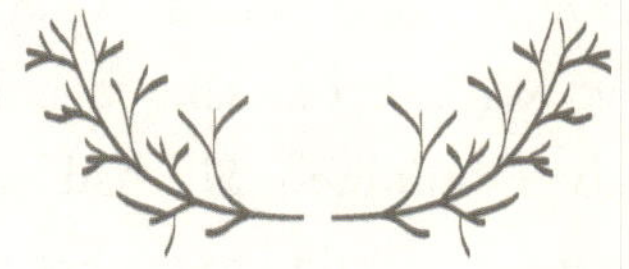

She woke up to sunlight streaming through her window. She rolled over to see Robert's pallet on the floor empty. *So much for watching over me*, she thought. It didn't bother her that much, though. She felt so much better after getting a full night's rest. Just as she was about to get out of bed there was a knock on her door.

"Come in," she said, and in walked Robert a tray of food balanced in one hand.

"Good morning, Lor," he said, a broad smile on his face. "Did you sleep well?"

"Very well, thank you," she said, smiling. "What is all this?"

"This is breakfast in bed," he said, putting the tray down on her bed with a flourish. "I'm afraid I'm not as good of a cook as William but I'm not half bad, if I do say so myself."

Florence looked at the tray in front of her. There was breakfast potatoes, eggs and sausage as well as bread and some fruit. It smelled amazing.

"Oh, but what about the customers?" Florence asked in a slight panic. "I wasn't there to help you with breakfast!"

She began to try and get out of bed, to really do who knows what, but Robert put a hand on her shoulder to stop her. "Whoa now, settle down! Breakfast was fine, Lor, we only had three people check in last night, so it was no trouble. Besides, I've closed the inn for today! I think it's time for a bit of a holiday."

"Oh," she said, settling back down. "What do you do on a holiday?"

"Do you mean to tell me you've never had a holiday before?" Robert asked in real shock.

"No, I guess I haven't," said Florence, fidgeting with her bed covers.

"Well, Lor, are you in for a treat!" he said, smiling. "Now first things first, eat your breakfast. I don't want it to get cold. I worked hard on it."

She obediently took a bite. It was delicious. "Good," he winked at her. "I'll be back in a bit for the tray." With that he saluted and walked out of a room.

She was touched by Robert's kindness. She had never had someone to take care of her in this way. She was beginning to get excited for the day ahead; she had no idea what he had planned.

A few minutes later there was another knock on her door. She wasn't quite done eating but that didn't matter. Robert came in carrying a huge kettle and walked straight into her bathroom. "What are you doing?" Florence asked, in between bites.

"I'm drawing a bath. I figured you could use a nice hot soak before we head out for today." He grinned at her and left the room. He came back with more hot water which he poured into the bath until finally it was full. So was Florence. She had finished her breakfast and Robert took the tray away. "Come down when you're ready," he said smiling at her and he closed the door behind him.

She had never been allowed to take a bath as long as she wanted to. It seemed like there was always something that needed to be done. The warm water helped her aching muscles and she fully relaxed for perhaps the first time since the Baron came in the picture. She stayed until the water began to get cold and then she finally got out.

She got dressed and came downstairs feeling completely refreshed. Looking around for Robert, she found him in the kitchen with his back to her. She peeked at him, marveling at how handsome he was. He was so tall and had broad shoulders and well-muscled arms that were currently doing dishes. As she studied him, she noticed he had a slight marking on his left forearm. She couldn't tell exactly what it was from this distance, maybe a scar? She felt a huge amount of gratitude fill her chest for this man who had taken such good care of her. She had never had someone do any of the things he had done for her, which made her want to find some way to repay him, but she wasn't sure how.

Just then he looked over his shoulder. She jumped, heat rising to her cheeks at being caught staring. He grinned at her embarrassment and said, "Hello Lor, enjoying the view?"

She stuck her tongue out at him and walked fully into the kitchen. "What is that?" she asked, pointing to the mark on his forearm.

"Oh! This is a battle wound; got it the first time I made a knife throw."

"What happened?" she asked, coming closer. Now that she was closer, she could see that it was indeed a scar. And a nasty one at that.

"Well, truth be told, I was being rather cocky," he threw her a sheepish grin. "I had seen my teacher do this knife technique where he flipped the knife around his forearm before throwing it. I thought I could do it too. I can't say it ended well for me," he examined his arm carefully.

"Did you ever learn to do the trick?" The scar was nasty. It zig-zagged down his arm, ending painfully by his elbow. It was thin though, not super noticeable until you were up close.

"Oh yes, it was the first thing I learned when I recovered."

"I'd love to see it."

"Sure," he said, smiling at her. "I'll show you sometime."

There was another moment where it was just the two of them in the room. Time seemed to stop and as Florence stared into his eyes, there was only one thing she knew for sure: she was in trouble.

"What is the plan for today?" she asked, breaking the moment but not even trying to mask her excitement.

"Well, the first way to start any holiday is to sleep in, which you have already done. Next is breakfast in bed, which I think we can check off the list. Then we have a good long soak which we can, again, mark as done. Let's see, what's next?" he asked, putting his finger to his lips.

"Come on, Robert," said Florence, not bothering to hide her impatience.

He grinned at her, enjoying the game. "The next thing we do is go out."

"Out? Out where?"

"Out. In this case outside the inn," his smile was contagious, and she couldn't help but smile back. Perhaps she should have been more nervous about someone recognizing her, but she wasn't.

"Well then follow me this way, Lor, and we will begin our adventure!"

With that he led her out the front door. As odd as it sounded, she had never been out of the inn this way. It was how she had arrived, of course, but she had never seen the front of the building in the daylight. It was a larger building with a sign over the door showing what it was. She had never noticed it before, but the inn's name was The Forest Maiden.

"Robert, why is the inn named The Forest Maiden?"

"Oh, well, that's actually my doing," he said, looking up at the sign. "I had a dream that a girl would someday walk out of the forest to me. I know it sounds strange, but I felt like she was the girl I was somehow destined for."

"So, then you believe in destiny?"

"Don't you?" he asked, looking over at her. "I believe that destiny plays a part in our lives. We can fight against it or release ourselves into it."

"What about your ability to choose? Doesn't free will have anything to do with it?" Florence had never thought about any of these things before, but something about Robert made her feel like she should.

"Aye, choice plays into it as well. When I say destiny, I mean the things we were truly meant to do, meant to become. I believe everyone on this earth has a gift that they are meant to share with the world. Sometimes it takes a while to find that gift, sometimes it takes someone special to bring that gift out in us. There are certain things that will happen in our lives. Certain beats and situations that we are meant to go through. I believe we can make what we will out of those situations. We have some say in our own destiny. But I don't believe it's very much."

Florence turned over what he had said. What did she believe about this? If random things just happened to her, that was easier to believe than everything having a purpose. If everything had meaning, then that was a lot to wrap her head around. And where did the Baron fall into that?

"You alright there, Lor?" Robert's voice pulled her out of her thoughts.

"Yes, I'm alright," she said, smiling. "Just got a little lost for a moment."

They continued walking past the inn and towards the market. Florence had only been to a market once or twice with her mother. It hadn't been a particularly pleasant experience either time. Her mother had seemed edgy and wasn't up for a whole lot of talking. She kept muttering to herself as they got closer to the market and had kept Florence practically glued to her side the whole time. Florence, while unsettled by her mother's mood, had enjoyed going to the market. There were so many sights and sounds and smells. The vendors all had colorful stalls and the food they were selling looked amazing. Florence had wanted to try some of it but had been afraid to ask her mother. She pulled herself back to the present. This time going to the market would be different.

After all, this time around she was older and had Robert as her guide. This market wasn't terribly big, consisting of maybe ten stalls in a semi-circle around the fountain in the middle of town. They stopped at every single one. Robert knew everyone which was unsurprising. He asked how their family was doing and if they'd be back in the inn for a drink soon. It was kind of amazing to watch him work. She knew she would not be that good at talking to people. She had never had much experience with people before, much less holding a conversation, and Robert was a natural. Just how he remembered all of those things about everyone was impressive.

As he talked, he began to buy her things from each of the stalls they visited. From the first one, he got her a silver chain. It didn't have anything on it, but she thought it was lovely.

At the next stall he got her a tiny green and pink flower; it was probably the last one of the season. When she looked at him, her mouth open as a question formed, he just winked at her and continued talking to the stall owner. She decided not to interrupt or ask why he was getting her all these things, trusting he would explain when he was ready.

They went to two more stalls after that; he got a blanket from one and then something secret from the other. He made her go and stand behind a tree with her eyes closed while he finished the purchases. She held her new treasures in her hands. She knew eventually the flower would die which made her sad to think about. But she ran the small chain necklace through her fingers, happy to have something to remember this day by.

"Hello Florence!"

She jumped, heart pounding as she looked around, wondering who had recognized her. Not seeing anyone nearby, she looked up. A pointy red face sat on a low branch above her.

"Hello there," she said, smiling at the red pixie above her. "What brings you here?"

"Two things," said the pixie in her high squeaky voice. "One, I have come to tell you that I'm leaving this place. Fall is officially over and so now my winter siblings will be coming."

"I see," said Florence, a little sad.

"Don't worry Florence! All of us magical folk are connected to you. If you don't see me again, at least you'll always have a pixie looking out for you!"

"What do you mean I'm connected to magic folk?" she asked, frowning.

"Oops! I've said too much!" said the pixie, looking embarrassed. "I can't tell you anymore right now. But I did have something else to tell you." She came down from the tree and hovered in front of Florence. "You are in grave danger." All the playfulness was gone from her face.

"What do you mean?"

The pixie put her tiny hand on Florence's knee. "Someone is looking for you. We are doing all we can to prevent this, but as the red moon grows near, so do his powers."

Florence's heart gave a stutter at her words. Could she mean the Baron? Before she could ask, the pixie started talking again.

"I must go now, but please, Florence, guard your thoughts. Don't let him in."

"Wait! I have questions," Florence started to say, but with a little pop the pixie disappeared. Florence stared at the space where she had been. What did all of that mean? Was the Baron coming for her now? Did he somehow know where she was? And what was that about her being connected to magic folk?

"Sorry to keep you waiting! I hope you weren't bored or anything."

Florence turned and saw Robert standing next to her, a cheerful smile on his face which began to fade when he looked at her. "What's wrong, Lor?"

"Nothing," Florence said, staring at where the pixie had disappeared. Looking over at him and forcing a smile. She didn't want to ruin their holiday together, but a cold feeling had begun to grow in her chest.

Robert had a bundle under his arm that she couldn't tell what it was, but it had a very odd shape. "Come on then," he said smiling and they began walking away from the town.

Florence was itching to know what was inside the package, but she knew Robert wouldn't tell her if she asked. She guessed she would just have to be patient, which was not a strong suit of hers, especially when she was excited.

He led her out into a big open field. There was nothing in it except for some wildflowers growing in the corner. Robert walked out into the middle of the field and laid the bundle down and began to unpack it.

Inside were two sticks that were polished and smooth, one piece of pale blue fabric, some string, and a green ribbon. He began to put the sticks together in a cross, then he tied the fabric to them, so it made a diamond. After that, he tied the green ribbon to the end of the diamond almost like a tail, and lastly, he tied the long string to the sticks in the middle. It was a very strange looking thing to Florence.

"This is called a kite," said Robert with a flourish. "Some of the children in the town play with them on windy days. Would you like to give it a go?"

"How does it work?" asked Florence, creeping forwards.

"It's pretty simple really," said Robert, taking the whole thing in his hands. "What you do is hold on to the string like this, then you have to run and then when the wind catches it, loosen the string and it'll fly up in the air. Think you can manage that?"

"Seems easy enough," said Florence, taking the contraption from him. She followed his instructions and, grasping the string in her hand, began to run. She ran around the whole clearing, but nothing was happening. No matter how fast she ran, the kite just kind of flapped around behind her.

"Let me try!" said Robert, as Florence handed the kite over, gasping only a little from her run.

Robert began to run, and Florence watched him. He was very agile, he reminded her of Ziv the way he majestically bounded through the clearing. She could see the muscles in his legs as they carried him over much more ground faster than she did. His reddish-brown hair looked redder in this light and he looked somehow magical in the open space.

After a few times around the clearing, he stopped running and came back over to her. "I'm afraid it's no good, Lor. I don't think there's enough wind today to make the kite fly."

"I want to try one more time," Florence said, taking it from him. She really wanted this to work, knowing how hard he tried to make this day special for her. Plus, she wanted to know what it was like to fly a kite.

She began to run and imagined a huge wind kicking up to take the kite into the sky. She felt a tingling in her hands, just like she had with the arrows. Just like she imagined, a huge wind came out of nowhere and she felt a tug on the kite. She kept running but gave the string a lot of slack, and then the kite flew up into the air. The wind swept it up into the open sky.

"Well done!" came Robert's voice from across the clearing. "You can stop running now! Just hold the string and the wind will do the rest."

She turned and did as he told her. The kite was soaring well above the trees and she had a proud and exhilarated feeling watching it, knowing she had contributed to its flight.

Her hands were still tingling but she wasn't really paying attention to them. Robert came to stand next to her and together they watched the kite soar in the air.

Florence felt herself being drained. She wasn't sure if it was all the running or what, but she was beginning to feel very fatigued.

"I think I may need a break," she said as the kite began to droop, slowly drifting back to the ground, the wind dying as well.

"Alright there, Lor?" Robert asked, looking concerned.

"Yes, I'm fine," she said, the sudden exhaustion continuing to grow.

Robert went to retrieve the kite and Florence sat down heavily on the ground. Her vision swam slightly but she held on to the ground in front of her. Slowly her vision came back and as she looked up there was Robert standing in front of her.

"Are you sure you're alright?" he asked.

"Yes, I just got really tired for a moment. But I'm feeling better now," she said.

Robert laid out a blanket for them to sit on and brought a basket she hadn't seen before. "In that case, how about a bit of lunch?"

He brought out a huge block of cheese, fresh baked bread, butter, fruit, and a canteen filled with water. Realizing how ravenous she had become, she dug in. They feasted until they couldn't eat any more and Florence laid back on the blanket, completely satisfied with the world.

She looked up into the clear blue sky and found herself imagining what it would be like to stay with Robert and William forever. She could go on holidays, learn how to cook from William, and spend time with Robert doing exactly what they were doing now. She knew it probably couldn't happen, but it was a nice thought.

"What are you thinking about?" She turned and saw Robert laying on the blanket as well, propped up on his side as he watched her.

"Well, I was imagining what it would be like if I was able to stay with you and William. I know it's probably silly," she said, realizing too late that Robert may not feel the same way. She shouldn't have been so blunt. She wasn't used to hiding her feelings and now here she was spilling them for the world to see.

She looked away. "I know it doesn't make sense and it's never going to work anyway."

"Why not?"

Florence's eyes snapped back to Robert's face. "Why not?"

"Why won't it work, Lor?"

She searched his face, looking for some sort of jest in his eyes, but he was serious.

"Oh, you know," she said, trying to play it off.

"No, Lor, I don't know. Why couldn't you stay with us?"

"I don't... I'm..." she trailed off, trying to gather her thoughts. Robert looked at her, no hint of a smile on his face.

"Lor, William and I want you to stay."

Her heart pounded. "What?"

"William and I want you to stay with us," Robert repeated.

"Why?" she asked, surprising herself again with her own boldness.

"Because we enjoy your company," said Robert, patiently. "We like having you here. We were going to wait and ask you together when William got back, but since you brought it up, I'll tell you now. Lor, we want you to stay with us."

It almost seemed too good to be true. She knew she was still waiting on Rasful, and she didn't know what the future would hold. But she felt like if she was with William and Robert, everything would be alright. The pixie's warning rang in her head. She didn't know what to do with that information, but she knew she felt safe with Robert and William. Maybe she could stay with them.

"I would like that," she said, smiling. He smiled back and she felt herself being pulled into those green eyes.

She was the first to look away, breaking the spell. She wasn't sure how she was feeling. She was happy, but something felt off. Maybe it was the fact that she may not be able to stay. She had never wanted something so much in her life, but she wasn't sure it could happen.

"Well," she said sitting up. "What happens next on a holiday?"

Robert continued to look at her, not saying anything for a moment. Just when she was starting to worry, she offended him, he said, "Next up is, going riding."

She practically squealed in delight. "I love riding!"

"Ah, then this is perfect," Robert said, smiling at her excitement.

Robert stood and they packed up their picnic making their way out of the clearing.

"You know the children around here really enjoy this toy. They make it in all different colors and the children get so excited anytime there is a super windy day. It's lucky that a burst of wind happened when it did, otherwise we would have had a flightless kite."

Florence, determined not to think about anything else that could spoil her day, asked, "Where did the kite come from anyway?"

Robert had finished packing up and began walking back towards the village. "Well, as a matter of fact, William invented it."

"William?"

He chuckled at her shock. "Oh aye, our William has more to him than meets the eye. He loves all the children in this village. They always used to complain when things got too windy. It would always blow over all of their toys so they couldn't play outside. So, William decided to give them a toy they could play with outside in the wind. He's actually pretty good with his hands, our William. He has made quite a few things in this town that otherwise wouldn't exist."

To say Florence was shocked would be an understatement. She had no idea William could invent things as well as cook amazing food.

"It seems as if William is more amazing than I thought."

"Oh, but Lor, you have to promise me something," Robert turned and looked her dead in the eye. "You have to promise that you won't tell him I told you. He would absolutely kill me. My life depends on your secrecy. Do we have a deal?" with that he held out his hand.

"Deal," Florence said, grasping his hand and shaking it. They let go and continued their walk. "You like to make deals a lot, don't you?"

"Oh aye," Robert said looking straight ahead. "You see there is something sacred about someone giving their word. I think sometimes people tend to forget that once they have given their word, they are verbally stating an intention. You can tell a lot about someone based on how they keep their promises. It's something so simple yet so complex. There isn't anything stopping that person from breaking their word. Nothing really, just the integrity of that person. To some that's worth more than all the money in the world, to other's it's not worth a thing. So, you see, making a deal with someone, or having someone make a promise tells you so much about them as a person."

"I see," said Florence, thinking it over. "But all of the deals we have made haven't really seemed that important. Some of them, in fact, seem a little silly."

"Which one seems silly?"

"Well for starters, the one we just made."

"Oh Lor, I am perfectly serious in that one," Robert said, looking at her with grave eyes. "William will kill me if he finds out I've told you anything. Even the children that he made the kites for have no idea he was the one who did it."

"What do you mean? How could they not know?"

"Well see, our William is a bit shy as well as modest. He doesn't want to do anything that will bring any sort of glory to himself. He wants to help make people's lives better, of course, but he doesn't want them to know he was the one who did it. So, with the kites, he saw there was a need. Children needed a toy to play with that would work on windy days. So, he created it, tested it himself in secret. Then when the time was right, he came to me."

"To you?"

"Well now, don't sound so surprised," he said, glancing over at her, a mock-hurt expression on his face. "I happen to be useful sometimes."

At Florence's eye roll he continued. "Anyway, I took the kites out to the children on the windy day. I showed them how to use them, just like I showed you. They were so excited, running all over town, getting the kites stuck in trees and on roofs. It was a little chaotic for a while. I ran around helping them, and William, he just stood at the front of the inn smiling the whole time. Taking such pride in what he had created and that it was so well loved. But no one will ever know it was him. At least no one else but you and I." He gave her a wink and they continued walking.

"But I still don't quite understand," said Florence. "Why didn't he want anyone to know it was him that solved their problem? What's wrong with them knowing it was him?"

"See that's part of the pickle that is William," said Robert, fondness and awe clear in his voice. "He doesn't want the glory, he doesn't even want people to know about him, that's why he hardly ever leaves the inn. You should be honored he left for such a long journey for you."

Yet another thing to think about. There was so much more to William than just the gruff cook she had originally pegged him for. He cared about people and yet most people didn't even know who he was. He wanted to help but didn't want anyone to know it was him. He was a strange one indeed, and Florence was honored that he had gone to such great lengths to help her.

"I want to do something special for him," she said with feeling. "Will you help me think of something he would like?"

Robert looked over at her surprised. "Of course, we can work on it now if you'd like."

"I'd actually like to go riding first," she said, sheepishly.

"Ah so the truth comes out then," he said, smiling at her. "Come on then."

CHAPTER NINE

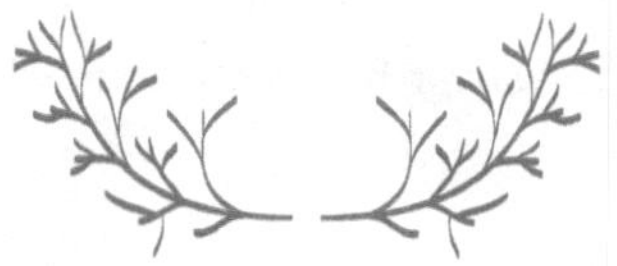

He led her to a big open space closer to the Inn. There were two beautiful stallions grazing in the field. One was jet black, and huge. The other one was smaller, a beautiful chestnut brown with a white streak down his nose.

"They're beautiful," Florence said, stepping into the pen where they were enclosed. Robert set down his bundle and joined her.

"Are these horses yours?"

"The black one is. He and I have been together for many years."

At the sound of Robert's voice, the black horse's ears pricked up and he stopped grazing to trot over.

"What's his name?" Florence asked, in wonder as the horse began to draw near.

"Duane," he said as the horse came right up to him, he stroked him gently.

"I've never heard a name like that before," said Florence, watching Robert's hands as he stroked his horse. "What does it mean?"

"The little dark one."

"He's not very little though," said Florence.

"No, I guess he's not, but he was when I first got him. As I said before, he and I go way back."

An immense sadness filled Florence. Oh, how she missed her horse, Beatrix. She had left her there with the Baron. She only hoped no harm had come to her.

"The other horse's name is Chestnut; you'll be riding him."

"Where did he come from?" Florence asked as Chestnut began to walk over, not wanting to feel left out.

"He belongs to one of the families in the village. He is a workhorse, so it'll be nice to give him a bit of a break from that. He is a wonderful horse to ride, I hope you'll enjoy him."

Chestnut came up to them, unsure of how they would treat him. Robert handed her half an apple to tempt him with while Duane nudged Robert for the other half.

Florence held out the apple with her palm flat, remembering how Beatrix thought her finger was a carrot when she was young. Chestnut came over, taking the apple from her hand. He crunched it noisily, and with her other hand, reached up to pet him slow and gentle. He didn't object so she put the other hand on him and gave him a good scratch.

"Let's get them saddled up," Robert said, pointing to a fence where there were two saddles and bridles waiting.

Florence went and got the saddle and began putting it on Chestnut.

"Well, I'm impressed," said Robert, smiling. "And here I thought I was going to have to help you."

Florence smiled at the compliment and kept working to get Chestnut ready for the ride.

Once he was saddled and the bridle was on, Florence saw Robert make his way towards her. Without looking at him, she put her foot in the stirrup and smoothly stepped up and over in the saddle. This stopped Robert in his tracks. "Lor, you are full of surprises."

She smiled, glad to have impressed him again and, with a click of her heels, she and Chestnut were off in a gentle canter across the small field.

Oh, to describe what it felt like to be riding again. Florence had the feeling of weightlessness and freedom somehow all bundled into one. Chestnut moved at her slightest touch and she was ready to make some ground with him and see how fast he could really run. Robert trotted up next to her, keeping her pace easily.

"Where should we go?"

"Somewhere with lots of space to run."

"Alright, follow me this way, if you can keep up," he shot off past the small enclosure with Florence following right at his heels.

The wind whipped her short hair out of the thong holding it securely and her hair whipped around her face. Oh, it was glorious being able to run like that. Feeling the horse's muscles move under her, feeling as if they were not two separate beings but one, reading each other's thoughts, each anticipating what the other would do next. It was a wonderful feeling; one Florence could only get while riding.

Robert was an excellent horseman. He was a black flash across the field ahead. Duane seemed to understand what he wanted him to do. It almost looked like Robert wasn't asking him to do anything, but rather he somehow knew what to do with being asked. Florence could only guess what kind of bond they had. She was curious though: what was an innkeeper doing with a horse as magnificent as that? Did Robert have some past he was keeping secret?

They rode hard; Robert almost seemed like he was trying to lose Florence. He took fast sharp turns, darting in and out of trees. Florence kept up with him, if not with ease, then well enough. She had never had anyone to ride with before. Her parents seemed to frighten the horses, so it was Florence's job to take care of them. She had grown to love them, and the stable became a safe haven for her. The horses on their farm always seemed to be drawn to her, and she to them. It was almost like she could speak to them. They understood each other, and she loved every single horse that she met.

Finally, her and Chestnut both panting, they came to a stop at a flowing river. Robert stopped next to her grinning like a schoolboy.

"Well, well, well, looks like our Lor can ride as well as he takes care of horses."

Florence grinned back, pleased with his praise. They both dismounted and took the horses' bridles off so they could have a drink. Florence sat down on the bank next to the running water. She was happy. Probably happier than she had ever been. Things were still complicated, none of her problems had gone away. But somehow being with Robert made all of her worries feel bearable.

Robert sat next to her, grabbed a stone, and threw it into the river. Florence counted two skips before it sank into the water. "Teach me how to do that," she said.

"Oh, it's quite simple," Robert said, handing her a stone. "What you need to do is look for a smooth stone like that one. Next hold it like this," he demonstrated by holding the stone out as flat as possible. "Next, toss it to the side of your body like this." He tossed it and Florence counted the stone skip three times before sinking.

She tried to mimic exactly what Robert did, but her stone sank into the river with a splash. Robert handed her another smooth stone and she tried again with the same thing happening. She huffed, and picking up another stone, felt the now familiar tingle in her fingertips. The stone skipped down the stream faster than what should have been possible. She counted ten skips before she lost sight of it.

"Remind me never to make you mad," he said, looking at her with admiration and a little wariness. "How did you do that?"

"I'm not sure," she said, looking at her hand. Why did weird stuff always seem to happen when her fingers tingled?

"Let's go back," she said, grabbing the bridle. "I think the horses have rested enough."

Robert nodded, not saying anything but still looking at her the same way.

They made their way back at a slow, comfortable pace; both of them were quiet. She wasn't sure what Robert was thinking but she was concerned that she might have scared him. If she was being honest, she was a little scared herself. She was trying to remember times when strange things like this had happened to her. For some reason she couldn't recall a time when anything close to this had happened.

"Have you given any thought to what you might like to do for William?"

"No," said Florence, glad for a distraction from her gloomy thoughts. "What does William like? You know, besides helping people and not telling anyone about it." She was glad Robert wasn't acting weird or treating her differently. She had been a little worried that maybe he would, with how quiet he had been.

His eyes sparkled mischievously. "You know, William really loves onions. You could make him a delicious dish just made entirely out of onions."

"Nice try," she said laughing. "First of all, William despises onions. I know because he won't touch them at all and always makes me chop them. Second of all, I'd be way too intimidated to make any sort of food for him. He's just too good of a cook."

"Oh, you're no fun," Robert said, pretending to pout. "Very well. Let's see, William loves artwork. Are you any good at painting?"

"I don't know. I've never tried."

"What?! You've never painted?" Robert asked, in genuine surprise. "Well, we will have to change that. After this we will go get some supplies!"

"Do you paint?"

"I have dabbled in my fair share of paints. Am I any good? No. No I am not," he said, with a laugh.

"I bet you are good!" Florence said, thinking maybe he was being modest.

"Very well why don't we put it to the test: you against me. Who is the better painter?"

"That's not fair! You've had practice, I've never done it before."

"Oh, but Lor, you have never seen me paint. I bet you are a natural. One of those people who picks up a brush and can paint circles around the rest of us."

Florence wasn't so sure. How could she be good at something she'd never done before?

They put the horses away and went back into the market. Robert picked out brushes of all different sizes, two white canvases, and paint that had been made out of an assortment of things. She was excited to see how bright the colors were.

They went back to the inn for a snack because Florence was starving once again. Then Robert took the paints and supplies and set up the canvases outside.

"So how do I do this?" Florence asked, excited at the idea of learning something new.

"There are several ways, the easiest is to pick up your brush and put it in the paint for starters."

"Yes, I figured that much," Florence said, huffing out a breath. "I mean what do I paint?"

"Ah, see, that's for you to figure out. I could tell you something to get you started but then where's the fun in that?" Robert grinned at her.

She rolled her eyes at him, feeling nervous and yet something else too. Her hands were all tingly again. She wanted to do well and sincerely wanted to wipe the smug look off of Robert's face. Hopefully he was as bad of a painter as he said he was.

She took up her brush and began to paint. It was a wonderful feeling of the brush sliding over the canvas. She didn't know what she was painting, she was just enjoying the feeling of putting different colors here and there. She was enjoying herself so much she didn't notice how much time had passed until it was getting too dark to see. Feeling the prickle of eyes on her, she looked up into Robert's eyes. He had been watching her.

"What?" she asked, blushing slightly.

He didn't look at all embarrassed about getting caught, he just said, "You look like you're in your element. It's a beautiful thing to watch."

She blushed again, unsure of how to take his words. "Well, it's getting too dark to see and I think I'm finished."

"Let's take them inside and do a reveal. I'm dying to see what you've painted."

They packed up and, keeping their canvases away from each other, brought everything inside. Robert lit the lights and started a fire in the dining room hearth. They set up their canvases ready for the big reveal.

"You go first," she said to Robert, her nerves coming back all at once.

"Alright, here is my masterpiece," he said as he turned the canvas around.

It was a good painting. He seemed to have a good understanding of color and technique. It was a painting of his horse. You could see the depth in the horse's eyes, its strong muscles. There was a green field behind him which was the same color as Robert's eyes.

"It's wonderful!" Florence exclaimed, meaning every word. "You were just being modest. This painting really is beautiful."

"Well thank you," Robert said, sheepishly. "Now I'm dying to know what had you so enraptured. Please show me."

Florence flipped around her canvas. Robert was silent for a few moments, just staring. She wasn't sure if that was a good or bad thing. She had never known Robert to be at a loss for words.

"Lor," he said, breathless. "I had no idea… Are you sure this is your first time?"

Florence nodded, still a little unsure of what his reaction meant. She had painted a forest, similar to the one she had grown up in, yet different. In the middle of the painting hidden behind the trees was Ziv. His pure white body completely contrasted the earthy forest tones. She also had added some pixies, different colors but in striking resemblance to the one she had met early that day. She also added a mischievous Rasful peeking out from behind a tree, grinning at her. She missed him so much, she felt like she had lost so much over the past few weeks, yet here she was gaining more.

She looked over at Robert, who was staring intently at her painting. "Well," she asked, feeling impatient. "What do you think of it?"

Robert continued to stare at the painting, still not saying anything.

"I know it's probably not very good. This was my first time after all. And—"

He turned to her, a serious look on his face for once. "Lor, this is the most beautiful painting I have ever seen."

Her mouth closed with a snap. She hadn't thought about what she was doing when she was painting, or thought of the outcome. But now standing next to Robert, she believed him. She hadn't seen him serious too often, so she knew what he was saying must be true.

She looked back at her painting. It was good, better than good. It almost felt like she could fall into it. She didn't know any techniques or tricks for painting, but it seemed like she somehow knew what to do. She was proud of her work and was glad she had done well.

"The only thing is, I'm disappointed really," her eyes snapped back to Robert at that comment.

"How so?"

"Well, you lied to me. You said you've never picked up a brush before, yet here you are."

"Wait just a moment!" she said, with feeling. "I never lied! This was my first-time painting. You on the other hand, saying you weren't very good and then wiping out a painting like that. You tried to make me look like a fool! You should be ashamed."

"Well see now," he said, hiding a smile. "I wasn't trying to make you look like a fool, you can do that on your own."

"Excuse me?" she asked, in a dangerous voice.

He laughed at this. "Come now all I meant was how little you know about, well everything. You don't need my help there, Lor."

She picked up the closest object and threw it at him. Which would have been impressive if that item hadn't been a napkin. It bounced off his head harmlessly and he began to laugh. Hearing his laughter made all of her anger melt away, and she joined in with him.

"You certainly are something, Lor. I did not see that coming."

"Clearly," said Florence, wiping the tears from her eyes. "Otherwise, it wouldn't have bounced off your head."

They continued to laugh together and yet again Florence was struck by how comfortable she was around Robert. It seemed strange that she had known him only a short while, yet she felt almost like she had known him her whole life.

After dinner they went upstairs and got ready for bed. "Are you sleeping in here again tonight?"

"Of course," he said, preparing his pallet on the ground next to her bed. "We can't have you having more nightmares when William is only one night away. I'll be here watching over you while you sleep. Unless you have any objections?"

"No, that is fine." Florence could in fact think of several objections, most of which had to do with him being a man and her being a girl. However, she was grateful for his kindness. "Thank you," she said as she laid down for the night.

"For what?"

"Everything. For today, for watching over me and just for being so kind."

"Of course. That is what friends do, isn't it?"

Florence didn't say anything to that. She wasn't sure if that's what friends did because she had never really had any. But she was grateful to him nonetheless.

As she drifted off to sleep, she couldn't help but imagine what life would have been like had Robert known she was a girl. Would he have treated her differently? Would he even have talked to her? She wasn't sure, but she imagined that he would and maybe they could be together in a way that was more than friends. She knew it couldn't ever happen. For now she would just have to imagine what that could be like.

It was dark. Florence couldn't tell if she was up or down, it was pitch black all around her. She held onto her knees for support, just to feel something real. Suddenly there was a light. Harsh and bright, only shining on her. She couldn't see past herself, if she was in a room or outside. She could see she was standing on something smooth and black. Heart pounding she stood, unsure of how she got here.

"Hello Florence."

Her blood ran cold at the sound of his voice. It was the Baron who came into her circle of light, smiling in a pleasant manner.

She didn't say anything. She held her ground, waiting for him to speak.

"You have been hiding from me like a little mouse. Hiding away in a hole that I haven't been able to find. Until now."

"What do you mean?" she asked, heart pounding wildly in her chest.

"Ah, she speaks," he said, beginning to circle her. She turned with him, always keeping him in her sight, never letting him get behind her. "Well my little mouse, it seems you have been careless."

"Careless? In what way?"

He stopped walking. "I know where you are."

Her heart almost seemed to stop. "You do?" she asked, trying not to sound panicked.

He smiled, seeing right through her. "I do."

"How?"

"You have given everything away. I have my ways of tracking you. See we are bonded in a way that you couldn't begin to understand. But thanks to you not being careful, now I know where you are."

She felt like she couldn't breathe. Was he lying to her? How could he possibly know where she was? And what did he mean she had been careless?

"Well, I should be going. I've got quite a bit of distance to travel," he said, turning his back on her and beginning to walk away. "Oh, and Florence? I'll be seeing you soon, little mouse."

He faded into the inky blackness in front of her. She didn't know where he went or if he would be popping out again in front of her somewhere, so she began to do a slow turn, continuing to move.

Then, she heard a strange noise. It was too quiet to make out at first, but as she listened it began to grow louder. It was odd, almost like a waterfall or a very quiet applause. Familiar yet different.

The sound was growing louder and louder. She was beginning to go mad; she couldn't tell where the sound was coming from. It sounded like it was all around her, digging into her brain.

The sound grew to a climax and then stopped. All she could hear was her own heart pounding and her ragged breaths. Peering through the darkness, she could just make out something moving, just outside her range of vision. It finally broke from the darkness and came into the light. It was a bug; the front half of its body was red which slowly faded into the black of its back half, which curved into a set of nasty looking pincers. It had glowing red eyes and long pointed legs that were carrying it closer to her. It had ridges all the way down its body and was roughly the size of her thumb. Without thinking about it, she squashed it with her booted foot. It ceased moving and lay still, making a huge mess on the floor.

"You're going to have to do better than that!" she shouted, into the air.

After the words had left her lips she saw a set of glowing red eyes in front of her, piercing through the darkness. These were answered by two more to her left and two more to her right. The eyes kept popping up and as she turned in horror, she saw there were thousands of them.

The bugs began to scuttle into the light one after another. She frantically tried to kill them but there were too many. They just kept coming and soon they were crawling up her legs and arms. She screamed in fear and pain, thrashing around, trying to get them off of her as their pincers sunk into her skin. She heard the Baron's laughter echoing around her.

Her eyes flew open, and she looked straight into Robert's eyes. He stood over her, shaking her awake.

"My god," Robert said, taking one of her arms in his hand. It was covered in blood, wounds from the pincers of the bugs in her dream.

She began sobbing in fear and pain. She felt hysterical as Robert continued to check her for wounds. Her shirt had been soaked through with blood and sweat.

He picked her up and gently placed her on the floor. She was shaking and sobbing, unable to get control of herself. He was searching her bed, pulling off the bloodied sheets and shaking them out. He came to the mattress and did the same thing.

When he couldn't seem to find anything, he came over to her and took her arm, turning it and looking at the damage. It could have been worse, but it was bleeding along with her other arm and her legs. He looked at her head and began shaking out her hair. She was confused at what he was doing but she let him. She didn't care what he did to her at this point. She was too shaken up to know what was going on.

He began to turn away from her, but she reached out her arm and grabbed his hand. "Please," she said, in a ragged whisper between sobs. "Please don't leave me."

He nodded and picked her up again, he took her to the kitchen. He placed her on the counter and began dressing her many wounds. The punctures seemed to be confined to her arms and legs. There weren't any on her face or torso. The wounds went all the way up to her shoulders on her arms. He started wiping off the blood and bandaging her with a tenderness she hadn't seen from him before. When that was done, he started at her feet and began working his way up her legs, cleaning the wounds and wrapping them in bandages. She saw him pause as he got to her knee, the muscles working in his jaw as he continued up her leg. She began to back away on the counter and opened her mouth to speak when he held up a hand in surrender.

"I'm not going to do anything to you," he said, in a tone you would use on a wounded animal. "Please trust me."

He continued working up her leg. It seemed like he would keep going forever and Florence began to worry. His touch was gentle and soft, she would have been enjoying herself quite a lot if it hadn't been riddled with pain. The marks stopped midway up her thigh; she thought she saw Robert sigh in relief when they stopped.

Tears continued to fall from her eyes, but she couldn't stop them. Robert finished up quickly and looked up at her.

"I'm not going to ask for an explanation," he said, softly. "Though I'm not going to pretend I don't want to know what is going on. I want you to know you can trust me."

"It's not about me not trusting you," Florence said, in a shaky voice.

"Then what is it about?" Robert asked, standing and moving closer.

She was quiet for a moment, trying to gather her thoughts. It was difficult with him standing so close. "I—" she broke off, looking for the right words. "I don't want to put you in danger."

"Ah, but you see," he said, moving in even closer, "I'm up for a little bit of danger."

"Not like this," she said, through her tears. "Look what's happened. Look what he's done," she said, holding out her bandaged arms as proof.

He looked at them carefully and then met her gaze. "As I've said, I'm up for a little danger."

As he looked at her, she almost told him everything right then and there. Why she was running, that she was actually a girl, that she had feelings for him.

She realized as soon as she thought it that it was true. She was beginning to fall in love with Robert and she didn't know what to do about it. That scared her almost more than the threats of the Baron.

She nodded, trying to decide what of the truth she should tell him. She was still crying, tiny sobs still hiccupping in her throat.

"Why don't I make us some tea?" he asked, turning away from her. "I'll give you a moment to collect yourself."

He turned and began busying himself in the kitchen. A delicious smell began wafting in towards her and she breathed it in. The scent helped calm her nerves and she was distracted enough that she was able to calm down.

A few minutes later, Robert handed her a mug. It was steaming but it looked nothing like tea. "What is this?" she asked, trying to decipher what it was she was holding. It looked very odd, being a dark brown color, but smelled amazing. It had a scent she couldn't quite place but she knew she had smelled it before.

"It's a drink that was in my family when I was a boy. My mother used to make it for me."

She blew on it and gingerly took a sip. Rich melted chocolate filled her mouth and rested in a delicious way on her tongue. She groaned a little in pure pleasure. It was hot and there was another underlying flavor she couldn't place.

"It has lavender in it," said Robert, seeming to read her thoughts as he took a sip of his own cup. "For your nerves."

"Thank you," she said, touched again by his thoughtfulness. She took another sip and let it rest on her tongue, enjoying the pleasure of drinking it. Holding her cup closer to her face, she began, "For your kindness, I feel you deserve some sort of explanation," she took a breath, gathering her thoughts. "I can't tell you everything, but I will tell you what I can."

Robert nodded, seeming to understand. He didn't look like he was impatient. He just waited for her to continue.

"I have been threatened," she said, slowly. "I had to run away because there is a man who wants me. I'm not entirely sure what he will do if he finds me. He's very powerful. I fear he will stop at nothing to find me." She looked down into her cup, shaking as the tears fell again. "I've been having dreams about him, and the things that happen in those dreams come true. The first time I dreamed there was a fire and my feet were burned. And then last night I dreamed about bugs." She shuttered the memory, still so fresh. "There were thousands of them, crawling all over me and pinching me with their pincers. I fear he's getting closer to finding me. I feel so trapped."

She heard Robert push off the counter and come over to her. His shadow blocked out some of the candlelight. He gently took her chin in his hand, tipping her head back to look at him. "I'm not going to let that happen. You are not trapped. You are safe."

She began crying in earnest again, not with fear but with relief. She had kept all these feelings inside of her for so long. If she could just stay with him and William, maybe everything would be alright. Maybe the Baron was bluffing. After all, it was only a dream.

"Oh Robert, I already lost so much. I feel like I've lost everything."

He took the cup from her hands and placed it to the side. Moving with slow measured movements, he wrapped his arms around her, holding her against his chest. She settled into his embrace, listening to his strong heartbeat beneath her ear. He didn't try to stop her, he just let her cry until all of her tears had dried up. Yet he still continued to hold her, his arms protecting and comforting her. They stayed like that until the dawn had broken, then he pulled back looking deep into her eyes. "It's going to be alright."

She took comfort in his words and wished she could believe him.

CHAPTER TEN

William was due back any moment. Robert wasn't sure of the exact time he'd be back, but he knew William didn't like to doddle. Florence was cleaning the kitchen, trying to make it spotless for William's return. The only problem was, she had to keep taking breaks. She was aching all over, and though Robert insisted that the wounds she had gotten from the bugs weren't poisons, she still felt weak.

She had put a cloth over her painting which she was both nervous and excited about, hoping that it was good enough to impress him. She wasn't sure why but she really wanted to get his approval. For once in her life there were two men whom she deeply cared about, and who cared about her. At least after what Robert said yesterday, it sounded like they did. She wanted to impress them and gain their approval, not for too selfish of a reason, but because she cared about them.

She finished cleaning just as the backdoor opened. There he was. It seemed like a lifetime ago since she had seen him but in reality, it had been two days. His stocky frame filled the doorway and as he squeezed in, he took a look around.

"Well, it looks spotless in here," he said with approval.

Florence beamed at him, happy that her hard work had paid off. He looked dusty and tired but alert which was why the slight smile he had on his face faded as he looked at her.

He came over to her in three quick strides. "What happened?" he asked, bending down and holding one of her bandaged arms in his large hands.

"Oh, well, I had another nightmare last night."

His eyes flashed to her. "You did?"

"Yes, but it was alright because Robert slept with me."

"He did, did he?" said William, in a dangerous voice. Right as he said that Robert himself strode into the kitchen a look of greeting on his face. He stopped short when he saw William's face. "Oi what's wrong with you?" he asked, not moving another step closer.

"Lor has just been telling me where you spent the last two nights," said William, in a low voice.

"It's not like that!" Florence exclaimed, feeling the heat creep up the back of her neck. "He slept on the floor."

William wasn't listening to her. He began to advance on Robert while Robert retreated, "You were in the same room with Lor?"

"Come now, old Willy," said Robert, a good-natured smile on his face as he tried to keep the counter in between them. "Nothing happened."

"I leave for two days. Two. And when I come back, I find out this?"

"What's the big deal?" Robert asked, dancing out of William's reach. "Lor is a boy after all. I mean it's not like he's a girl, is he?"

William stopped short at this, giving Robert a chance to put more space between them. Florence's heart was pounding, hoping against hope that they didn't get any closer to the truth.

"Right," William said, slowly. "But that doesn't mean you should sleep in the same room together."

"What would you have had me do, William?" Robert asked, in complete seriousness. "Lor wasn't going to sleep until you came back."

"Well then Lor did sleep and look what happened?" William said, pointing at Florence. "Look at those bandages! Some job you did looking out for Lor."

"I have something to say," Florence said, loud enough for them to hear her. They both turned to her, and she had to fight to keep a straight face at how similar they looked. "Now I have your attention, I would like to say I am a grown person. I can make my own decisions, and though I am truly touched that you care so much for my safety William, if I didn't want Robert there, I would have made him leave. I had all the say in this matter and like Robert said, I was afraid to sleep. Yes, I did end up getting hurt regardless, but I felt safe with Robert in the room. Now I am hungry, as I'm sure you are too after being on the road. So, I am going to make dinner with Robert, and you are going to go upstairs and get cleaned up. Are we settled?"

Both men looked at each other and then back at her and nodded their agreement. "Good, then let's get to it," she said, making a shooing motion with her hands.

They listened to her and twenty minutes later they were sitting in the dining room around three bowls of steaming stew.

"How was your trip, William?" Florence asked, as they began to eat.

"It was fine. Not too much to speak of," he said, but he continued to glare at Robert. He hadn't stopped since he came down from his bath.

Robert, for his own part, was looking anywhere other than William's face. He looked at the ceiling and the walls, even at Florence, but he was avoiding William's eyes. In fact, he was almost acting like William wasn't there at all.

"Alright that's enough," Florence said, making her voice stern. Both men looked at her again in the same way, heads cocked to the side, a confused expression on their faces.

"Pardon?" asked Robert, confused.

"You two need to make up. You're being ridiculous."

"What's ridiculous is Robert," William jabbed his spoon in Robert's direction as he said his name. "Making this inn his personal plaything. He hasn't paid attention to any of the rules that were set in place. I leave for two days, and when I come back, things are in shambles."

"We didn't burn down the inn, old boy," said Robert, finally acknowledging William's presence in the room.

"Oh, well, that's about the only thing you didn't do! All you did was sleep around and be lazy! At least the inn was generating income while I was gone."

"About that," said Robert, starting to look nervous now.

"What about it?" William growled, beginning to rise up from his chair.

Robert visibly gulped. "Now see what happened, little Lor here wasn't feeling his best. He hadn't slept in days so I decided to close the inn—"

"Close the inn?" William thundered. "What do you bloody mean, close the inn?"

"Robert, you didn't tell William?" Florence asked, aghast.

"Oh no, not you too, Lor," said Robert, exasperated. "I thought you were on my side!"

"I'm not on anyone's side! I just thought William knew what you were doing! Hang on," said Florence, realization dawning on her. "I thought you both owned this inn."

William stopped advancing and Robert turned to look at her. "Oh no, definitely not," said Robert. "Can you really see me owning an inn?"

"What gave you that idea?" Asked William, freezing where he stood.

"Well, I just assumed since both of you were here working that you owned it together."

Robert and William looked at each other and both burst out laughing. Florence had no idea what was so funny but she was glad at least they were getting along again.

Robert was gasping for breath and William had returned to his chair for support.

"Can you imagine me owning an inn?" said Robert, between laughs.

"You would never be open! Your meals would be terrible." William laughed along with him.

"Wait, I don't understand," said Florence trying to keep up.

William turned to her and said, "I own this inn, Lor. Despite Robert's greatest intention otherwise, it's running quite smoothly."

"But you never come out of the kitchen," Florence said, her head spinning.

"No, I suppose that's true," said William, giving her one of his small smiles. "But that's simply because I choose not to. I really am a better cook than I am an innkeeper. Just having a restaurant doesn't make enough money, though. So, I had to get creative. Thus, the inn was born."

"But Robert told me the name was his idea."

"Ah, yes, that it was. As I said I really am better in the kitchen. I had just called the inn, The Inn. Not a particularly clever name, so when Robert came aboard, he suggested we change it. I wasn't going to. The name was fine. Simple. Told you exactly what you needed to know. But Robert eventually convinced me to change it. And I'm glad he did."

"Why is that?" asked Florence.

"It gives people something to talk to him about. He's able to make a connection with people that he still would have done somehow, but it just makes it easier. Also, it gives people a place to come back to. If we were just called The Inn, people wouldn't know what inn they were talking about, if others tried to recommend a place to stay. Now if that inn had a name, and a good story that goes with it, that's how we get more customers."

"So would you say that's a good thing Robert is here?" asked Florence, in a timid voice.

William shot her a look, and then one at Robert who tried his best to look uninterested and innocent. He wasn't doing that well.

William chuckled and said, "Aye, I'm mighty glad Robert is here." There was a nice moment of peace where both men were looking at each other. "He's a good man, even if his cooking is awful."

"Aw you can't mean that!" Robert said indignant, the moment broken. "Look, you've cleaned your plate!"

"Nonsense," said William, stroking his beard. "You said Lor helped you make it, so that's why it's swallowable."

Florence rolled her eyes but was happy they were back to their normal banter. She had been worried when William had come after Robert. She knew Robert was a skilled fighter, but William had several inches on him, and she didn't want anyone to get hurt on her account.

When they had finished eating, Robert took the plates into the kitchen and looked at Florence giving her a wink. "Well," he said, unnecessarily loudly. "I'm going to go wash the dishes now."

"You do that," said William, in an annoyed voice. "And don't shout we are right here."

Robert gave Florence an exaggerated look which she replied by waving him on. They had made a plan for Robert to go do the dishes so she could present her painting to William. They both thought he might be less distracted if Robert wasn't around.

Florence walked over to where she had placed the cloth over her painting, taking William's hand to lead him over to it as well.

"William," she said, her nerves tight as her bow string. "I made this as a thank you. You have taken me into your home and business without a second thought. You've fed me and taken care of me. Now you've just gotten back from a two-day ride to get me something to help me sleep. I wanted to pay you back in one small way that I could. Here," she said, losing her nerve and taking the cloth off the painting with a flourish.

William stared at it, his facial expression unchanging. Florence was beginning to get nervous. He wasn't saying anything, wasn't moving a muscle. Did he even like it?

He stepped closer, getting a better look. After what felt like an eternity, he said, "You painted this?"

Florence nodded, too nervous to speak. What if Robert had been lying to her and William hated paintings? Or worse, what if the painting wasn't any good at all?

"It's alright if you don't like it," she said, trying to cover up her disappointment. "I mean I only had one afternoon to do it and—"

William held up a hand for silence. "Lor, art is something I take great pleasure in. I have traveled all around the world to study and admire some of the greatest artists in the world. However," he said, seeing her deflate as he talked. "I have never seen such a painting as this. Your use of color and shadow. The way your eye travels up and down around the forest scene. I feel like I can fall into it if I look too deeply." He continued to lean in closer to it. "Lor, it's lovely. Never have I had someone paint such a glorious picture for me. You have my deepest thanks."

He bowed to her, his eyes never leaving hers. Florence momentarily choked up, took a few breaths to try and get control back over herself. "Thank you, William. Your approval means the world to me."

He nodded, straightening his shirt. They looked awkwardly at one another for a moment, and then with the sound of a crash they looked over to the kitchen door. Robert was sprawled out on the floor rubbing his head.

"What happened to you? How did you end up there?"

"I was trying to fix this door, see it's terribly squeaky."

"Oh, likely story!" exclaimed William. "You were eavesdropping, weren't you?"

Robert stood up and looking offended said, "I would never eavesdrop. Unlike some people I could mention that are in this room."

"Watch it," said Florence.

"Don't listen to him Lor, he's just trying to push the blame off of himself."

"I would never!"

"Oh yes you would! Don't you remember the time that one customer was in the inn, and you were dying to know what her secret was?"

"That is a completely different story," said Robert marching back into the kitchen.

"Is it really that different?" asked William following him.

Florence heard their voices rising and falling in the other room, though she couldn't make out anything they said. She smiled, completely and utterly happy. She looked back over at her painting. She was so pleased that William had liked it. And she was happy Robert hadn't lied to her. She knew he was a trickster but she did trust him. Just like she trusted William. Maybe she could stay here, maybe she was once again safe.

"Lor," Robert said as he stuck his head out of the kitchen. "Come in here. We need you to settle an argument."

Florence rolled her eyes but went into the kitchen anyway.

Florence heard a knock on her door. It was later and she was getting ready for bed, feeling exhausted after her sleepless night last night. She opened her door and saw William's timid face looking at her.

"Good evening," he said, awkwardly. "I came to give you this."

He handed her a small package which she promptly unwrapped. A small metal ball about the size of a marble fell out. It had a small hook at the top of it to be threaded through a chain. The ball itself was smooth and had tiny holes that made a pattern. She couldn't quite tell what was inside the ball, nor could she make out any feasible way something could be put inside. Yet it rattled a little when she shook it. It smelled like herbs as well, something earthy and faint, something she had never smelled before. Not unpleasant, just different.

"Thank you, William," she said, smiling. "How did you find this anyway?"

"I had a friend that couldn't sleep. She was plagued by horrible nightmares, to the point that she was terrified to go to bed. One day she decided that enough was enough and went to see a healer. This healer was an interesting man," William smiled at the memory. "I went with her, skeptical of what this so-called healer could do. He asked a whole lot of questions that didn't seem related at all. But then handed her a necklace very similar to this one. She wore it every day after that and never had another nightmare again."

"What is it made out of?" Florence asked, looking down at it.

"I'm not sure. The man said that it was full of some kinds of herbs, but it was the intention he placed in it that will make the difference."

"What's the intention?"

"Light and love," William answered.

"I hope this works. I would hate for all of your hard work to be in vain."

"Nothing I do for you will be in vain, my dear," he said, quietly.

She nodded, taking the charm in her hand.

William cleared his throat and then said, "Now, it's best if you put it on a chain. It's not as easy to lose. I think I have one somewhere."

"Oh! I just remembered," she said and running over to her drawer she pulled out the silver chain Robert had given her the day before.

"That will do nicely," said William with one of his rare smiles. "Where did you get it?"

"Robert gave it to me."

His smile faded. "Did he?"

"It's not like that. He got it for me at a stall in the market. He must have known that what you were bringing back needed a chain."

"Yes, he must have," said William, letting the frown in his face pass.

"Anyway," he continued. "All you need to do is wear the chain with the charm on it while you sleep. It should prevent whatever it is that is causing these nightmares."

"Thank you, William," she said, putting the charm on the chain and fastening it behind her neck. "For everything."

William bowed again and, taking the door in his hand, said, "Good night."

"Good night, William," she answered.

He smiled again and shut the door behind him.

Florence settled into bed, hoping and praying that the charm would work, and she would have a good night's rest.

The next morning shone bright and clear. Florence got out of bed, feeling unusually refreshed. She looked at the charm around her neck. Maybe there was something to it after all.

She went downstairs to prepare for breakfast. As she was walking, she heard William's and Robert's voices talking in whispers. She didn't want to interrupt but she was getting hungry, so she quietly crept downstairs.

She tried to listen through the closed door, but she still couldn't make out any of the words they were saying. She put a little more of her body weight on the door, leaning in and trying to make out something. But as she did the door swung open and she fell into the room.

"Well, well, well," came Robert's voice. "Not trying to spy on us, were you?"

Florence scowled at him. "Don't be silly," she said, standing and brushing herself off. "I just stumbled a little bit coming into the room, is all."

"I hope it's not because you're tired," said William, looking worried.

"Oh no! It's not that! I actually feel pretty wonderful today. I've slept the best I have in a very long time. And it's all thanks to you, William."

"Well," he said in a gruff voice, "Since you are feeling better, how about helping Robert with the chores."

"Yes sir!" she said with a small salute. Just then her stomach gave out a huge rumble.

William rolled his eyes as she smiled sheepishly. "Oh, very well. You can have breakfast first then."

CHAPTER ELEVEN

Florence felt the bite of the frigid winter air on her face as she went outside to gather water for the morning. It was going to be a beautiful winter. She had just walked over to the water pump when she heard:

"Hello Florence."

Her blood ran cold. She turned around slowly hoping she was imagining things but she knew that voice. The Baron was there by the Inn wearing a huge fur lined cloak. He had found her.

"It seems my little mouse has found herself a hole to hide away in."

"How did you find me?" she asked, unsticking her vocal cords.

"Let's just say I have my ways," he said with a pleasant expression that was anything but pleasant. "Your disguise is very clever," he said, looking her up and down. "I'd say it's a good look for you. It shows off quite a bit more of you than those bulky dresses."

She shivered which had nothing to do with the cold air. This was her worst nightmare coming to life around her.

"Oh except for your hair," he said, tsking. "That is a shame to have lost. No matter I'm sure it'll grow back quickly."

He waved his hand in a circular motion and Florence felt a tug on her head. She reached up and felt that her blonde hair had grown back the exact same length it had been before she had crudely cut it. She gasped, terrified. If the Baron could do that without even trying, what else was he capable of?

He laughed at her discomfort. "Oh yes, my little mouse. I am a very powerful sorcerer. Did I not mention this earlier?"

He took a slow step forward and she countered with a step back. She didn't want to get cornered again. She remembered all too well the feeling of helplessness which was one she was not eager to go to.

"Did you get lost or something?" Robert had stepped out of the inn; the smile faded from his face.

"Now what do we have here?" asked the Baron, smiling. "Is that Robert?"

Florence's heart almost gave way. "How do you know him?" she asked, not bothering to hide her panic.

The Baron's smile grew at this. "What a small world! It looks like we have some explaining to do, don't we Robert?"

"How did you find me?" Robert asked, taking a slow step forward.

"Don't flatter yourself," the Baron said, in a bored voice. "I'm not here for you, I'm here for her." He pointed to Florence to further prove his point.

This was very bad. Florence didn't even know what to think, or who to trust at the moment. Why had Robert never mentioned this?

"Well, that's a different matter then," Robert said, still slowly moving forward. "However, it doesn't change the fact that you are on my property and I'm going to have to ask you to leave."

The Baron laughed at this. "Do you really think that's going to work? Haven't you seen me, seen my power? You of all people should know what I'm capable of, Robert."

Robert nodded his head looking away. "This is true, yet for someone so powerful, you've managed to underestimate me." He was in front of the Baron now which both the Baron and Florence who were so busy listening to him talk had failed to notice. He drew back his fist and gave the Baron a solid punch in the jaw. Florence heard the crack of bone hitting bone and the Baron, surprised, went down.

Robert ran back to Florence and grabbed her hand, pulling her around the side of the inn before the Baron could recover. They dashed into a door leading into another part of the inn, closing it behind them.

Robert dashed into the laundry room, not letting go of her hand. He grabbed clean clothes for each of them and shoved them into a bag. He also grabbed something else Florence couldn't make out and put that in the bag as well. Running back out of the laundry room he took her hand again and led her into the hallway.

They were just about to make it to the kitchen when there was a horrible boom. It shook the whole inn and knocked both Florence and Robert off their feet. Dazed, Florence raised her head and felt a horrible heat like she was standing too close to the oven. She looked over at Robert who shouted, "William!" He went to open the door but jumped back when he saw the flames that were curling around the door. They started to lick up the wall and Florence knew they would soon be surrounded.

Robert grabbed her hand again and began running towards the dining room. "No! What about William!" Florence screamed over the sound of the fire that was gaining on them.

"There's no time! We need to move now!" Robert yelled back, dragging her along.

The flames seemed to chase them as they rushed to the front of the inn. They stumbled out the front door coughing from the smoke that had begun to fill the place. Once her eyes had cleared from the tears from the smoke, she saw a figure standing a couple of paces off.

It was her mother. "Florence!" she said in a happy voice. "I've found you at last! Come and give your mother a hug. I've been so worried about you." She opened her arms towards her, inviting.

Florence almost rushed to her, but something stopped her. Something felt off. "How did you know where I was?" she asked.

"The Baron told us of course. Now don't be silly. Come here you've been gone long enough," her voice had gotten the parental edge that always made Florence feel like she was doing something wrong.

She looked over at Robert who was looking at her mother, his jaw clenching. He was still holding her hand which gave her the strength to say, "I have no intention of going back with you."

Her mother's face contorted. She had pushed her before but never like this.

"Is that anyway to treat your mother?" her mother spat; her eyes glowed a faint red.

"No, it's not," said Florence, in a calm voice that didn't match her heart pounding in her chest. "However, I'm not sure you're really my mother."

Just then there was a terrible sound of wood breaking. She and Robert turned to see the whole roof of the inn collapse on itself.

She turned back to her mother and saw something very strange. Her mother had begun to convulse and twitch in a way she had never seen another person move. Robert took a protective step slightly in front of her as a shield as she watched in mute horror as the figure that was once her mother began to change shape. She heard joints and bones cracking and shifting. Her mother's skin had begun to turn gray, and her arms and legs were lengthening. Her skull slowly became longer and where her nose and mouth used to be was now a snout similar to a dog's. She was beginning to get patches of fur all over her body.

Then the convulsions stopped. The creature in front of her was just like the one that had attacked her the night she ran away. This was the thing that had raised her. It's true form.

The creature gave a horrible howl, making Florence's eardrums hurt. Robert had taken out two short swords, ready to defend her. That must have been what he had put into the bag earlier. She turned and saw in horror that a second creature of the same kind had come around the side of the inn and was making its way towards them with the Baron.

The creature in front was slowly advancing, growling and snapping its jaws. "Robert," Florence said in warning, not sure if he had seen the other two behind them.

"I'm aware of them," Robert said, not taking his eyes off the first creature. He began to step back, angling his body to run parallel to the other two so he could keep his eyes on all three of them.

"Well done, that was very clever of you Robert," came the Baron's deep voice. "It's good to see you in your natural form," the Baron smiled pleasantly at him, but Florence felt Robert stiffen beside her. "Now, I'll be taking back what's mine."

"I don't think she is yours," said Robert, keeping his sword up. "As far as I'm concerned, she's free to make her own decisions."

"Ah, see, that's where you're wrong," said the Baron, still advancing. "She doesn't get to make the decision here."

"And why is that?" asked Robert, never taking his eyes off the creatures advancing on them. "Why do you get to decide what her fate is?"

"Because I own her," the Baron growled. "She is my property. I had her raised for a purpose and now it is time for her to fulfill her part. No more games, Robert. Give her to me or suffer the consequences."

Florence was desperately trying to figure a way out of this. This looked like it could be the end. Helpless and frustration swelled in her chest. The tips of her fingers began to tingle. She was desperate for some way, anyway out of this. She felt a strange energy shoot out of her hands as a huge wooden beam from the burning inn behind the Baron, began to streak towards him and the two creatures. The Baron, hearing the noise, turned just in time to get knocked off his feet as the beam fell on top of him and the two creatures.

Robert didn't waste any time and pulled Florence down the street at a dead run. He gave a long whistle and out from behind a house came a black streak, Duane. Without waiting another moment, he threw Florence on top of Duane and jumped up behind her. They galloped out of town at a breakneck speed. Florence clung to the horse, feeling an exhaustion like never before come over her. The last thing she felt was Robert's strong arms around her and then she blacked out.

Florence woke with a start, looking around wildly.

"Shh," came Robert's voice as he put his hand on her shoulder, pushing her back on her blankets. "It's alright."

Florence put her hand to her head trying to steel herself. Her hair was back to short. Was the whole thing with the Baron a dream?

She took in her surroundings. They were in the forest, surrounded by snow. She wasn't cold, because of the fire near her and the huge skin lying over her. Robert was leaning over her, grave-faced.

"What happened?" she asked, fearing the worst.

Robert sighed and ran a hand through his hair in a gesture she was beginning to realize was a sign of stress. "Well, I'm afraid the Baron found us." Florence sat up, struggling under the weight of the skin, trying to stand. "Take it easy. He's not here now, we lost him. You need to reserve your strength."

Florence's head began to spin, so she leaned back on the roll. "I thought it was a dream," she said, putting her head in her hands. "I didn't think he would find me."

Robert nodded, "I'm afraid he did."

"And the inn?"

"Gone," Robert said, heavily. "It was burning when we fled."

"Poor William, his home was destroyed."

Robert looked away at this and Florence got the most horrible feeling.

"Robert," Florence said, the urgency sounding hysterical in her own ears. "Robert, where's William?"

He was quiet for a moment staring into the fire. Finally, he said, "I don't think he made it."

His words hit her like ice water being dumped on her head. "What do you mean?"

He shook his head, trying to gain control of himself. "He was in the kitchen, Lor. That's where the fire started. I don't see how he could have made it out in time."

Florence buried her face in her hands, letting out a sob. William, who had been so kind to her. William who had traveled for days to keep her from having nightmares. He couldn't just be gone.

She cried for what felt like a long time until all of her tears had dried for the moment. She raised her head and looked at Robert, who had shed as many tears as she had.

"It's all my fault, Robert," she said, choking up again. "It's all my fault."

"You couldn't have controlled what the Baron was going to do. You couldn't have stopped it." Robert leaned over and took her hand.

"You don't understand," she said bitterly. "I put him in danger. I put you in danger! I should have left a long time ago. I shouldn't have stayed for so long. Then the Baron never would have found me."

"He would have probably found you anyway, Lor," Robert said in an intense voice. "He has his ways of finding people."

Florence nodded but took no comfort in his words. She felt like it was all her fault. And she didn't know how to carry the burden of what she had lost. She would never forgive herself for what had happened.

But there was something nagging at the back of her mind. Something she couldn't quite shake. A memory of something the Baron had said.

Florence took a deep breath. "Robert, I need you to tell me exactly how you know the Baron."

Robert heaved a heavy sigh, running his hand through his hair again. "Look, I know you probably need to know this, but I need you to make me a promise."

He looked her dead in the eye, making sure he had her full attention. "You have to promise me that you won't think differently of me after what I tell you." He held out his hand to shake on it. Florence took a moment before shaking his hand. What could be so bad he had to start with this?

She locked eyes with him. "I promise."

He held her hand a moment longer before letting go. "Once you asked me how I knew so much about weapons," he began. "As a young boy, I was always interested in weapons and fighting. I was like most young boys, I guess, wanting glory and honor for what I had done."

He sat back staring into the fire in front of them and continued. "The only difference between me and other boys is that I had some actual skill with weapons. I could somehow feel a strange energy when I held them. It was almost like they could talk to me, tell me what it was they wanted me to do. I know it sounds crazy saying it like this, but that is the best way I can describe the feeling. One of my teachers said I had something special. I instinctively knew what to do, it seemed. I kept getting passed on to more and more teachers until finally someone met with me to discuss my future. He took me under his wing and trained me personally. It seemed like I really could go somewhere far with him, and so as the years passed, I grew to love and trust him. When I had found out what he had been training me for, it was too late."

Robert paused, unsure of how to go on. Florence knew this was hard for him and didn't want to interrupt. She sat, without saying a word, waiting.

"He was training me to be an assassin and a thief. He wanted me to steal artifacts that had to do with the most horrible kind of magic. I didn't learn this until later because I just blindly did what he told me too. I've killed so many people, Lor. I don't even know if they were guilty or not of the crimes he said they were. Finally, the night came where he said he had a special mission for me. He said it was time to prove my loyalties once and for all. He had me blindfolded and took me on a long journey. Eventually we made it and he told me to kill everyone in this one house. The blindfold came off and I was inside. Slowly I started making my way through the rooms. There was something strangely familiar to me about this house, but I couldn't quite put my finger on it.

"I began to work. As I may have said, I was good at my job. I hardly made a sound, and no one was aware of what I was doing. My job was almost done, I had pretty much wiped everyone out that was in the house except for one room. I usually got pretty laser focused when I was working. I didn't really look around at my surroundings but there was something tickling at my subconscious. Something I just couldn't quite shake. It only hit me when I got to the last room. There was a little girl sleeping, she looked like she was about six with bright red hair spilling over her pillow. I had a brief thought that I had a sister who was probably about her age, and she had hair just like hers.

"The truth of where I was and what I had done hit me and I collapsed on the floor. This was my house from childhood. The people that I had just killed were my own family. I didn't even know what I was doing. I was so blindly trusting. I had done something unforgivable."

Robert stopped, overcome and unable to continue. Florence was shocked and disgusted. Not by Robert and what he had done, but by the Baron and all the lives he had torn apart. Tears began to fall from Florence's eyes, for all that Robert had lost and all he had been forced to do.

"What happened to your sister?" she asked, quietly.

Robert sighed. "I don't know. After I fell to the floor, I heard the Baron's laughter in my head. It was too much to take so I blacked out. When I came to, I had been living in the wilderness for some time. It was too much to deal with, so it was almost like my brain had completely shut down in self-defense. I had no idea how much time had passed, but now that I was back, I knew what I had to do. I searched and searched for her. I spent years, Lor, years searching. I can't say I searched in the best way either. I was desperate to find her, so I killed and tortured many people, trying to find answers. That's when I came across William.

"I had heard that the Baron may have been in a town called Torrine. I had stopped at an inn and sat down at a table. He had served me the most delicious stew I had ever had. Something about it had melted my icy heart. Sometimes food has that effect on people, I've learned. I told him everything. Everything that had happened, everything I had ever done. He listened without saying anything, until I finished. I'll never forget what he said. "Robert, you need to heal. I don't know if your sister is alive or dead, but do you think this is the right way to find her? What makes you different than the Baron if you use the same methods as him?"

"It stopped me in my tracks. I did need healing, I needed to step away from all the killing and torture. It was time to figure out who I was without all of that. So, I stayed. I put the weapons in a chest in the woods and started learning the craft of running an inn. William saved me. Now there are two people in my life that I couldn't save."

They both stared into the fire, overcome with sadness, mourning the loss of William.

"Now you know everything. Yes, I know the Baron, maybe even better than you. That's why he needs to die, and I would love to be the one to give that final blow."

Florence saw a hardness in his eyes that scared her. The Robert she had learned from and maybe even grown to love was not this man sitting in front of her. She wasn't sure what to do with this information, she didn't know how to process it. She didn't see Robert as a killer. If you had told her a week ago all of Robert's history she would have laughed. But the way he looked now? She could believe he had done all of those things. Which scared her. She was not scared of him, but of what he could become.

She tentatively reached over and took his hand. He seemed to snap out of whatever dark place he had been, and he looked over at her in surprise. "You saved me," she said quietly, looking deep into his eyes. "That's got to count for something."

He seemed to deflate, all the anger and hardness leaving him. "You're the only one, lass. The only one." He moved closer to her, seeming to see her for the first time since he started his tale. "Why the tears, lass?" he asked, softly.

"They're for you and everything you've been through," she said, new tears falling at his question.

He lifted a hand and brushed a tear off her cheek. He cupped her face, looking into her eyes. His hand was warm, and she leaned into it, enjoying the feeling. Then, he began to lean in closer, until they were mere inches away now. Florence knew what was happening. She realized she had been hoping this would happen since she had met him. Their breath mingled in white clouds in the cold winter air.

Someone cleared their throat behind them. They both jumped, springing apart and whirling around.

"Rasful!' Florence cried, springing up and rushing over to the little blue fairy.

"I hope I'm not interrupting anything," he said, grinning from ear to ear.

Florence felt her whole face grow hot at his words. She looked back over at Robert who was looking at the fairy, questions swimming in his eyes.

"I'm sorry Robert, his is Rasful, he's my childhood friend," at her words, Rasful took a bow, still grinning.

"Ah, well that clears everything up, doesn't it?" Robert asked, sarcasm dripping from his words.

She made a face at him and turned to Rasful. "I'm so glad to see you! What news do you have? And Rasful why did it take you so long to come for me?"

Rasful looked down at her words. "I wanted to come for you, honest I did, Flor. But I was told to wait."

"Who told you to wait?"

"My boss, Flor. I can't disobey him even if I wanted to. I had no idea this would happen though." He looked up at her, sadness in his eyes. "I truly am sorry for all you've been through and all you've lost."

"Thank you Rasful," Florence said, choking up again. At least it seemed like he cared about what had happened to her. She had felt so abandoned by him, but maybe it wasn't by his choice. "What happens now?"

"Well, that's somewhat up to you. I do think my boss would like to meet you."

"Your boss? The guy who has been keeping you from me and making all these decisions about me and my life without consulting me? I'm not completely keen on the idea."

Rasful shrugged. "It's up to you, Flor. Is there something else you had in mind?"

Florence wasn't sure. After all, she had been told what to do her whole life. First by her parents now by some strange fairy boss whom she had never met. She wasn't sure what to do or how to react to the fact she hadn't been given control over her own destinations.

She looked over at Robert. "What is your plan?"

Robert looked at her strangely. She wasn't sure what the look was for, but she decided to let it go as he answered, "I have nowhere else to go. The inn was my home. Now that it's gone, I don't really have any plans."

"I see," she said softly, Rasful looking between them. "Well, if that's the case then there is nothing holding you here. You can go and make a life for yourself, continue your search."

"What about you?"

"Oh, I'll be fine. Rasful is here so I'll be safe."

Robert snorted at this. "Right, the tiny blue man can protect you. Need I remind you, he left you at the inn with no protection or answers?"

"That's not fair!" Rasful said, stomping his tiny foot. "The person I work for has his reasons. I was just following orders!"

"And the other thing," Robert continued as if Rasful hadn't spoken. "Who is this mysterious boss he has? And why don't you know anything about him?"

"Enough," Florence said, holding her hand up to Rasful who was about to retort. "Look," she said, trying to keep calm. "I don't have many answers and it's true Rasful has been less than forthcoming with the information he possesses. However, for a while I knew nothing about you or your past, yet I trusted you."

"That was different," Robert protested.

"Was it that different? You withheld information from me about how you knew the Baron. Sure, you didn't think it was relevant at the time, but you still didn't tell me. Now Rasful," she said, turning to him. "I will need some information from you. I think this has gone on far enough, and since we are already in the mood for truth telling, let's continue."

She led him over to the fire and they all sat down around it, trying to keep warm in the freezing snow. Rasful sat and after producing some food for all of them, he began by asking, "What do you need to know Flor?"

"Well for starters, who is your boss and what is his interest with me?"

Rasful gathered his thoughts for a minute before speaking. "He's a bit hard to describe, Flor. He's a very powerful magician. The most powerful in the world actually. And as for his name, he goes by many. It's hard to settle on just one thing about him. I can tell you he's good, I can tell you he's a little dangerous but most of all he's the representation of love."

"Please explain: what do you mean he's the representation of love? How can there be such a person?"

"Ah see now things get a bit tricky here. My boss not only loves but is love. Love is a powerful thing. It can move mountains, stop waterfalls and perform amazing miracles. However, love is also as gentle as a butterfly's wing, as soft as a rose petal. It's thoughtful, it thinks not of itself. It's slow to anger and does not boast, yet it is almost proud. It's very complicated and intricate. That is what my boss represents. He is the king of this world and other worlds. He is a lot of things but most of all he is good."

"You have somehow managed to tell us nothing about him," said Robert frustrated. "What does all of that mean?"

Rasful shot Robert a look. "It means that he is complex, maybe even more complex than some people can understand."

"Alright, that's enough you two," said Florence, sensing a fight brewing. "What is your boss's interest in me?"

"Ah, see, this is an easier question. He has been watching over you since birth Flor. You have a special place in his heart, and he cherishes you greatly."

"If he cherishes her, why can't he get involved with the Baron? Why doesn't he step in and rescue her?"

"I feel as though you may be asking this for yourself as well. I know all about what you've been through. My boss does as well, and we are both greatly saddened by the horrors you have had to go through."

Robert clinched his jaw. "Then why didn't you do anything?" he growled.

"We did," said Rasful, quietly. "Who do you think got you out of that house? Who looked after you and kept you from starving when you went mad in the woods? Did you really think you just got lucky?"

Robert for once was silent. His eyes had grown hard and unreadable at the mention of his past.

"He does bring up a good point though, Rasful. Why doesn't he step in? Especially if he's as strong as you say he is."

"Well, there are rules. Even for my great boss as well. He can only interfere so much. He can send his servants to help you when needed. Servants like me and Ziv for example. Or even servants like William."

"William?" exclaimed Florence. "You and William have the same boss?"

"Of course, we do," said Rasful, impatiently. "Isn't that what I just said? He took people into his inn, he fed and clothed them. Everything he did was for my master."

Florence and Robert were both quiet for a few moments. Florence was trying to process all this, but she wasn't sure how to. It somehow seemed like she knew nothing about William at all. Everything he did in his life had a purpose, yet she had never gotten a chance to talk to him or really get to know him.

"Any other questions?" Rasful asked. Florence shook her head, too tired to do any more thinking. "Then let's get some rest. We should be safe here for the time being."

With that, Rasful began making rolls for everyone to sleep on. It was almost like he was getting the supplies out of thin air. One minute he'd be placing something down that she didn't remember him picking up. She was watching him intently trying to see where he was getting all this stuff from, when she felt Robert move closer to her.

"By the way, Lor, since we are in the mood for truth telling, why pretend to be a boy?"

She gave a start and looked over at him. "How long have you known?"

"It was pretty obvious from the start, lass. I mean that is why I gave you the room I did. I figured you didn't need to be sharing a bathroom with the rest of us."

Florence shook her head, rolling her eyes heavenward. "Did William know?"

"Of course, he did! Why do you think he got so mad when he found out we slept in the same room together?"

Florence laughed at the memory. But then her smile faded when she remembered what had happened to the kind giant who almost never smiled.

"What's your real name?"

"Florence," she said, looking over at him.

He held out his hand. "Nice to meet you, Florence."

She took it and shook his hand, "Likewise." They didn't stop holding hands as they watched the last of the fire fade. It was nice to have something to hold on to.

CHAPTER TWELVE

The next few days passed in a bit of a blur. Florence was still recovering from escaping the Baron at the inn. She found herself very weak, and they had to constantly take breaks for her. It was infuriating to go so slow, but she knew she shouldn't push herself or there would be worse consequences.

She also still hadn't decided what to do about Rasful's offer to take her to his boss. It wasn't that she wasn't curious, but there was something holding her back. Maybe it was that Robert was with her. She didn't know what his plans were, and she was worried that if she made a decision to go and meet the boss, that he would go a separate way. She wasn't quite ready to say goodbye.

Travel was hard and slow with just one horse. Even though Robert's horse was huge and strong, he could still only carry one person for any great length of time. At both Rasful's and Robert's insistence, Florence was the one to ride him while the other two walked.

The weather had grown fierce. It seemed like Mother Nature herself was fighting against their progress. The wind blew hard and cold, bringing with it snow and sleet. They all hunkered down against the wind, but it was no use. Most days they were worn out by nightfall and had only traveled a few miles.

They also didn't have a destination yet, so it felt like they were traveling in aimless circles. It felt pointless and Florence found herself becoming more and more depressed. She was worried about the future, especially if her future didn't involve Robert. It wasn't that she needed him to do things for her or that she was incapable on her own, even though she did feel that way sometimes. She had come to care for him, and she hoped he felt the same way.

But that was the thing, she didn't know how he felt, and she wasn't sure she could handle it if he didn't feel the same way. The not knowing was killing her, but so was the idea of knowing. She was also confused about what she wanted to know.

One evening when they had made camp for the night, she found she did need the answer to something.

"Rasful, what happened to my parents? When the Baron was there, they turned into these strange creatures, did he do that?"

Rasful nodded. "In a way. See, those creatures were that way to begin with. The Baron made them look like people and that's who raised you. I knew the people raising you weren't your parents, but I had no idea they were those creatures."

"You knew they weren't my parents?" Florence asked, shocked.

"Of course, I did, Flor. Why do you think I played with you every day? Not only because I enjoyed your company, but also because I was watching out for you."

"I see." Florence wasn't sure how she felt about this new information. It wasn't like Rasful had flat-out lied to her, yet it felt like a betrayal in its own way. It seemed like everyone was in the know about her life. Even Robert hadn't been fooled by her disguise as a boy. Everyone seemed to know more than her and she wasn't sure how to take that.

"So, you lied to her?" Robert asked in an indifferent voice.

She didn't like this new version of Robert. He seemed cold and unfeeling. Not the fun, energetic person she had gotten to know. Just yet another thing that had changed.

"No, I didn't lie to her," Rasful snapped. "I couldn't tell her. Can you imagine how she might have reacted if I had told her everything she knew to be true was a lie? That could destroy a child."

"He's got a bit of a point though," Florence said in a quiet voice. "How did you know how I would react? You didn't even give me a chance to! You just made the decision for me. That makes it hard for me to trust you, Rasful."

Rasful nodded looking down. "I wanted to tell you, honestly I did. I just didn't know how you would react."

Florence looked into his sad blue face. She knew he hadn't meant to hurt her and that he'd thought what he was doing would protect her. "I understand," she said, putting her hand on his shoulder. "Next time there is valuable information that, I don't know, could change my life, please tell me."

Rasful nodded enthusiastically. "I will, Flor! Promise!" he said, jumping up and crossing his heart in a swear. Florence laughed at his silly antics, glad at least one of them was acting normal again.

She looked over at Robert, who was frowning. He had been rather quiet these past few days. She wasn't sure what to do about his moodiness. Perhaps if she talked to him, he'd snap out of it.

"You doing alright, Robert?" she asked, coming a little closer to him.

Her question seemed to snap him out of his moody thoughts. "Oh, aye," he said with a smile that didn't quite reach his eyes. "I'm doing great."

"I'm having a hard time believing you," she said, timidly. "You've seemed a little off since we left the inn."

He looked away from her and stared instead into the fire. "I'm fine Lor. Don't worry about me. You've got enough on your plate without adding me to the mix."

She wanted to ask him more, ask him how he was truly feeling and to tell him that she did worry about him. She wanted him to talk to her, but if he wasn't willing to do so then there wasn't much else she could do. She nodded at him but continued to sit close, hoping against hope that he would reach out and tell her what was wrong.

⌒⌒

The days continued to pass, slowly turning into weeks. The lack of real destination made time pass that much slower. The weather was at least cooperating a little better than before. It wasn't fighting them the whole time now, though it was still cold and snowy.

Rasful seemed to somehow have everything they needed. When things got really cold, he would produce another blanket or animal skin, and when they were hungry he would pass around food.

"How are you doing that?" Florence asked one day after Rasful had produced bread and cheese for their lunch.

Rasful grinned, showing his tiny, pointed teeth. "Magic," he said, simply and continued to hand over the food.

Now that Florence took a closer look, it did seem like he produced the food out of thin air. Perhaps it was magic after all.

She had never given much thought to magic. It was something she had always known existed, but no one had ever answered her questions about it. Most people were somewhat afraid of magic users, and they were shunned by normal society. Often, they went to live in the forests by themselves. She only knew this because when she was a child, she had seen a magic user.

She had gone to the market with her mother, who she now knew was a strange beast parading as a human. She was trying not to think too hard about that. Anyway, she had gone to the market, and there had been a crowd around someone. He was tall and wore a long cloak with a hood that covered most of his face. He was dressed in the colors of the forest and was pulling flowers out of thin air. The children were ecstatic and kept cheering and asking him to do more tricks. The adults, on the other hand, had grown restless. They began shouting at the man to leave them in peace, and soon a riot had started. People were shouting and gathering old rotten food to throw at the man. The children, confused by their parents' reactions, either began to join the adults or simply cry in fear and confusion.

The magical man turned his back on the crowd and began walking towards the forest. As the crowd departed, her mother began to pull her away. Florence had looked over her shoulder to try and glimpse the magician, but he was gone.

Florence shook away the memory. She didn't want to think about her old life; it had all been a lie anyway. What she did need to decide was what to do with her future, and that was difficult enough without lingering on all her jumbled childhood memories.

She gathered wood with Rasful while Robert stayed behind to tend to his horse.

"Where did you get that Flor?" Rasful asked, pointing to her neck. She looked down and saw that her necklace had come out from under her shirt where she had kept it.

"William got it for me," she said, fingering the charm. "I was having really bad nightmares, so he traveled and got this for me. Since wearing it, the nightmares have stopped."

"What kind of nightmares were you having?" Rasful asked, suddenly serious.

"They were about the Baron. It was strange, though. One time I dreamed he set fire to the inn's kitchen and when I woke up, I had burns. Then I dreamed he set some bugs on me and I had bug bites all over me when I woke up."

Rasful had frozen in place. "Why didn't you tell me about this sooner?"

"What do you mean?" Florence asked, starting to worry.

Rasful shook his head and began pacing. "This is bad Flor, really bad. The Baron is growing even stronger than I feared." He looked up at her and said, "It's a good thing William got that charm for you. You may not realize it, but that charm will protect you from any of the Baron's advances."

"Why does he want me so badly? Why is he seeking me out?"

Rasful sighed, taking his time in answering her. "I don't know all the answers, but the Baron wants power. He is already powerful, but he is hungry for more. All I know is that he thinks if he has you, that will increase his power."

"I see," said Florence. "Then how do we fight him?"

"Is that the path you will choose?" Rasful asked.

Florence thought about it. "I'm not sure."

Rasful nodded, not concerned. "Let me know if you want me to take you to my boss. He will have a lot more answers for you."

Florence nodded and they continued gathering wood in silence, both lost in thought. As they made their way back to camp, they heard a commotion. They looked at each other, and Florence took off at a run, bursting through the trees.

Robert was locked in combat with a huge wolf. Florence had never seen anything like it before. It was roughly the size of Robert's horse. It was jet black with teeth the size of her forearms. It was growling and snarling, snapping its teeth at Robert, who was trying to fend it off with his two short swords. The wolf's eyes were glowing red.

Robert looked back at her and shouted, "Stay back, Florence!" The wolf took that opportunity to strike at him. Florence cried out in warning, but too late; the wolf had knocked Robert to the ground.

He lost his swords and with the massive body of the wolf on top of him, he was somewhat lost from sight.

Rasful rushed in and, with a tiny sword he had pulled from somewhere, he leaped up onto the wolf's back and began stabbing at it. The wolf cried out in pain and began trying to turn and snap and Rasful but he leaped out of the way which had given Robert a chance to pick up one of his swords.

It looked like the battle would be won with both Robert and Rasful hacking away at the huge wolf. But then Florence spotted something that made her blood run cold. There were five more huge wolves, their red eyes peeking out from among the trees surrounding them. Florence knew from her time in the forest that wolves usually hunted in packs. It seemed that these huge wolves were no exception.

Panicking upon seeing the wolves and guessing their intentions, she looked around for a weapon. All she saw was the fire burning merrily in the center of the camp. She knew, somehow, what she had to do. She felt the now familiar tingling in her fingers as the fire began to spark and grow larger. She saw the fire slowly licking toward the wood she and Rasful had gathered, igniting it easily. The logs, once ignited, flew through the air and landed on each wolf. The wolves' thick fur caught fire and they cried out in pain and fear. They fled, running in circles and crying out in pain, trying desperately to try to get as far away from the fire as possible. Robert and Rasful had finished off the first wolf in the meantime and were now looking around in confusion as the wolves on fire ran past them. Florence briefly noticed that Robert was bleeding from a wound in his shoulder, but then everything went dark.

She awoke to the sound of a crackling fire. She opened her eyes and groaned, her head pounding. She saw Robert sitting on one side of her and Rasful on the other. She covered her eyes with her hand, trying to gather herself.

"The way you both are looking at me, you'd think I'd died or something," she meant it as a joke, but neither of them laughed.

"Florence, what was that?" Robert asked with a worried look on his face.

"What do you mean?" Florence asked, not even trying to hide the weariness in her voice. She could feel a pounding starting in her head, thumping to the beat of her heart.

"Flor, you set logs on fire and sent them shooting across the forest. Do you remember any of that?"

Florence shut her eyes. She vaguely remembered seeing the wolves and knowing that Rasful and Robert were in danger, so she had wanted to protect them, but she didn't remember what happened after that.

"Slightly," she said, rubbing her forehead in an attempt to stop the headache before it started. "But I feel a bit of a headache coming on."

"I can help with that," came an unfamiliar voice.

Florence stopped rubbing her head and looked over toward the fire. There was a woman sitting there. She looked to be around Robert's age, maybe a little bit older; it was hard to tell in this light. She had on a black cloak, the same color as the wolves' fur, and beneath it she wore a dark green dress. She moved closer to Florence; in her hand she held something strange. It was a piece of bark and something that looked like cotton, which she held out to Florence. "Here, put this under your nose and breathe in. It should help get rid of the headache."

Florence took it but didn't otherwise move. "I'm sorry, but who are you?"

"Oh, sorry Flor, this is Lydia. We kind of found her after you passed out."

"What do you mean you found her?" Florence asked, confused.

"Well," said Robert, looking to Rasful for help.

"We were fighting that huge wolf and just as we were about to kill it, she sort of crawled out of it? It's hard to explain."

"Allow me," said Lydia, removing the hood of her cloak. Her hair was light blond, almost white, which stood out in stark contrast to the blackness of the cloak. It was in a long braid which draped down in front of one shoulder. "I was a great herbalist, which is what I love most in the world. In my studies I had come across a reference to a rare herb in a faraway land. I was determined to find it. You see my, well, my friend had grown very sick and the only way to save him was with this herb. Before I could go in search of it, I ran into a sorceress. We had a bit of a… history together from my past, years before the horrible disease took root in my village.

"I was prideful. I thought I could outsmart the sorceress since I knew her. But I was wrong. In the middle of the night while we were camping together, she called to the woods. From behind some trees came those huge black wolves you saw. I was terrified. I didn't know what was going on. She called the leader over and as it neared me, I screamed. The wolf basically ate me in one bite, almost like a fairytale. When I was inside the wolf, I somehow didn't need food or water, I was just stuck in an in-between place. I heard the witch say: 'Only when all the wolves are dead will you be set free.' I screamed and cried out to her, cursing her name. But all I heard was her laughing as the wolves set out on their hunt, and I have been in there ever since. When you killed all the wolves, I was set free. Now, as I was saying, those herbs will help stop the headache, so if you don't mind following my directions?"

Florence obeyed, and a minty scent filled her nose. It wasn't peppermint, exactly, but it was something similar. As Florence breathed it in, she did feel her headache begin to lessen.

"What happened to your friend?" she asked, through the bark and cotton pressed to her face.

"I'm not sure," said Lydia, quietly. "I'm don't know how long I was in that wolf. It could have been days or years for all I know. I'm trying to keep hope, but he was very sick. He probably didn't make it."

"We are so sorry for your loss," said Robert, putting a hand on her shoulder. Florence's eyes were drawn to his fingers on her shoulder. She felt a tightness in her chest at the gesture.

Lydia smiled at him. "It's possible he's still alive or someone else has found the herb. I guess I will know for sure only when I get back to my village. I'm hoping I can find my way, but I have no idea where I am. You can stop inhaling that now," she added, and Florence handed the bundle back to her.

"We will help you in whatever way we can," said Robert, with a smile. This was the first time Florence had seen him smile since what happened at the inn. She wasn't happy it was towards another woman.

"Thank you for your kindness," she said, smiling back at him. A heavy feeling began to settle in the pit of Florence's stomach.

"Robert, did the wolf injure you?" Florence asked, remembering something else from the wolf attack. "Are you alright?"

"Yes, it did injure me, but Lydia fixed me right up. She's a magician when it comes to healing."

"Oh, no, I've just done a lot of research," she said, modestly. Somehow that made Florence like her even less.

She decided not to try and worm her way into whatever was going on between these two. Perhaps it would all work out and Lydia would soon be on her way. It was worth hoping anyway.

The next day, Florence woke to the sounds of Robert and Lydia talking. She couldn't make out what they were saying but that somehow didn't make it any better. She wasn't sure what she was feeling about the new member of the group. It seemed Lydia hadn't gone off to find her herb in the middle of the night that Florence had been hoping she had.

She rolled over and saw them sitting together a little way away with their heads together. She didn't know what was going on between the two of them, but she didn't like it.

She sat up and began rolling up her sleeping mat. "Good morning, Flor! Did you sleep well?" came Rasful's cheerful voice.

She looked over and smiled at him. "I did, thank you Rasful."

"I'm glad. I've been thinking about those nightmares you mentioned."

"What about them?"

"Well, when did they seem to happen? It sounded like you only had two from what you told me. What happened the day before those dreams happened?"

"Let me think," she said, trying to remember. "The first time I had a nightmare, I learned how to shoot a bow and arrow. Well, I sort of had been practicing for a while but there was a weird moment where I finally made a bullseye. Robert was impressed so I did it a few more times."

"You made a bullseye a few times in a row?"

"Yes… is that unusual?"

Rasful scratched his head. "For the amount of time you had to learn how to shoot, yes. It takes most people years before they are able to shoot like that. No wonder Robert was impressed. What happened the next time you had a nightmare?"

"Robert showed me how to fly a kite. But I remember there wasn't any wind, and then all of a sudden a huge gust of wind kicked up and we were able to fly the kite."

"I see," he said, thinking hard. "Flor, did you feel anything out of the ordinary when these things happened? A strange sensation maybe?"

"Now that you mention it, there was. There was a tingling in my fingers right before the strange things happened. Do you think it's related?"

"I'm afraid so Flor," said Rasful, looking serious. "Flor, I think… Now bear with me. But I think you may have magical powers."

Florence was silent for a minute. Her first reaction was to deny it. There was nothing super special about her at all. But then something in her brain clicked;

magic made perfect sense of the strange things that had happened. She thought back to the first incident with the knife she had dropped and recalled how it flew back into her hand. These strange happenings only seemed to occur when she was stressed or upset.

She looked at Rasful, who looked back at her waiting for her reaction. "Maybe," she said, slowly. "But why is this only coming up now? Why wasn't I magical from childhood?"

Rasful shrugged. "I don't have all the answers, Flor. I just know magic when I see it and what you did last night, that was magic. Maybe that was how the Baron was able to track you."

She hadn't thought of that, but it somehow made sense. "I probably shouldn't do any more magic then, should I?"

"I don't think so, not if you can avoid it. You'll need to learn to control it and I may be able to help you there."

"How?"

"I have my ways, Flor. Leave it to me!" With that, he bounded away into the forest.

Florence watched him go, a smile on her face. She really had missed him and was glad that he was with her again.

Just then Robert looked over at her and, seeing she was awake, made his way over to her. "Good morning," he said pleasantly, running a hand through his hair.

"Good morning," she replied, in a soft voice. She had noticed that when he ran his hand through his hair it was usually because he was stressed. There had been a time at the inn where the dining room was completely full. She and William were in the kitchen cooking like crazy, and Robert was moving faster than she had ever seen him. He had run his hand through his hair to the point it was standing up at odd angles, making him look like a porcupine. Already she was missing her time at the inn. Just when she started to get used to things, there were even more changes.

"So, I'm thinking Lydia needs our help. I got a lot of information today from her about what her village looks like. We still don't know how much time passed when she was in that wolf, but she wants to go ahead and get back, even without the herb. Do you feel up to a bit of an adventure?"

She looked over at Lydia, who was sitting on the other side of the fire pit. Her pale braid was still draped over her shoulder, and she looked hopeful. Somehow Florence knew she was waiting on her answer. She was grateful to be given a choice, but she just wanted to be wherever Robert was.

"Yes," she said, making Lydia's face light up with a smile. "Let's go on an adventure."

CHAPTER THIRTEEN

They set off after lunch, heading north this time. Florence didn't have any clue about geography or directions. She had only been on that small farm her whole life, and then at the inn for a few months after that, so there was a lot to learn. She didn't know how to tell north from south, but Robert showed her an easy way to remember. He said if there was moss on rocks or trees that the moss always grew on the north-facing side of the rock. If she remembered that, she could find her way back if she ever got lost.

As they were walking and he was pointing out all of this, Florence saw something white in the corner of her eye. She heard Lydia gasp and Robert jumped back a pace or two. Looking over her shoulder, Florence saw Ziv standing there, looking majestic and blending into the white surrounding him. She cried out in joy and ran over to him, throwing her arms around his neck. She was so happy to see him that she didn't notice the others' reactions to her cry. She stroked his long neck and said, "Thank you for all of your messengers, Ziv. It's so good to see you!"

Ziv looked at her with his big brown eyes, seeming to understand her as he always did. She looked into his eyes a few minutes longer and then heard a coughing behind her. She turned, remembering the others who were now looking at her with questions swimming in their eyes.

"Lor, who's this?" asked Robert.

"Oh! This is Ziv, he's the king of the forest. He was actually the one who took me to the inn. He let me ride on his back and took very good care of me."

Robert nodded. "Interesting. He wouldn't have had anything to do with all the tiny white creatures I saw you talking to while we were at the inn, would he?"

"Yes, that was Ziv," she said, never taking her hand away from him. He leaned down allowing her to scratch him behind his ears. "They were bringing me news and messages from Rasful."

"How fascinating," said Lydia, taking a few curious steps forward. "What kinds of other animals would he send to you?"

"One time a bird and a rabbit," Florence answered, still petting Ziv.

Ziv inclined his head to Lydia, bowing slightly, but he kept his eyes on Robert. He didn't bow or do anything other than stare. Florence thought he might be as curious about Robert as Robert was about him.

"Why is Ziv here, Rasful?" asked Florence, knowing that Rasful knew how Ziv felt about things and what he was trying to communicate.

"Well… Flor I don't think you're going to like it."

Florence's heart raced. "Why? Tell me what he wants."

"Flor… he's been sent to take you to my boss."

Everyone was quiet for a few moments. They were all watching Florence waiting for her answer. She tried to take the news calmly. The truth was, she trusted Ziv. He had always looked out for her and seemed to know what she needed before she did. However, she didn't want to leave Robert. She was worried about Lydia and didn't want to leave them alone; they were getting a little too comfortable together, she felt.

Turning back to Rasful, she asked, "How long will we be gone?"

"I'm not sure, Flor. Sometimes it can take a few days, other times it'll take a lot longer. It depends on what my boss wants to teach you."

She looked up at Ziv and then back at Robert. Addressing Rasful, she said, "Do I have a choice in the matter?"

"There's always a choice. You can decide not to go. My boss doesn't force people to come to him."

She looked around, trying to decide what to do. Rasful, seeing her distress, continued, "I know I'm biased in this, Flor, but I think it's in your best interest to go to him. I don't know what the future holds, but I do know that you can use all the help you can get."

Florence nodded, and though she didn't like it, she made her decision. "I'm going to go, then," she said, trying not to sound upset or conflicted about it. "If whoever Rasful's boss is can give me some answers, then I'm going to meet with him."

Robert nodded a small smile on his lips. "I thought you might decide that lass. I think it's the right thing for you to do. I can get Lydia back home and then you and I can meet up again when you're done."

Her heart swelled at his words, and it made her feel much better. Just knowing he wasn't planning on staying with Lydia once he got her back to her village made Florence feel like she could float on air. Anything could change between now and then, but she would hold this memory in her heart and hope he still felt the same when it was all over.

"How will I find you?" she asked.

"Oh, you know," he said, shrugging, "I'm sure you can send one of your animal friends over to find me. I'll follow anything you send me," he added, winking at her.

She nodded with a smile, trying not to run into his arms for one last embrace before she left. She climbed up on Ziv's back and looked at Lydia. "I hope you make it back to your village. Thank you for healing us."

"The pleasure was all mine, Florence. I hope we meet again someday, and I wish you a safe journey."

Florence nodded, still smiling and feeling much more positive towards Lydia. And with that, Ziv took off at a run in the northern direction. She turned and looked over her shoulder and waved to both Robert and Lydia, hoping she would see both again soon.

They traveled through the forest for what could have been hours or days. Florence couldn't be sure because the light never seemed to change, but she found herself growing weary at regular intervals. Ziv soared through the forest on agile feet and, just like last time, Florence hardly felt any bumps.

At last, they came to a clearing in the forest. Florence dismounted and Rasful appeared next to her. "How did you get here so fast?" she asked.

"I have my ways, dear Flor," said Rasful, mischievously. "Come on, it's this way."

As they walked, her breath began coming out in gasps and she was growing tired rapidly. Her head grew too heavy to lift and drooped to rest on her chest. Her legs and feet felt as though they were made of lead, yet she still shuffled one foot in front of the other. The weariness was like nothing she had ever experienced before. Every cell in her body hurt and cried out for sleep, yet she walked on.

Just when she was thinking she had a handle on her exhaustion, a huge and fast wind kicked up, blowing against Florence and causing her to almost lay flat and crawl on all fours in an effort to not be blown off-course. It seemed like the wind had a mind of its own. Anytime she tried to move out of its way it seemed to follow her.

"Come on Flor, you can do it," said Rasful's encouraging voice. Oddly, he didn't sound like he was struggling, nor did Florence have a hard time hearing him over the wind.

Florence was sobbing with exhaustion, yet she pushed on and managed to find the strength to continue. She tripped over a fallen branch and began to fall. Thin strong arms caught her and as suddenly as it began, the wind stopped. Florence looked up into the face of the ugliest man she had ever seen. "Well, it's about time you got here." he said in a kind, deep voice, smiling. Her body hit its max and she felt herself slip into unconsciousness.

CHAPTER FOURTEEN

Florence awoke in a four-poster bed. The bed was very comfortable if a little extravagant. There was a strange pattern on the bed hangings, which matched the covers she was wrapped in. She sat up, trying to remember what happened. The last thing she remembered was seeing that very strange man. How she got to the bed she had no idea. She crawled out from beneath the covers, trying not to make a sound, and peeked out past the drapes surrounding her.

She found herself outside, which was a definite surprise. She was surrounded by trees, and as she listened there seemed to be a brook bubbling somewhere to her left. She got out of the bed and the grass beneath her bare feet felt like carpet. It was strange, when she had left Robert, she could have sworn it was in the dead of winter. Now here she was in what felt like spring. There were wildflowers everywhere, birds were chirping, and the leaves on the trees were the brightest green.

She had always felt at home in the forest, and even though she had never been here before, it somehow felt familiar. Stepping away from the bed, she began to walk towards the sounds of flowing water to see what was there.

Walking beneath the trees and ducking under branches, she realized she felt better than she had in months. It might have had something to do with getting a good night's sleep, but there was something else to it. Like all the tension she had been feeling for the last few months had melted away like snow.

There were squirrels running above her head playing tag, and birds were swooping and soaring. There were sleepy rabbits coming out of their nest with all their little babies running around. Florence shook her head at their silliness and continued on her way. The forest seemed to open up in front of her and there was the stream she had heard. The water was so crystal clear that she could see the stones and pebbles beneath the current.

Sitting off to the side was the strange man she had seen last. He was on a log by the stream, surrounded by animals of all different kinds. He was talking to them, and they seemed to be talking back. As she came farther into the clearing, he said without looking up, "Hello Florence. Glad to have you back."

"Back?" she asked, coming closer.

"But of course," he said, smiling and looking up at her. "All living creatures start here in this forest. It's only afterwards that they are sent into the world of man, that which you know as your home. However, this is your true home."

Florence walked closer until she was right in front of him. "I'm afraid I don't quite understand you, sir."

"And you may not until the end. Now, why don't we have a spot of breakfast?"

As he said this a beautiful doe came forward, balancing two leaves on her back. The man took one and handed it to Florence while he took the other for himself. Florence looked at the food with curiosity. It seemed to consist of only vegetables without any meat in sight. There were many different kinds of vegetables; some she could name, like carrots and potatoes, and some she had never seen before.

The man was watching her and wasn't eating. He almost seemed to be waiting on her, so she picked up some of the food and placed it in her mouth. It was delicious. Everything tasted so fresh, and she found herself trying not to wolf down the whole lot in one go. Once she had finished trying not to lick the leaf clean, she looked up. The man was smiling at her, having finished his food as well.

"I take it the food was to your satisfaction, then?"

"Yes, thank you," Florence said, a bit sheepish.

The man chuckled and took her leaf from her. Now that she was closer to him, she really could see how ugly he was. He had a huge nose that seemed to curve down his face. His hair was stringy, and he was balding in some places. He had warts and pustules all over his face. His lips were cracked and thin, covering jagged, spaced-out yellow teeth. His eyes met hers and she should have been embarrassed for staring, yet somehow, she just felt as if she knew him from somewhere. His eyes were strange. They didn't seem to stay one color for long as they switched from one color to the next. One moment they were a striking blue, the next a purple slowly melting into brown and then back again. They even seemed to be colors that Florence couldn't name, colors she had never seen before.

He grinned at her, showing his crooked teeth. "Well then, I'm sure you're wondering why I've brought you here."

"The thought had crossed my mind," said Florence, thoughtfully. This comment got her a chuckle from the strange man.

"Very good, glad you're thinking," he said, smiling at her. "First allow me to introduce myself: my name is Eli."

"That's an interesting name."

"I go by many names, but that is the one you can call me," he said, with a wink. "Now down to business. It seems to me you have a bit of a problem on your hands."

"What do you mean?"

"The Baron, for one. I'm afraid he seems to have his eyes set on you, my dear."

"But why? Why does he want me of all people? I'm nothing special," she said. Her voice held no bitterness; she spoke as if stating a fact.

"Ah, you see, my dear Florence, he has seen something in you that you have perhaps not even seen in yourself. You have a gift, and a powerful one at that. And the Baron wants to use your gift for his evil gains."

"Gift? What are you talking about?"

He leaned forward closer to her. "You have magic, my dear."

Florence didn't say anything for a minute. She had experienced some weird things around her. From the wolves catching fire to the wind suddenly kicking up when she needed it to, and all those things making her fingers tingle. Rasful had suggested as much. Maybe she shouldn't be shocked by this. She looked up into Eli's kind face, wanting answers.

"How?"

"That could be a long story, Florence. Magic came into your world back when it was created. Some of the magic that made your world managed to creep into it as well. The magic flows to the person it deems fit. It's almost like magic has a mind of its own, which in a sense it does. The magic can come to a child whose family has never known it before and can skip children in a family full of magic users. It's a mystery with no apparent rhyme or reason.

"Magic is different for each person who wields it. Some can levitate things, others can manipulate dreams, some work in different elements and yet others seem to not fit into any one category but can wield all kinds of magic. It depends on the person.

"Now when magic comes to that child, you can tell pretty quickly. Strange things will begin to happen around the child, things that can't be explained, when the child is distressed in some way. Parents tend to react one of three ways: they will either try and encourage the child to get the proper training and support them. They reject the child and send them away, or in extreme cases they try to kill the child, believing they are riding the world of one less evil."

"That's horrible!"

Eli nodded sadly. "I agree. However, there isn't much we can do about it. There is a choice to be made in all matters, so I'm afraid I can't interfere."

Florence thought for a moment, then dared to ask: "Which of the three reactions were my parents?"

"I'm afraid your parents were never given the chance to react. You were taken from them when you were barely born, a tragedy they have never gotten over."

This news Florence had not expected. "Is the Baron responsible for that?"

"Yes, child, I'm afraid he is."

"I see," she said, pondering this. She had always known deep down that something about her life on the farm was off. She had thought it was all in her head but now, after hearing this news, she wasn't crushed. She was relieved. She had always thought there was something wrong with her, but now she was finding out that there was nothing wrong with her. It had been her circumstances that were wrong.

Eli was looking at her thoughtfully, not saying anything. "Thank you for telling me this," she said in genuine gratitude. "So, you know who my parents are?"

"Yes, I do."

"Can you tell me who they are and how to find them?"

"I'm afraid that's something I can't do," he said, holding up a hand at her protest. "I can't just give you all the answers. There are some things that you need to find out on your own."

"But why? If you know, why don't you just tell me? It would save me an awful lot of trouble."

"Sometimes trouble is good for you. It teaches valuable life lessons that could not be learned without going through it. Would it save time and maybe even some painful experiences for me just to tell you now? Sure, but why would you want that? Wouldn't you rather learn the value of seeking out your own answers?"

She thought about his words, she really did, but she wasn't convinced she would want the harder way when she knew there was an easier one.

"You humans are all the same," he said, throwing up his hands in mock exasperation. "Always looking for the easiest way out."

"Aren't you human?" she asked, curiously.

He laughed at this, a big belly laugh. "No child, I'm not the slightest bit human. I have been around a lot longer than a human could."

"So can you change your appearance?"

"Why? Is there something wrong with the way I appear now?"

She wasn't sure how to answer him, or what to make of this man who wasn't actually human.

He chuckled again. "We have gotten off topic, my dear. Now my reasoning for inviting you here is to teach you magic."

"I thought I already had magic."

"Oh, she's a clever one now, isn't she?" he was smiling again. "You have magic, but you don't yet know how to control it. Just because you were born with a gift doesn't mean you know how to use it. That's why I brought you here."

"Why me?"

He looked at her thoughtfully for a few moments. "Florence, you are special. You have an amazing amount of magic for a human, and that is something rare. The amount you have would destroy another human, yet here you are, seeming as normal as the next. I'm afraid that this amount of power, my dear, comes with great responsibility. People will want to use your gifts to their own means. I don't think you want that, do you?"

"No, of course not," she replied. "But if I have had all this power inside me from birth, why didn't I started showing signs before now?"

"That is the Baron's doing again. He saw the kind of magic that you would someday possess, and he wanted it for his own. When he took you to that farm, he placed a magical barrier over it. That meant that no one inside the farm could use magic. That included him as well."

"But what about those creatures? They paraded as my parents for years without changing shape into their true forms."

"Did they? It may have seemed that way, but every night they turned back into the beasts they truly were. Enchantments are different, my dear. They are a form of magic that continues to work until the magician decides it's time to stop. It's powerful magic, that's the truth, but because it was cast outside the barrier, it could continue inside the barrier."

"I see," said Florence trying to wrap her head around what he was saying. "The barrier only worked for magic being cast inside the barrier, not specific spells that could be brought inside it."

"Precisely," he said, smiling again. "Well done. There are a lot of rules when it comes to magic. You see, magic always comes with a price. It's not something that anyone can do whenever they want. Otherwise, there would be no balance and the magicians would rule the world you live in. There is a check-and-balance system already in place with magic, and magic users know this system and rules well."

"What are the rules? What kind of price does magic ask for?"

"The price depends entirely on the type of magic. For example, if you wanted to levitate something, let's say a kitchen knife for our purposes, you could do it without too much trouble. You may feel hungry or a little tired afterwards, but because it was a small thing and for a short amount of time, it wouldn't drain too much of your energy. Now let's say you cause a fire to jump out of its pit and onto some ravenous wolves surrounding you. That would take quite a bit more energy and may even cause you to pass out."

"Does magic always use up a person's energy?"

"Not always," he said, thoughtfully. "It depends not only on the magic but the magician as well. Some magicians are able to do magic without having any sort of negative effect on their bodies. However, if magic is used, something does have to be paid. This could mean the loss of a relationship, memories, or the life of another being in extreme cases. These are just some of the side effects that can happen if you don't know what you are doing."

"What does the Baron use as his power source? I don't see him fainting all the time for the magic he uses."

"He, unfortunately, is a special case. He keeps humans around and uses their lives to pay the price of his magical use."

"He kills people?"

"I'm afraid it's even worse than that. Magic, as I've said, has rules. He can't just kill people by his own hands, or the price will not be paid. He uses others for that purpose, assassins that he's trained to do his bidding."

"Like Robert," Florence said, understanding dawning on her.

"Yes, unfortunately like our Robert. The Baron made a fatal mistake, though. He lost Robert, who was one of the best assassins he had. He was hoping to turn him into an unfeeling killing machine. That's why he had him kill his whole family. He wasn't anticipating what happened next."

"What was that?"

He smiled again, not unkindly. "That's not your story my dear; that's all I can tell you on the matter."

This seemed a little unfair considering all he had told her about the Baron. Seeming to read her mind, he continued, "But the things I have told you about the Baron are directly tied to your defeat of him. Robert's story doesn't have anything to do with this matter. Well, maybe a little," he conceded. "But that's for him to tell you, not me."

Florence nodded, deciding she wouldn't get any more answers out of him on the matter. "What happens now?"

"Now? Well now what you are going to do is explore, rest, and take the day to yourself. Tomorrow we will begin training."

She nodded again, rising to leave. "Before you go," he said, motioning behind her. "Allow me to introduce my son. This is Joshua."

From past the tree line came another man. He was tall, with broad shoulders. He had long dark hair and a beard. He wasn't particularly handsome, and his nose was a little off center, but for some reason Florence felt her breath being taken from her. It was his eyes, she realized as he came closer. Those which first seemed dark were in fact a multitude of colors, ever shifting and changing, just like his father's. She found herself at ease as he approached. It was like he had a calming effect and she found herself wanting to be near him.

"Hello, Florence," he said in a deep, comforting voice. It was like being wrapped in a warm blanket.

"Hello," she said, unsure of how to act around him.

"Well, you two have fun," said the old man, laughing. "Joshua, be sure to show her around."

Joshua led the way down a path that she hadn't seen before. It wasn't large by any means, and it had a winding nature to it. As they walked different animals could be seen coming up from the forest. There were rabbits with tiny bunny babies, all different kinds of birds in different colors and sizes. There was a doe and her baby, and Florence swore she saw a perfectly white lamb walking beside them in the trees.

She wasn't sure how to act or what to say so she just walked quietly next to Joshua without speaking. Just enjoying the beautiful forest around her. It was strange though. This forest was brimming with life, animals and plants alike. Everything was lush and green.

He led her to an opening in the trees, where there was a field which seemed to go on forever. Florence couldn't see the end of it, and she felt so small surrounded by so much open space. There were a few scattered trees dotting the field of what looked like barley and there was the sound of running water coming from somewhere to her left. The sun was shining and there was a slight breeze blowing, keeping Florence at the perfect temperature. She found herself smiling at the beauty of the field surrounding her and the utter feeling of freedom that grew inside her.

"I see you are enjoying yourself," Joshua said, pulling her from her thoughts.

"Yes, I very much am," she replied, looking over at him and smiling.

"What is it about this spot you find so enjoyable?" he asked, continuing to lead her through the field. The tall grass brushed up against her legs tickling them, which reminded her she wasn't wearing her normal dress and petticoat. Now that she thought about it, she hadn't worn a dress in months, which she wasn't particularly upset about.

"I forgot what you just asked me," she said, somehow being completely honest and unafraid of hurting his feelings or sounding rude.

He just laughed and repeated himself.

"I think the reason I find this place so enjoyable is the feeling I'm getting the longer I'm here."

"What feeling is that?"

"It's somewhat hard to explain," she said, taking some time to think before answering right away. "I think it might be the complete sense of freedom. I feel like I could run if I want to, and nothing would hold me down."

"And is that a feeling you don't usually have?"

"I guess I don't," she said, thoughtful. "I always had to do what my parents told me growing up, and then I had to run away, which led me to the inn. I feel like I haven't been able to choose what I want."

"And what is it that you want?" he asked in a quiet voice.

This question gave Florence some pause. She had never thought about what she wanted. The past few months' decisions had been based solely on survival. Now it seemed that this perfect stranger had somehow come to the heart of the matter. "I have no idea," she found herself answering.

"Well, perhaps part of your time here will reveal that to you."

She looked up at him and into those ever-changing eyes. It was strange for her to be alone with a man, a man that somehow seemed to know her intimately well, yet she had no romantic feelings towards him. What she did feel was curiosity and something else she couldn't quite place.

"Why am I here?" she asked, continuing to look at him.

"To learn," he answered, simply.

"I see," she said, continuing to walk. "What is it I'll be learning?"

"That's for you to find out tomorrow," he said, with a smile that made Florence feel somehow at peace. That was the feeling she had been trying to name since she got here. She felt, for perhaps the first time ever, at peace.

They continued walking, this time in comfortable silence. It was strange, but even though they had only just met, Florence felt like she had somehow known Joshua her whole life. She had never been given the opportunity to be quiet with those around her. Yet somehow this came naturally with him.

Beyond the field there was a trickling river that flowed straight through the forest. It didn't seem deep, so Florence immediately kicked off her shoes and went wading into the water. It was cool and smelled fresh, and she just wanted to feel the water on her bare feet and shins. However, after two steps the river bottom went at an incline and Florence slipped, water completely covering her head. The current began to take her downstream, but she fought its pull and managed to get her head above water.

Coughing and continuing to fight the current, she tried to make her way back to the shore. Just then, Joshua was beside her, unaffected by the current. He held out his hand and Florence clung to it, grateful for the help. A tingle shot up through her arm at his touch, which was a feeling she had felt before.

146

He pulled her out of the water in one simple motion. She looked up at him sheepishly, water streaming from her hair into her eyes.

He looked back at her with laughter in his eyes. "You need to be careful here, things are not always what they seem."

"Could you not have given me that helpful warning before I fell headfirst into the river?" she asked, with a playfulness in her voice.

He laughed, the sound of it filling her up. "Sometimes, people need to learn the hard way. Would me telling you to be careful have stopped you from going in?"

"Probably not," she reflected. "But I may not have gotten so wet or been swept downstream."

"True. But isn't having the freedom to make your own mistakes something you've never been given before?"

"No, I guess not."

"Well maybe I wanted to give you that chance. Plus, you were never in any real danger. I am here to catch you when you fall."

With those words he gestured in front of them, and they continued walking. As they walked, Florence reflected on what Joshua had said. While a warning would have been nice, it was also nice being able to make her own decisions for once, without thinking about the consequences. When she was growing up, she was so worried about pleasing her parents, and over the last few months she was worried about her cover being blown. It seemed that all her past decisions had been to avoid some sort of consequence, which seemed weird now that she had a chance to think about it. However, being here had somehow changed that for her. She felt safe here; even when she had taken a tumble in the river, she had never felt like her life was in danger.

Joshua led her to yet another clearing, this one filled with flowers. Their scent filled the air with a sweet, natural perfume and Florence felt a little dizzy with it. There were roses and daffodils as well as some flowers she had never seen before. They were all colors of the rainbow and Florence was happy just to admire them all.

A soft buzzing filled the air and as they got closer, she saw tiny bugs flying around. At least that's what she thought they were until one flew right up to her. It was a pixie exactly like the one she had seen in the forest when she was training with Robert. It flew up to her and squealed in delight. "Florence! See, I told you we would meet again!"

It was the same pixie! "Hello, it's so good to see you!" Florence said, sharing her excitement. "But what are you doing here?"

"I live here in the off seasons," she said breezily, as if this made perfect sense. "There are only so many falls happening around the world, so when they're done, I get a much-needed break and come here!"

"How wonderful," Florence said, meaning it. It was strange that this little pixie was here, and that Florence knew her. What were the odds of that happening?

"I want you to meet my family, Flor," said the little pixie in excitement.

She flew down and took Florence's finger in both of her hands, dragging Florence along with a surprising amount of strength for such a tiny being. She led her around the clearing, introducing her to all the pixies. They were all the colors of the rainbow and more. There were bright blue and dark forest green, as well as pink, purple and white. The fall pixie explained that the different colors represented the different tasks the pixies were meant to do. The light blue pixies were in charge of the warm summer breeze, and they had to chase away the clouds to leave the sky clear. The dark green ones were in charge of helping all green foliage to grow. The pink and purple ones were in charge of flowers and making sure they grew, and the white ones were in charge of snow and anything icy. The pixies chattered excitedly when she approached them. They all wanted to give her a gift of some kind, so by the end of the greetings she was practically covered in flowers and leaves and even beautiful intricate snowflakes that glittered in the sun. She looked behind her at Joshua, who was also being adorned in this way. The pixies seemed to give more gifts to Joshua than to her, which he accepted with great fondness and laughter.

After some time had passed, Joshua approached her and said, "We should be getting back so you can rest."

Florence looked up and saw the sky overhead was beginning to darken. She had no idea how much time had passed, although with all the walking they had done she supposed it made sense.

Joshua led her out of the clearing as all the pixies waved and called out their goodbyes. He led her into another part of the clearing instead of back the way they had come, which confused Florence. How long would it take them to get back to where they started if they went this way?

"Shouldn't we go back the way we came from?" Florence asked tentatively, not wanting to offend him but genuinely curious.

He smiled as he looked back at her. "Sometimes, the easiest and quickest way back is not the way you came."

Florence pondered this as they continued. But wasn't going in the exact opposite direction going to take them farther from where they started?

They walked a few steps more and, just as the sun was setting, they stepped out into the same clearing they had started from. Florence blinked and looked at Joshua with a skeptical eye. He laughed at her expression and then said, "If you follow me, things may not always be what they seem. But I promise to get you where you need to go."

"I'm not sure I completely understand you," she said.

"I'm not sure you ever will. But there's nothing wrong with trying. Perhaps the more you get to know me, the better you'll be able to understand."

"Understand what?"

"That's for you to find out, isn't it?" he said, smiling at her.

She wasn't sure how she felt about Joshua or his father. It wasn't that she thought they were bad people, or that they meant her any harm, but there was something strange about them, something she couldn't quite figure out. Maybe she wasn't supposed to figure them out, like Joshua said. She had only spent a single day here with them, and still had no idea what she was doing here. They also seemed to know a lot about her, which was also odd.

Joshua led her over to Eli and he smiled a crooked smile at her. "Well now, how was your day?"

"It was fun, I really enjoyed it," Florence said.

"That's good to hear, now let's eat!" he said, passing her another leaf filled with food.

They ate and a comfortable conversation began. They talked about many things and yet somehow about nothing. It was not that the conversation was meaningless, or that Florence wasn't interested in the topics, they were just whatever came to mind. It seemed like no time at all had passed, but it must have been quite late because Florence found herself growing tired.

"Ah, I believe it is time to rest now. Why don't we call it a night? You go and get some rest and be ready for a day of training tomorrow!"

Florence smiled and said her goodnights. As she crawled into bed that night, she began thinking and wondering about this strange man and his son. She somehow felt comfortable around them despite their strangeness. She wasn't really sure why that was either. If anyone else had treated her the way that these two did, she would have been genuinely freaked out. Yet something was different with them. She pondered all of this as she fell into a deep dreamless sleep.

CHAPTER FIFTEEN

The next day dawned bright. Florence woke up slow, enjoying the feeling of being outside. The cool breeze tickled her face. The warm sunlight filtered through the trees warming her. This was the way to sleep, and to wake up for that matter. Never before had she felt so well rested or awake. She couldn't remember a time when she felt this good.

She got out of bed and stretched, taking in big breaths of the fresh morning air. She decided, after a moment of taking in the day, that it was time to find breakfast. She walked through the curtain of trees and found herself in a new place. This was odd, because she was sure she went through the exact same trees the day before. She looked around, feeling a little lost and unsure of where she was. She turned back to try and walk back through the trees she had come from, but when she did so the trees she had just walked through weren't there. She had no idea where she was.

She looked around, trying not to panic. This whole forest was weird; yesterday just turning a different direction got her back where she had started, so maybe it was something similar now. She decided to just continue in the direction she started and began to walk.

At first the forest seemed the same in front of her as it did behind her. It was almost like she hadn't moved at all, even though she was walking forward. Her surroundings didn't move, which was unnerving. She decided to continue and not change directions so that she could, hopefully, find her way back if she needed to.

After what felt like an hour of walking, her surroundings abruptly changed. One moment she was in the forest, but then she blinked and all of a sudden she was walking on a cliff's edge. She stopped, a little thrown at the sudden change of scenery. She looked over the edge of the cliff and a wave of dizziness threatened to take over. She swayed and took a few deep breaths as she waited for the dizziness to subside. She was up so high. She had never had a fear of heights; she was always able to look down from the many trees she had climbed in her childhood, but this was different. The highest thing she had ever climbed was a tree that overlooked the whole forest. It was probably around 100 feet tall, which in hindsight was pretty high. But she knew the tree well and had something to hold on to. That was the difference with this situation; she was up much higher than she had ever been before and she had nothing but her own will to stay on the clifftop to help her.

The dizziness passed and she decided to continue forward, praying that the wind wouldn't come up and blow her into the water below. The view was beautiful once she kept her eyes away from the water crashing against the side of the mountain. It was cool, but not cold, and all around her was the brightest green grass she had ever seen. The grass was the only color, everything else was in different shades of grey, from the rocks on the cliff below to the sky above as far as she could see. It was a strange contrast to all the colors she was usually surrounded with in the forest.

She continued walking and eventually found a small dirt trail. Here she paused, unsure of her next choice. She could follow the trail in front of her or continue on in the direction she was already going. She debated for a minute, and then decided to take the trail. After all, she reasoned, a trail at least went somewhere. Who knew where she would end up wandering around the way she had been?

As soon as her feet touched the trail, she found herself in yet another new place. This one was hot, dry, and had bright yellow sand dunes that stretched as far as the eye could see. Maybe she had made a mistake. The sun was already beating down on her, making her sweat, and she had only been here for a minute. Oh well, there was no turning back now. At least the trail was still visible.

She began walking in this new place, feeling the weight of the heat surrounding her. Sweat dripped off her body in places she hadn't even known she could sweat. The sand and the sun burned her eyes and she didn't know how long she would be able to keep this up. Her feet dragged onwards, pure willpower being the only thing keeping her going.

Finally, she saw something in the distance. It was a tiny speck that she almost couldn't make out except for one thing: it was blue. That must be water, she thought and her throat cried out in misery at the thought of fresh cold water. She found the will to keep going somehow, and she slowly continued her march forward.

After what felt like a good two hours, she was close enough to the blue speck to be able to tell what it was. It was a forest, somehow out in the middle of the desert. She had no idea how this was possible but she continued walking anyway, hoping to find a pond or a river or something that could quench her thirst.

As soon as she made it under the first branches of the trees, the air cooled, and she felt like she could breathe again. She turned to glance behind herself and, instead of a huge desert, all she saw was a small square of sand, probably about three feet wide and across. Had that been the desert she had been stuck in? What was going on?

She had started this journey, so she might as well continue in the direction she was already going. She followed the trail and, after about ten steps, she found herself in a familiar clearing. There was Eli, sitting comfortably on a log with a jug beside him and a happily crackling fire.

Florence stopped for a moment, trying to make sense of all that had just happened to her. "Hello my dear!" said Eli, cheerfully. "Come join me and we'll take a look at your results."

"My results?" Florence asked, making her way across the clearing to sit next to him. He offered her the jug which she gratefully took. It was delicious cold, clear water, and she had never tasted anything so thirst-quenching before.

"Your results for the test you just took," he said, smiling.

She almost choked on her water. "I'm sorry?"

He chuckled a little mischievously. "Didn't know you were being tested, did ya? One of my more brilliant ideas, if I do say so myself. You see, every choice you made brought you to a different location, which in turn brought you to another and another until you made it back to me."

"Well, how did I do?"

"What do you think?"

"I suppose I didn't do all that well," she said, a little sad. "I didn't make it back here as quickly as I would have liked."

"Don't be so hard on yourself," he said, laughing. "First of all, this isn't a win or fail type of test. The only way you could have failed would be if you'd stopped moving and sat down or something. But you did very well, you made choices and stuck with them. You'd be surprised how long it has taken some people I've given this test to. They try to backtrack, which will get them into even more worlds and leave them twisted around even further. I was impressed with your determination to stick with the course you started with."

Florence blushed a little at that. She wasn't used to getting such high praise so she wasn't sure how to react.

"Moving on! Your first choice was to continue forward. This brought you to the cliff, which means that you aren't afraid of a challenge. This is a good thing but beware your need to be in control. This was represented by the vertigo. Part of the reason you want to be in control is because so much of your life is out of your hands. Here is some harsh love for you," he said, as he leaned in closer to her. "You won't be able to control most things in your life. There will be things that happen to you and your only option is to move on," he looked her in the eye for a moment to make sure she understood what he was saying. Then he leaned back and continued. "Then you found the trail. This represents the literal path that is laid out before you. Sometimes we make choices based on what we think will be easy. While this is human nature, it can sometimes get you into trouble. Sometimes the way that seems the easiest from the outside, is much harder than the road that looks more difficult."

"What was the goal of this whole test?" Florence asked.

"Well, the goal was me," he said, grinning again. "Or rather, it was reaching me. Sometimes the goal isn't always the destination but the journey you take to get there."

"This is all a little confusing still," Florence said, trying to piece it all together. "I'm still not sure why I had to take it, especially without knowing about it first."

"That's simple! If you knew it was a test, would you have made different choices?"

"I suppose I would have," she said.

"And then we would have gotten different results. You did just fine, Florence. You did as well as any human can do."

Florence nodded as she felt sleepy. Maybe the test had taken more out of her than she originally realized.

"And now, another day is behind us. Tomorrow is when the real training begins. For now, why don't you go on off to bed?"

Florence nodded and stood up slowly, her legs feeling like lead. As she made her way back beneath the canopy, a question suddenly popped in her head that she couldn't quite shake. She knew she had to have it answered or she'd never be able to sleep.

She turned back around and there was Eli smiling at her. "Yes, my dear?"

"I was just wondering," she said, wondering if she should ask the question. She decided she had already come this far so she might as well continue, "Has anyone ever gotten the test done perfectly?"

"Interesting question. Just one," he answered, smiling again at her.

"Who was it?"

"My son, Joshua."

"Oh, so he's human then?" she asked, trying to make sense of it all.

"He was, but he's not anymore."

"I see," Florence said slowly, trying to wrap her brain around the crazy sentence he'd just uttered.

He laughed a huge belly laugh. "No, you don't," he said, still chuckling. "But maybe one day you will. Now off to bed with you! The real training begins tomorrow."

Florence nodded and turned, walking back through the now familiar trees to her bed. She didn't understand this strange man at all. She wasn't even sure if he was being serious with her most of the time. But she didn't have much choice. If she had any intention of learning who she was and what her purpose was, then she would have to stay and face whatever challenges he put before her.

Another bright and beautiful day dawned the next morning. Florence woke early, anticipation for what lay ahead keeping her from sleeping in too late. She walked out from her canopy of trees, half expecting to end up in another place again. However, she walked into the same clearing that she first met Eli. This time he wasn't sitting but was standing and waiting for her. She walked up to him and as she got closer, she realized for the first time how tall he was. Any other time she had seen him, he had always been sitting. Now that he was standing, she felt incredibly small in comparison. He must have been at least seven feet tall, which would have sounded ridiculous if she hadn't been standing next to him herself. She had to tilt her head right back to even see his face when she was directly next to him.

"Good morning!" he said cheerfully, seeming to be unaware of her amazement. "Shall we?"

She nodded and he turned, leading the way through a cluster of trees into a new place. Florence felt like she should have seen that coming with all of the weirdness that had surrounded her over the past few days, but it still took her by surprise.

Once she had passed through the trees, she found herself in a rocky terrain.

Everything around her was grey and stone, from the ground she stood on to the walls that surrounded her. She could see a sliver of sky peeking out from the massive rock walls around her. She had never been anywhere like this before.

"Florence!" She looked over at him and he threw something at her. She caught it, the impact stinging her palm. She looked down surprised at her own reflexes for catching the thing. It was a small stone, probably about the size of one of the flat stones Robert had taught her to skip. It nestled in her hand perfectly.

She looked up and said, "Did you just throw a rock at me?"

He laughed, the sound echoing off of the walls around them. "Come now Florence, you caught it. There was no harm done."

Florence looked at him skeptically. "I wouldn't be so sure," she said remembering the stinging in her hand.

He shook his head, smiling. "What is there to be gained if there isn't anything at stake?"

"What does that have to do with you throwing stuff at me? Why did you throw it, anyway?"

"To test your reflexes," he said, walking a little farther away and looking around on the rocky floor. "Congratulations, you passed. Now enough chit chat! Let us begin," he straightened and looked over at her. "What do you know about your powers?"

"Not too much," she answered. "I know I've made some things move on their own. But I have no idea where the power comes from or how to use it."

"Well, that's why you are here. Let's start with something simple. What I want you to do, Florence, is take that stone in your hand and make it float. Just a few inches above your hand will be fine. And begin."

Florence looked down at the stone in her hand. How was she supposed to make it do anything? Usually when things happened to her before she was stressed or frustrated. She wasn't sure she could do it just on her own.

"Concentrate now," she heard Eli say from a short way off. "All you have to do is make it float."

"But you haven't told me how to do it," she said. She looked up, only to realize he no longer stood in front of her. She glanced around but he was nowhere to be seen. "Eli?" she called, starting to feel a little anxious.

"I'm here," his voice seemed to call from all around her. His voice was bouncing off the rock walls, making it impossible to tell which direction it was coming from. "Deep down, you know how to do this. It's in the very seams of your being. It's part of you. Trust it, let it guide you."

She looked back down at the rock, feeling foolish. What if she couldn't make it do anything? What if Eli told her he couldn't help her and she was a failure? She shook her head, trying to get rid of the negative thoughts. She couldn't start thinking like that. That kind of thinking didn't help anything and she needed to concentrate.

She closed her eyes, forgetting the stone for the moment, and as she cleared her mind of all thoughts, looking deep down inside herself. At first nothing happened, but then she began to feel the strange energy. It was soft at first, she just barely felt a pulsing kind of vibration in her chest. She focused on it, and it began to get louder and stronger. It expanded, the vibrations and energy moving into her shoulders, down her arms and into her hands, causing that now familiar tingle. She opened her eyes and there was the stone, hovering two inches above her outstretched hand.

She let out a whoop of celebration and looked around, wanting to share her success with Eli. "Well done," he said, his voice echoing across the rock faces. "Now see if you can maintain it."

Out of nowhere something came whizzing towards her at an unthinkable speed. She yelped and moved out of the way just in time. It hit the rock face beside her and fell to the ground with a thud. She looked down and saw it was another rock, roughly the same size as the one she held in her hand, which had of course fallen back into her palm and was no longer hovering. "You're throwing rocks again! How am I supposed to concentrate if I don't know where the rocks are coming from?"

"That's the point, my dear," came his echoey voice. "You must hold your concentration, keep that stone levitating no matter what is thrown at you."

"What exactly is it that you're training me for?" Florence asked, suspiciously. "I thought you were just training me to use my powers."

"You will see when the time comes. For now, what I need you to worry about is keeping that rock in the air."

With that he refused to continue speaking, no matter how many more questions Florence asked or how many choice words she used to describe this sort of training.

She sighed and began to concentrate again on making the stone levitate. She felt the familiar energy flowing down into her fingertips, making them tingle. Then the stone floated the same two inches above her hand, taking much less time than it had before. She heard a whizzing sound and, anticipating it this time, she stepped to the side just as a small stone came hurling towards her from her left. The stone hit the wall behind her harmlessly and she smiled, thinking she knew exactly where the next stone would be coming from that direction. Suddenly a stone came from off to her right, which she wasn't anticipating. It hit her shoulder and she lost concentration again. The levitating stone clattered to the ground.

"You shouldn't ever assume you know where the next stone is coming from," Eli chastised her. "Concentrate but don't anticipate. Trust your instinct and the energy inside you to be your guide."

Florence rubbed her sore shoulder irritably. She could already feel the bruise beginning to form. She said a few more choice words, just so Eli would know how she felt about this whole situation, and then got back to concentrating on the stone in her palm.

This pattern continued for what felt like hours. By the end of it, Florence was covered in bruises, but she had learned how to channel her energy the right way to anticipate the next thrown stone. She was hurting but proud of her progress.

"I think you've had enough for today," Eli said, coming out from behind a stone wall to her left. "Well done."

She smiled at him, and then remembered she wasn't happy with him and scowled. His laughter filled the space around them, echoing off the walls once again. "Well now, there is no reason for that! No real harm has come to you, which is not something I can promise in the future."

"But it hurt," Florence knew she was sounding a little pathetic, but she really didn't know why this was the best way for her to learn concentration.

"As many things in life do, my dear," Eli said, softly. "The lessons you learned today came with a price. This is a price that was paid, and these lessons won't be easily forgotten."

Joshua appeared beside her and put his hand on her shoulder. A pleasant warmth spread all the way from where his fingers touched her down her entire body. She felt herself releasing a breath and leaning into him. He smiled at her and then let her go. She found that all of her aches and pains were gone. Somehow Joshua had healed her.

"Also, physical pain is just temporary, my dear," Eli said smiling at her. "Now you and Joshua spend some time together. I know he has some things he wishes to teach you as well."

Florence blinked and Eli was gone. She wasn't sure how he managed to disappear while she was looking at him but she decided not to question it too much. She was learning that Eli was a slippery one, and she wasn't sure how to feel about him. It wasn't that she disliked him by any means, but she wasn't sure how to put it into words. She felt safe around him but knew she could get hurt. She knew she wouldn't get seriously injured around him, but she also knew he wouldn't make things easy for her.

"Shall we?" asked Joshua's soft voice, pulling her out of her thoughts. She smiled at him, nodded, and began to follow him. One thing she was sure about was that she liked Joshua. Not in a romantic way, but she knew she could trust him entirely. She felt at peace around him, even when they weren't talking, and she had never been so comfortable around anyone before.

He led her through the rocky expanse and into yet another forest. This one was different from the ones they had been to before. Florence wasn't sure how she knew that other than it sounded different. She could hear different animals than the ones she had heard before.

She took a deep breath in, her chest feeling light and free. Feeling eyes on her she looked over and saw Joshua smiling at her. "What?" she asked, hoping she didn't have something on her face or anything.

"Just admiring your loveliness," he said, still smiling.

Florence rolled her eyes and shook her head trying not to blush. Lovely? Her? That she wasn't so sure about.

"You don't think you're beautiful, do you?" Joshua asked, quietly.

Florence didn't answer. She thought the answer to that question was pretty obvious. It wasn't that Florence thought she was bad looking, just certainly not beautiful.

"I want to show you something," Joshua said, holding out his hand.

She took it and felt warm as that now familiar energy moved into her. This was something she was getting more used to when Joshua touched her. He led her out of the garden and down a path she had never seen before.

"Where are you taking me?" she asked, a little trepidatious.

"You'll see," he answered, not really giving her an answer at all.

They chatted as they walked about anything and everything: the trees surrounding them, flowers, birds, painting… The conversations just seemed to flow with him. It was almost like she had known him her whole life. After about half an hour, they came to the mouth of a cave. It wasn't very large or small, but somewhere in between.

He led her inside and, as they walked in, torches that Florence hadn't even noticed, lit up along the walls. A warm light cascaded down and revealed a long hallway ahead of them. Florence looked over at Joshua, who smiled encouragingly, and together they walked forward. Right when they were about to run out of light another set of torches would burst forth, lighting their way.

This continued for what felt like an eternity but really might have only been twenty minutes. The cave opened up and they came to a round chamber. There wasn't much in it, just a small stand in the middle of the room. Florence could hear the musical sounds of water trickling nearby, but she couldn't tell where it was coming from. Joshua led her forward, towards the table in the middle of the room.

As they got closer, she saw that the stand had a large wide rimmed bowl on top. He stopped leading and gestured for her to go on without him. She set up the small step and leaned over the basin. The bowl itself was made out of metal that was silver and shiny. It had no design on it other than a delicate roping along the outside rim. Inside the bowl there was water, it was moving gently even though the bowl was completely still. This led her to believe that there was a water source that was feeding into the bowl somehow, but she didn't see any other sign of it besides the movement of the water.

At first, she didn't see anything besides the moving water, then all of a sudden the water stilled and looking up at her was a girl. She had golden hair that lay in perfect ringlets across her shoulders. Her face was heart shaped and she had a slight blush to her lips and cheeks. She had light brown eyes flecked with gold, matching her golden hair perfectly.

Florence looked back over her shoulder at Joshua. "What is this?" she asked, heart pounding. "Is that really me?"

Joshua nodded. "This mirror shows you most clearly how you are. This does not reflect your physical form but what you look like on the inside, how you look as a person. The most beautiful person in the world could look into the mirror and see an ugly hag staring back at them. Outward beauty can come and go, but internal beauty is something that stays the same."

Florence looked back into the mirror at the beautiful girl. "So, I don't really look like this?"

"That's not necessarily true," he said, gently. "Beauty is in the eye of the beholder. To those that love you and see you for who you truly are, yes you look like this. To those that can't see past their own insecurities or selfishness, you may look different."

"I'm not really understanding you," said Florence, beginning to feel a little insecure. She wanted nothing more than to look like the girl in the mirror. She had always been plain and had been accepting of that fact, but now that she had seen what she could look like, knowing she didn't look that way was almost more than she could bear.

Joshua looked at her in a way that made her feel like he was looking into her very soul. "Let me ask you something. What would being that beautiful in your world get you? Why do you want it so desperately?"

Florence had never thought of this before. Why did she want it? Was it for power? She knew that if she was beautiful then she could bend people to her will. No that wasn't it. She didn't want it for a manipulative purpose. Ah that was it. "If I were beautiful, I would have a purpose. I would feel like I could do anything."

"Do you think, perhaps, that you already have a purpose?" Joshua asked, quietly.

"I'm not sure."

"Then let me help you here: your beauty or lack thereof has absolutely nothing to do with who you are as a person or what your purpose is. Most humans put way too much worth in beauty or what they perceive as beautiful. Many people use it for their own selfish purposes while others spend all their time trying to achieve it. Beauty has nothing to do with looks. All that truly matters is how you treat others and how you live your life. It may sound like I'm backtracking here, but Florence you are every bit as beautiful as that girl in the mirror."

Florence wasn't completely sure how to take all this. On one hand she was glad to know that beauty wasn't as important as it had seemed to her before. Beauty was something she had wanted so badly and for so long, but knowing it didn't really matter in the scheme of things made her feel immensely better. Also knowing that what Joshua said was true, that perhaps she was beautiful, made her feel so much better.

"So, this mirror shows ourselves, our truest selves, correct?"

"That would be a safe assumption," Joshua smiled, kindly at her.

"Then what happens when you or Eli look into the mirror? After all, your father said you weren't human."

"Interesting," Joshua rubbed his hands together, for the first time looking just as mischievous as his father. "Care to find out?"

He stepped up to the platform and gave her one last grin before leaning over the mirror. Florence eagerly looked in the mirror too, and at first she didn't see anything. She was about to express her disappointment when a light started. At first it was dim not doing much of anything, but as time went on the light began filling outward, growing brighter and brighter.

Florence stumbled back off the platform, as the light continued ebbing out from the mirror. It lit up the entire chamber, this pure white light, like nothing Florence had ever seen before. But it kept getting brighter, and brighter, until Florence had to shield her eyes.

"Florence? You can open your eyes now," came the sound of Joshua's voice. She did so but it took several minutes before her eyes adjusted to the now dim cave.

"That was... unexpected."

Joshua chuckled, "Be careful what you wish for. Now that is settled, let's get you some rest. You've got another busy day tomorrow."

Joshua led her out of the cavern. For maybe the first time in her life, she wasn't worried about what she looked like or how people may perceive her. She knew deep down that she was beautiful, she had seen with her own eyes how beautiful she was. Now that she had accepted that, she would never have to worry about being beautiful again.

CHAPTER SIXTEEN

"Again, Florence!" came Eli's sharp voice.

Florence was on her knees with sweat dripping off her face. She had never worked this hard in her life and she was becoming exhausted. Wiping the sweat off her forehead with her shirt sleeve, as it was trying to drip into her eyes, she got back to her feet. Her legs were shaking. Every day for the past few weeks, Eli had created a new challenge for her to conquer. Similar to the rock throwing, Eli had asked her to keep the stone hovering above her palm while she stood in the middle of a stream. She was fighting the current as well as fighting to keep the stone under control. Eventually, the things he made her levitate had become bigger, which led them to today's challenge: hold a tree trunk roughly double her size. Nothing was currently being thrown at her, but that didn't make it less of a challenge.

She stood and began to levitate the tree again. Her whole body was shaking; she had only lifted something this big one other time, and directly afterwards she had passed out.

"Concentrate, Florence," came Eli's voice from beside her. She made the mistake of looking over at him and lost her hold on the tree once more. It hit the ground with a boom.

She fell to her hands and knees again, black spots dancing in front of her eyes. She sucked in a breath, trying not to give in and pass out. She knew that if she did give in, she wouldn't have to work anymore and could take a sweet break from all this work. But she also knew that wouldn't truly help her in the long run.

She felt Eli sit on the ground down next to her. Once the spots had passed, she looked over at him. He was just looking at her, waiting for her to catch her breath. "Why isn't this working?" she asked once some of her breath had returned. "I've been able to get every other lesson up until this point. What makes this one so difficult?" she sat back, still on her legs looking at him.

"It is because this test is not like the other ones," he said, simply. "This one was designed to test your strength, not your concentration. I can see we have a long way to go in this area."

Florence bristled at this. "Are you saying I'm weak?"

"Of course not! A weak person would never have been able to make it this far. You are incredibly strong, but there are always areas of improvement, yes?"

Florence nodded, calming down. She was hot and tired of failing. It made her irritable, but she hadn't meant to take that out on Eli.

"Now, Florence," he said, rising to his feet and holding out his hand, "Shall we continue?"

The training did not get better. She was now given multiple tasks to do at the same time which she was able to handle somewhat well. However, when it came to lifting the tree, she still failed every time. It wouldn't have been so bad if she had been able to make some progress, but she hadn't. Every time she came to that task, she choked and continued to fail. All she had to do was keep the tree in the air for an extended period of time. She didn't have to focus on anything else or do anything besides keep that stinking tree in the air. Yet she couldn't do it. She still found herself in the dirt on her hands and knees trying not to lose consciousness. It was the only thing holding her back, the one thorn in her side.

Getting things to levitate around her had become easy, almost like second nature to her now. She had gotten to the point where she didn't even have to look at things to make them move. As long as she knew they were there, she could manipulate them to her will, which was extremely satisfying.

She sat on her bed making flowers weave themselves into a crown in front of her. She had just gotten the shape right when a shadow crossed over her. She didn't have to look up to know who it was. "Hi, Joshua."

"Hello Florence," he said, warmly. She and Joshua had gotten very close over the past few weeks. They spent almost every moment together when Florence wasn't training or sleeping. She was completely comfortable around him now and could tell him whatever she was thinking about at any given moment, something she hadn't felt with any other person before.

"That flower crown is lovely," he said, coming closer. "But I think it's missing something." With that, another flower came out of thin air and floated in between them. It was a deep red rose, beautiful and full. It matched well with the other color flowers she had picked out and it weaved itself into her crown, making it seem like a jewel for the front. Florence smiled as Joshua plucked the crown out of the air. He placed it gently on her head. "There, fit for a princess."

She smiled at him, pleased at how well the crown had turned out. "Won't you walk with me?" he asked, holding out his hand. She took it, almost not feeling the surge of energy going up her arm from where their hands met. She could almost forget how powerful Joshua was when she was with him, but the truth was she didn't actually know how strong his powers were. She had never seen him use them other than for silly things like the flower crown. All she knew was the power she felt surging into her if he touched her.

They began their walk through the trees and out into the unknown. It was strange how normal it seemed to Florence now, the way the world shifted and changed around her. She almost didn't see the scenery around them anymore because she was usually so caught up in their conversations. Today, however, their surroundings looked strangely familiar. As Florence looked around, she realized she recognized the place that Joshua had taken her. She looked at him, unsure, but he gestured for her to continue moving forward.

This was her home, or what had been her home for so many years. It was the farmhouse, and Florence was surprisingly glad to see it. She walked forward, remembering all the times she had run through this field just for the sake of it. She walked up the couple of wooden steps to the front porch and hesitated before opening the door.

She looked back over her shoulder at Joshua, who was still standing where she had left him. He gestured for her to continue without him, so after one more deep breath, she opened the door and entered.

The house was the same as she had remembered it: the small kitchen with the window overlooking the yard, the living room fireplace with ashes in its grate and the hallway just beyond it.

Florence looked around cautiously. The last time she had been here was the night she had made a run for it. The Baron had ruined everything, shattered the perfect life she'd thought she had before he showed up. Just then the realization dawned on her that she wasn't alone; her mother stood in the kitchen, stirring something over the stovetop. Her back was to Florence as she slowly approached her.

As she drew closer, she heard animalistic sounds coming from the woman in front of her. "Mother?" she asked tentatively. Her mother froze, the spoon in her hand poised above the pot and no longer moving. She turned and Florence tried not to scream. The thing in front of her had the body of a woman but the face was that of the creature that had terrorized her at the inn.

"Ah, my Florence," came its raspy, hoarse voice. "I was hoping you would come here. Do you see what I've become? A servant!" she spat, anger causing her dog-like lips to lift in a snarl. "I was one of the most feared creatures for my master and now here I am! Forced to stay in this stinking house with this horrible body, cooking for the rest of my days. And I have you to thank for it!"

"Me?" asked Florence, finding her voice. "What do I have to do with it?"

"You killed me of course! What do you think happens to those that die? We come here! Forced to relive the worst times of our lives," the creature sat down heavily, and it was only then that Florence saw the chain wrapped around her wrist, keeping her locked to the stove. "You see?" said the creature, noticing Florence staring at the chain. "I built this chain myself, link by link creating the very prison for myself that I most hated. This is what happens to those who have died. We must live out our days in our own form of torture. And now," the creature said, coming into a crouch on all fours. "Now my dear Florence, I think you'll join me here."

With that she lunged. Florence fled, turning her back on the creature and sprinting towards the door. She could feel the creature's hot breath on her neck, her teeth almost closing in. Florence pushed harder, reaching the door handle and yanking it open. She stepped over the door frame and heard the sound of metal pulling tight. There was a strangled yelp and Florence turned to see the creature that used to be her mother clawing at her throat. The chain was constricting her, similar to a dog leash. An overwhelming sense of pity came over Florence as she looked at the creature in front of her. The creature continued to writhe around teeth snapping, trying to break free from the chain and come after Florence.

"I'm sorry," said Florence softly, tears filling her eyes.

"I don't want your pity," spat the creature still trying to break free from the chains holding her in place. "I want your life! You did this to me Florence and I will never forgive you."

Florence turned away from the sickening scene of the animal that she once had called mother, the person she had spent most of her life with. The person she had believed had loved her and protected her. She stepped out of the house and let out the sobs that had been choking her these past few months.

She cried for the life she had lost, the one she could never go back to. She cried for the idea of her mother and having that reality shattered. She cried for the creature and the fate that she now had to endure for the rest of eternity.

"Come now, what's all the tears for?" asked a familiar voice.

Florence's head snapped up. She was no longer at the farm but instead in the inn. The one she had watched burn down. The tables were gone, leaving the space open except for one table and a comfortable-looking chair by the fire.

William was smiling down at her. She cried out again, this time with tears of joy, and threw herself into his waiting arms. She hugged him and cried, feeling better after seeing so much pain. She looked up at him, breaking away and smiled up at him through her tears. "Oh, William! It's so good to— but how did you—"

"Slow down, Florence! Come now, let's have a bite to eat. You must be starving."

Florence's stomach grumbled in response to this, making them both laugh. They sat down at the table, where laid out before them were steaming bowls of stew, the same stew that he made for Florence the first time she ever had his cooking. There was fresh bread and big mugs full of something frothy that Florence had never had before but was delicious. It felt so normal, that for a moment, Florence forgot that she wasn't back at the inn.

Once they had eaten their fill, William sat back in satisfaction with his hands resting on his stomach. He looked over at her, smiling, and said, "I imagine you have some questions for me."

"That's an understatement," said Florence as all the questions she had swam in her mind. William laughed at this, which she couldn't help joining in. Finally, she decided and asked, "How did you get here?"

"Well, that's a bit of a story. You see, once that fire started, I had no way of getting out."

"Wait," Florence said, dread setting in on her. "Then how did you survive?"

"I didn't, lass," he said, looking at her.

Florence's stomach dropped at his words. She had somehow known that he hadn't, no one could have survived a fire that hot, that unexpected. Yet she had still held the hope inside of her that maybe, somehow, he had.

"It's all my fault," she said with despair, tears falling from her eyes. "If I hadn't been there, none of this would have happened."

"Come now, you don't know that," he said, taking her hand in his own. "Anything could have happened. Who knows? That fire still could have taken me, or it could have been bandits, or really anything. It was my time to go, Florence. You had nothing to do with it."

Florence nodded, trying to shake the guilt that had placed itself heavy on her shoulders.

He gave her hand a pat and continued, "Now then, I'm sure you have plenty of other burning questions for me. Let's hear them."

Florence took a shaky breath trying to get control over herself. "So why are you here?"

"This is where I will spend the rest of my days," he said, simply. "This is the place that I've loved most dearly. This inn I've built from the ground with my own two hands. There is no place else in the world I've ever wanted to be."

"So, you're happy here? This isn't some kind of punishment?" Florence asked, thinking of her fake mother stuck in the world over.

"Of course, I am! I couldn't be happier."

"Does Robert know?"

"I think he has an idea of what happened," he said, thoughtfully. "But like you, he is holding on to a false hope."

"I see," she said, as a heaviness settled on her heart. "If I'm here does that mean I'm dead too?"

"No lass," he said, with a chuckle. "It means you've been given an opportunity to get some closure. Not many people get an opportunity like this, you are very lucky."

Just then something came hurling out of the kitchen and launched itself directly at William. Florence jumped up, thinking it may have been attacking him, but William was laughing. "Florence, allow me to introduce to you my daughter, Caroline."

The little girl in his arms was probably about six years old from what Florence could guess. She had the same dark hair as William, but it was in a curly mess around her face. She smiled a toothy grin as she hung upside down from her father's arm.

"You have a daughter?" Florence asked, shocked.

"Caroline? Where are you, love?" called a voice from the kitchen. "There you are!" A beautiful woman stepped out of the kitchen. She was of average size and average build. Really, most things were pretty average about her. The thing that made her so gorgeous was her eyes. They were a deep violet that crinkled at the corners as she smiled at Caroline.

"And my wife, Irene," William finished, smiling at her.

"A pleasure to meet you," Irene said, pulling Florence into a hug. "I've heard so much about you that it's so nice we finally got the chance to meet."

She released her and walked over to stand behind William, placing a hand on his shoulder.

"Wait," Florence said confused. "You have a family? When did this happen?"

"Oh, many years ago," said William, placing his hand over Irene's. "I lost them in a fire many years before I met Robert. It's almost poetic that I would go in the same way."

Florence was unsure how to feel at that revelation. Sad that William had lost so much, yet that sadness was mixed with a feeling of joy for a family being reunited again. It explained so much about William's stoic nature.

"This is why you took us in, wasn't it? This is why you helped all those people in the village."

"Yes," he answered, simply. "It brought me joy to see others happy. I had lost so much that the only way to get through it was to take care of others. I never wanted credit for it because that's not what it was about for me. It was about bringing joy to others' lives in little ways so I could bear the burdens I was dealt. It also might be why I somewhat adopted two lost kids who didn't know what to do with their lives and may or may not have been in some kind of trouble," he said, giving her a wink.

"You knew about that?" she said, sheepishly.

"Come now," he said laughing. "Why else would a girl come into my inn disguised, poorly I might add, as a boy looking for work?"

"Was it really that obvious?"

"Yes, my dear," he said, with a laugh. "Now, Florence," he continued, on a more serious note. "I have something I need you to do for me. When you see Robert again, tell him that what happened wasn't his fault. His family is waiting for him here when it's his time."

At that little Caroline hopped off of his lap and ran into the kitchen. She came back a few moments later carrying a huge book which she handed to Florence. "This is for you," William said, as Caroline ran back to his lap.

Florence looked at the book in her hands. It didn't look particularly special. It was a brown hard-cover book with no ornate designs on the cover and no words on the spine. There wasn't even a title. She opened it and nearly dropped it in her shock. Inside were dozens upon dozens of recipes. They were handwritten all in the same blocky handwriting. "Are these your recipes?"

She looked up into William's smiling face. "They are. I began your training. Now the rest is up to you."

"Thank you, William!" she said, rushing over and giving him a hug. When she pulled back, she saw that he had tears in his eyes, and she suddenly just knew what that meant.

"It's time for me to go now, isn't it?" she said, sadness threatening to overtake her.

"Yes, lass," he said, sadly. "But this isn't goodbye forever."

She nodded, tears in her eyes yet again. "I'll miss you," she said, in a shaky voice.

"And I will miss you," he said, putting a hand on her shoulder. "Be strong, lass. Robert needs you more than either of you know right now."

She stepped back and had one last glimpse of William with his beautiful family. Then she blinked and was out in a field once more, clutching the book to her chest. She wasn't alone.

CHAPTER SEVENTEEN

"Joshua," she said looking up into his strange colored eyes.

"Hello Florence," he said, softly. She couldn't read the expression on his face. It was somewhere between empathy and sadness.

"Why did you bring me here?" she practically screamed. "I didn't ask for any of this!"

"No," he answered, entirely calm in the face of her yelling, "You didn't. However, this was necessary."

"Necessary?" she spat. "In what way is something like this necessary?! I've been to two different places, and I have no idea which one is right or if they were even real."

"I think holding that book in your hands is all the proof you need."

Florence looked down at the book she hadn't realized she was clinging to, her anger fading away into sadness. "But it was a reminder of all that I've lost. William—" Her voice broke into a sob. Getting control after taking a few deep breaths, she continued, "William is dead. I'll never see him again."

"Do you really believe that, though?" Joshua asked in the same soft voice. "Do you truly believe that you'll never see him again?"

Florence thought about it while the tears streamed down her cheeks. "Perhaps not," she answered after a moment. "Maybe I will when I've passed on as well. But I have no guarantee that I will."

"No, you don't," he said, thoughtfully. "But if you believe deep down that you will, then you will."

"You make it sound so simple."

"Maybe that's because it is simple. Most things in life, and death, are."

She looked up at him, questions swimming in her eyes. "Why did you bring me here? What was the point of all of this?"

"You hadn't given yourself time to mourn, Florence," he answered. "You have lost two people who were very impactful to you in the past few weeks, and you haven't given yourself any time to miss them."

"Even my so-called mother?"

"Especially her," he said, surprising her. "She was someone who was very important to your upbringing, someone who shaped you as a person. You needed to see her for what she truly was in order to release the hold she had on you. You were always striving for her attention and approval, and you truly cared about her, only to find out everything about her was a lie. You needed to mourn that loss of the idea of your mother. This gave you the freedom to do so."

"Oh," Florence said, unable to think of anything else to say.

"Seeing William was a different matter," he continued. "With him you still had a hope that he was alive. Unfortunately, that hope, as well as the guilt you felt for dragging him into trouble, was holding you hostage. Those two things holding you back are why your training has been so difficult."

"You mean to tell me that if I'd just let go of these two things that my training would have been easier? Wait, does this mean that these two meetings were a part of my training?"

At Joshua's affirmation Florence exclaimed, "Then why didn't you just tell me? I could have done all this work on my own and been much farther in training without having to go through all of this!"

"Would you have done it though? You were given all the tools you needed to make it through these two issues that have been holding you back, but you didn't do them on your own. Do you really think you would have gotten over this just because one of us told you that you needed to?"

"No, I suppose not," Florence answered, in a soft voice. "But you could have tried it!"

"We both know that wouldn't have made that much of a difference," he answered, simply. "You needed to be there physically, to experience those two things, or else you may have never dealt with them on your own."

They both were quiet for a few moments, Florence lost in thought and Joshua giving her the space she needed to do so.

After a few minutes he said, "Are you ready to continue your training?"

Florence took a deep breath and released it slowly. "Yes, yes I believe I am."

Training was a breeze after that. Anything Eli asked her to do, any task he gave her, Florence found herself completing with ease. They moved on from the tree strength test and were now working on much more complicated things. Not only could she now hold things with her gift that were much heavier than anything she could carry in real life, but she could now do that while wading through deep water and dodging stones being thrown at her. She no longer had to move out of the way, she could block projectiles only with her own will. She could even make those things change direction mid-flight, which was an interesting bonus.

She was feeling better, not just mentally but physically as well. She was gaining muscle in her arms and shoulders as well as her legs and core. She was feeling strong and powerful, which was a nice change to the helpless running and hiding she had been doing before. She felt like Joshua and Eli were training her for something, but she wasn't quite sure what it was.

The days passed quickly, with each day bringing its own challenge that Florence now felt like she had the ability to accomplish.

As they were in the woods training one day, Florence heard a rustling in the trees to her right. She had been working on holding a boulder over her head which she put down when she heard the noise. It wasn't a normal rustling, like one of the many creatures that lived in these woods. It sounded like something much bigger. She picked up a pebble and held it in her hand, ready to shoot it towards the sound, when out of the trees stepped none other than Lydia.

She looked around, almost in a daze, and when she saw Florence, she rushed over only to collapse at her feet.

"Lydia!" Florence cried, bending down towards her. She was still breathing but seemed exhausted. She felt Eli's presence behind her and then he lifted Lydia up in his arms with surprising strength and carried her to the clearing.

Florence followed close behind him and noticed something fall from Lydia's hand. She bent down to pick it up; it was a small piece of paper. She intended to return it immediately, but something on the paper caught her eye. It was addressed to Florence, and it was written in a handwriting she did not recognize.

Heart pounding, she slowly began to unfold the paper. Just when she had one more fold to go, she heard, "Florence?" She realized she had stopped walking and looked up to see Eli several paces away. "Are you coming?"

She nodded, putting the paper in her pocket, and followed him into the now familiar clearing. There was a fire in the pit, which was always burning even though Florence had never seen Eli or Joshua feed it. This time when they walked into the clearing, instead of the normal log and seats waiting for them, there was a bed made out of leaves and moss. Eli laid Lydia down on the bed and Florence saw that she had started shaking. Florence came to her side and placed a hand on Lydia's forehead. She was burning up.

Eli bent over Lydia and peeled one eyelid open. Florence jumped back in shock; Lydia's eyes were completely black. There was no color or white in them at all, just pure black. It looked almost like her iris had bled into the rest of her eye. Eli nodded, not seeming at all surprised by this new development.

"What's wrong with her?" asked Florence, in horror.

"I'm afraid she's had a touch of dark magic," he said, sadly. "She's going to need special care. The next twenty-four hours are crucial to her survival."

"Who did this?"

Eli looked over at her. "Can you think of no one, Florence?"

Her heart sank. "It was the Baron, wasn't it?"

He didn't say anything, he just looked at her with his color changing eyes. "What can I do?" Florence asked, and with that they got to work.

The next few hours passed quickly. Florence spent the entire time gathering herbs and water, as well as blankets when Eli sent her for them. He didn't leave Lydia's side the entire time and remained seated on the mossy bed beside her.

At first nothing seemed to be happening. Lydia was still burning up and sleeping fitfully. Then, after about five hours, she began to show signs of getting worse. Black began to seep into her veins, making inky trails down across her face from her temples. Unfortunately, they didn't remain only at her head and face but soon began to cover her arms and legs as well.

Florence began to shake with nerves, her whole body being tense for hours. What kind of creature would Lydia become if they weren't able to get the curse out of her? Eli didn't look worried. He just continued to hold his hands over her body in what Florence assumed was his way of healing with magic.

Finally, after the sixteenth hour, the black veins lacing Lydia's body began to recede. It took several more hours for all her veins to return to normal and for her fever to break, allowing her to finally drift into a peaceful sleep. Florence sat heavily on the ground, exhausted.

"Lydia will make a full recovery," said Eli. His voice broke through her exhausted fog with ease. "Why don't you go to bed?"

Florence nodded, slowly getting to her feet and making her way to her bed. She was asleep before her head hit the pillow.

The next morning, Florence woke with a start. She sat up, rubbing her face and trying to figure out what time of day it was by the height of the sun. She wasn't sure what had woken her up. She didn't have dreams while she was here in the forest. She always slept peacefully and deeply, but she had the strangest feeling she was forgetting something.

She swung her legs over the side of the bed and as she did a piece of paper fluttered to the forest floor. She bent down to pick it up, trying to remember where it had come from. Everything from the day before came rushing back to her: Lydia, her sickness, and the mysterious paper addressed to Florence. Now, alone and without a crisis hanging over her head, she unfolded the letter and read:

Dearest Little Mouse,

I'm not sure where you scampered off to, but I hope you have been doing well. I wanted to inform you that a friend of yours has decided to pay me a visit. He came willingly and, while he is alive, he may not be for much longer. Perhaps you would be so kind as to pay us a visit and we can discuss the terms of his release.

Lovingly,

The Baron

Florence's blood ran cold. She jumped out of her bed and ran full force into the clearing. Eli was sitting at the fire enjoying what looked like a cup of tea.

Running up to him and panting she said, "The Baron has him! The Baron has Robert!" She thrust the short note into his hands and put her hands on her knees as she tried to catch her breath and calm her racing heart.

"I'm afraid this is not news to me, my dear," he said, solemnly.

Florence's head snapped up to stare at him in shock. "How is this not news to you?! You knew that Robert was taken?"

Eli nodded. "Not much goes on that I'm not aware of. In fact, I'm aware of everything that you humans decide to do. It's one of my many gifts."

"How could you not tell me?" she asked, trying to remain calm.

"My dear, it wasn't my story to tell."

"But it directly involves me!" she yelled, finally losing her temper. "It involves someone I— someone I care about! You willingly kept it from me!"

"Florence, listen to me, I've been preparing you for this moment."

Her raging came to an abrupt stop, replaced by pure confusion.

Eli stood, towering over her. "What do you think all this training was for? Did you think that it was for fun? It was so you could fulfill your destiny and fight for the one you love. Because you cannot deny, Florence, that you love this man."

Florence, despite her shock, felt the need to defend herself. Before she was able to gather herself enough to speak, Eli continued, "Now that is out of the way, let's continue. The Baron has Robert and I assume the only way you will be able to free him is if you agree to marry him. This can happen under no circumstance can happen."

"Why do you care who I marry? What does that have to do with anything?"

"It has to do with everything. Florence, do you know why the Baron wants to have you as his wife? It has nothing to do with love, and everything to do with power. The Baron is very power hungry, and he will stop at nothing to have you as his wife for that reason. He wants to take your powers for himself. While you may not yet know this, your powers are extremely important for your world."

"For the world? How can I be important? I don't even know how to do much!" She was starting to get frustrated at this point. "Eli, you aren't making any sense."

He sighed and gestured for her to sit down. When they both had, he handed her a cup of the same steaming liquid he had been held, before continuing, "I can't tell you everything, all I am able to do is awaken your powers. You have not scratched the surface of what you are capable of, nor do you understand the need the world has for your powers."

"Then why don't you just tell me? It seems like that would be a lot easier than beating around the bush."

"Sometimes, it's better for you to learn these things on your own. I know that sounds as though I'm trying to get out of answering your question," he said, smiling at the look she sent him. "Trust me, I would answer your question if I thought it would in any way benefit you. In this case, I believe it would cause you more harm than if you discovered it on your own."

It still bothered her slightly, but now really wasn't the time to push the issue. Right now, she was more concerned about Robert.

"How do I find the Baron?"

"Rasful can lead you there," he answered, simply. "I need your word though, Florence. No matter what he threatens, no matter how appealing he makes it sound, you must stand firm and not marry him."

"Even though I don't understand why this is so important to you, I promise."

Eli nodded, seeming satisfied with that. "Now let's go see Lydia. She can explain more of the situation to you."

Lydia was laying on a bed made out of moss and leaves, similar to the one she had been laying on when Eli healed her. She turned her head and looked over at Florence as she walked into the clearing. She tried to sit up, but Florence pushed her shoulder back down. "Shh," Florence said, gently. "Don't sit up, you need to preserve your strength."

Lydia took a shaky breath and relented, laying back down on her bed.

"I'll leave you two to talk," Eli said, turning away from them. Florence blinked and then he was gone. She had no idea how an old man could move so fast.

"Oh, Florence," said Lydia, beginning to tear up. "I'm sorry, I'm so, so sorry."

"It's okay!" Florence said, trying to calm her. "What is there to be sorry for?"

"I couldn't stop him. I tried, I promise you I did, but it was almost like he was in a trance."

"Hold on," said Florence, lifting a hand to stop her. "Why don't you start at the beginning?"

Taking another breath Lydia began again. "After we left you, we were on our way to a village so we could find directions. Unfortunately, I was in that wolf for a long time, so I had no idea where to begin to find my village.

"One night while we were camping, something woke me from a deep sleep. I wasn't sure if it was a noise I heard or something subconscious that pulled me from my sleep. As I rolled over, I happened to glance over at Robert's bedroll. He wasn't there.

"I jumped up and looked around wildly for him, fearing the worst. I saw him walking into the forest a few paces off from where we had made camp. So naturally I called out to him, but he either didn't hear me or he ignored me. I followed him.

"The closer I got to him the faster he would walk. It was almost like he knew I was following him, and he was trying to lose me. I kept calling out to him, but he never answered. Up ahead I saw something red flash behind a tree. Curious, I tried to see it from a better angle. It was a little girl, probably about six or so."

Florence's stomach dropped at these words. The Baron wouldn't. Surely, he wouldn't use a trick to get Robert to go back.

"After what felt like hours, the girl led us to a castle. I was out of breath but Robert, who never seemed to get winded in our whole trek through the woods, continued forward. I watched him get to the gate and before it lowered, he seemed to disappear. I ran up to where I had last seen him and there was a man there. He gave me a note and told me to deliver it to you and then he touched my face. I felt dizzy and then found myself at your feet. The rest I don't remember."

Florence was quiet for a full minute after Lydia had finished speaking. So, the Baron had known where she was the whole time. She wondered briefly why he hadn't just come here to kidnap her but dismissed the thought as soon as it formed. Even though Eli looked frail, Florence had the idea that he was far more powerful than he appeared.

"Thank you for telling me all this," said Florence, taking Lydia's hand in her own.

"I'm just sorry that I couldn't protect him," said Lydia, tears filling her eyes.

"No! Don't even think that!" said Florence, taking her hand in both of her own. "I know you care deeply for Robert so this must be incredibly difficult for you."

"Well, yes, but I'm more worried about you."

"Me? Whatever for?"

"Aren't you in love with him?"

Any potential response fled Florence's mind at that. That was not where she thought Lydia was going with that. "Aren't you in love with him?"

"Oh, please," said Lydia, laughing out loud. "Not at all! He's an amazing man, but to tell you the truth, I'm in love with someone in my village."

"The man you were getting medicine for?" Florence said, starting to piece it all together.

Lydia nodded, blushing. "He… He may not be alive."

"Lydia, I am so sorry I misunderstood you and your situation."

"That's alright. Water under the bridge now," said Lydia, giving her a sad smile. "Wait a minute. Is that why you were so cold to me all that time? You thought I was in love with Robert?" Lydia asked, snorting.

"I guess it does seem a little silly now that you mention it," said Florence, giggling. Who would have thought that they would be laughing over something so silly? Florence had really blown it out of proportion. Maybe they would be friends after all.

"So, who is the man that you love? Tell me about him," said Florence once the laughing had stopped. She was genuinely interested in Lydia's relationship and what her type was.

"Now that I'm not a threat you want to hear about my romantic life?" she asked, with a grin. "I know that's not what you meant," she said, holding up a hand to stall Florence's protests. "Just for the record, there was never any competition, not just from me but from Robert too."

"What do you mean?"

"Oh, come now, Florence," she said, rolling her eyes. "Because he's in love with you too, of course!"

Maybe Florence shouldn't have been surprised by this news, but somehow, she still was. She felt the shock from her heart run all the way down to her toes. "How do you know this? Did he tell you something?"

"Well of course he did! What did you think we were whispering about all that time? It was you!"

"I can't believe it," said Florence, still trying to work through it all. "I thought you two were planning a getaway or something!"

"That is ridiculous," she said, laughing again. "Trust me. Robert is great and all, but he's certainly not my type."

"Which brings us back to this subject," said Florence, now really wanting the attention off of her for a few minutes. "And what is your type? Enough stalling!"

"Oh, very well. My type is…" Lydia trailed off looking over Florence's shoulder.

Joshua was standing behind her. She wasn't sure how long he had been there, but it must not have been long.

"Oh, let me introduce you two—"

"Lydia?"

"Joshua?" Lydia asked, her face a mix of confusion and shock.

CHAPTER EIGHTEEN

"I take it, you two know each other?" asked Florence. This was somehow the least surprising revelation of the day.

"How?" Lydia asked, sitting up.

"I live here now," said Joshua, coming closer. "I can't believe it's you."

He came closer and took her hand very gently in his own. He cradled it almost like he was afraid to hurt her.

"I thought I'd lost you and I'd never see you again," she said, reaching a hand up tentatively to his face. He leaned into her hand and placed a gentle kiss on her palm.

"I'm sorry to interrupt, but how do you two know each other?"

Joshua and Lydia looked over at Florence, having seemed to forget she was there.

"This is the man from my village," said Lydia, smiling at him.

"Instead of clearing things up, I'm beginning to get more confused," said Florence, trying to keep all the pieces straight. "So, you were from her village originally or you moved there? And how does this tie in with Eli?"

"It's a bit of a long story," said Joshua, slowly. "They were having an outbreak of a terrible disease. I ended up getting it too, that's part of the reason why I went there. Eli sent me to take on the illness so the rest of the village could live."

"But you were so sick when I left! What happened?" Lydia asked, searching his eyes.

"Well, and here's where it gets complicated," he said, taking her hand in his own. "I died. That was part of the plan. What wasn't part of it, was falling in love with you. No one else was supposed to get hurt."

"I guess I have another thing to be sorry for," Lydia said as tears began to fall from her eyes. "I couldn't save you."

"You were never meant to," Joshua reached up and brushed her tears away. The tender way he was looking at Lydia was making Florence's heart ache.

Lydia took a deep breath, calming herself. "So where does that leave us now? Do I have to go back?"

"That's up to you," he answered. "What do you want?"

"I want to be wherever you are," she said, instantly.

Joshua's laugh filled the clearing. "In that case," he rested his forehead against hers, "You'll stay here with me."

"I guess I have a wedding to plan," Lydia said, causing another laugh from Joshua.

"We have plenty of time for that, my love," he pulled back, giving her the softest kiss on her forehead before saying, "However, I came here to fetch Florence," he looked over at Florence with his strange colored eyes. "It's time."

Florence nodded, standing. "Thank you for everything, Joshua," she said, meaning it with her whole heart. "Will I see either of you again?"

"I'm sure you will," said Joshua, smiling kindly at her. "And maybe next time, Robert will be with you."

She nodded again, hoping the fear she was feeling wasn't showing. She needed to be strong and, after saying goodbye, she turned to the woods, ready to face her next challenge.

⌘

"Well, this is a castle alright."

She and Rasful were standing outside of a building that could only be classified as a castle. It was huge with many different buildings and towers. The only strange thing about it was that it was pure black. The stones and the gates as well as the glass all were as black as night.

Florence wasn't sure how she was feeling about her approaching encounter with the Baron. She would love to say that after all her training with Eli she was feeling beyond prepared. However, she wasn't entirely sure what she had been training for. She had learned how to let things go, she guessed. But most of her training seemed to be about levitation, which she supposed could help her in any situation. But really, how was levitating an object going to help against someone who could make her worst nightmares a reality?

"Are you staying with me, Rasful?" she asked, trying not to sound as desperate as she felt. The last thing she wanted was to go in there alone.

"I'm with you 'til the end, Flor," came Rasful's strong voice.

Taking great comfort in that statement alone, she said, "Let's go then."

They slowly crept forward, hiding in the shadows and trying to blend into their surroundings. Florence wasn't sure what to expect so they kept their eyes out for the basics: traps, alarms, or guards. However, as they got closer, they saw that the castle almost seemed abandoned. Florence didn't see anything that could alert the Baron to their presence. They also didn't really have a plan going into this, so Florence wasn't sure why they were sneaking. Making the decision to stop hiding, she stood up tall and strode towards the front gate.

"Flor, what are you doing?" Rasful asked, in a harsh whisper.

"There really isn't a point in sneaking around, Rasful. The Baron already knows we're coming, so we may as well go in with our heads held high."

"I'm not sure that's the wisest thing," said Rasful, keeping up with her easily as the front gate grew nearer.

"Well, I'm done hiding and sneaking around. No matter what happens, this ends tonight."

They reached the gate. Florence knocked and stepped back, imagining the worst. Nothing happened. Her whole body was tight with nerves as she waited for something horrible to happen. But still nothing. She gave it a full two minutes before stepping forward and knocking again. Still nothing. She knew this was a power move from the Baron. He was trying to show her that she couldn't do anything unless he gave her permission to.

Well, that's what she got for trying to be polite. She took a deep breath and, without too much effort, tore up a tree behind her. She drew it back maybe fifty feet and then hurled it towards the gate. It slammed into the gate with such force that it actually shattered the tree and the gate into splinters.

It might have been a bit much, but Florence was angry at feeling like she was at the Baron's mercy. Also, making things fly around was a lot easier when she didn't have Eli throwing things at her. Maybe her training would help her after all.

"Wow," said Rasful, staring at the mess before them. "I think you may have overdone it."

Florence rolled her eyes, although secretly she did agree with him. Then, squaring her shoulders, she strode through the wreckage she had made.

She found herself not in the courtyard but somewhere in the castle itself. It must be some kind of transportation magic. She was determined not to let the differences between the Baron's magic and her own scare her.

She looked around and saw that she was in a huge room. The ceiling seemed to go on forever and there were banners of all kinds lining the black walls on either side of the room. Even with all this space she almost felt claustrophobic. After spending so much time outside, she wasn't used to having anything above her head

"Where to, Flor?" asked Rasful, as they paused.

"I'm not sure," she said, turning in a circle. It was dark. The pitch-black stones seemed to absorb any light from the torches dotted along the walls between the banners. She could only see a few feet in front of her in any direction, and from what she could see, the hallways were identical, leaving no clue as to which way they should proceed.

She looked around, thinking hard. What did she know about the Baron? He was manipulative and, unfortunately for her, cunning as well. Since she wasn't sure which direction to take, she picked one at random and made her way forward, Rasful following close behind.

As they walked, she tried to come up with some kind of plan. After all, she was currently going into this blind, which may not help her in the long run. The Baron was full of tricks. What could she do to combat him or level the playing field a bit?

They had been walking for a long time but the hallway in front of them didn't seem to be changing. They were moving, the walls were moving with them, but they didn't seem to be going anywhere. Florence stopped and the walls stopped moving as well.

"I don't like this, Flor," said Rasful, looking around.

"I can't say that I do either," she said, inspecting one of the walls for a mark or any sign that it was different from the others. There was nothing that she could see. Then suddenly an idea struck her.

"You know something about the Baron, Rasful," she said, continuing to walk forward. "He tries to be clever and is full of deceit and trickery. However, there is one way to beat him."

"And what's that?" asked Rasful, keeping close to her side.

"He only has the power you give him. If you believe you are walking down a hallway that never ends, then you will continue to walk down a hallway that never ends. However, if you stop believing in his power, he will lose it. So, you have to see through his disguise." With that statement, she knew what it was she had to do. Fully believing that she would see something different and without stopping or slowing her stride, she turned around and walked in the opposite direction.

Florence blinked in the sudden light that surrounded her. Once her eyes had adjusted, she saw they were in a wide-open space. There was light filtering down from the ceiling where parts of the roof had collapsed.

"Where are we?" asked Rasful.

"I believe we're still in the castle. I think I broke the spell," Florence said in slight astonishment. She looked behind her but there was no longer a hallway. Just more of the huge space they were in. She looked at Rasful, who nodded at her, and they continued forward.

There were puddles of water on the marble floor which must have been from rainwater when the roof had fallen in. There were large marble pillars as well, also broken and cracked, scattered about the floor. They came to part of the roof that hadn't fallen in and were in a patch of shadow.

Florence started. There was a person standing in a strange position just up ahead. She wasn't planning on seeing anyone else here and she paused for a moment, waiting for her heart to stop pounding. The person didn't seem to have seen them because they didn't move. In fact, they were unnaturally still. Deciding there was no way around it, Florence moved forward with slow, measured steps. The figure still did not move. It seemed to be a woman, standing with a slight bend in her waist, holding her arms out at right angles. One was bent downwards and the other was to the side of her body. It almost looked like she was in the middle of a dance. As they got closer, Florence noticed that it looked like the woman was made of plaster.

Florence breathed a sigh of relief, knowing it wasn't a real person. She wasn't sure what she would have done if there had been a person there. She wasn't very good at hand-to-hand fighting, though she did have her bow as well as a small knife Eli had given her for protection.

Turning away from the sculpture, she and Rasful began to walk forward once more. After a few steps, she heard a strange noise. She and Rasful looked at each other; he had heard it too. Heart in her throat, she turned slowly towards the sculpture behind them.

"Is it just me, or did that sculpture move?"

"I'm not sure," she said, answering Rasful's question. It seemed like the sculpture was the same as it had been before they passed it. The arms were in the same position, she was sure. Had her right foot always been in front of her left, or did they somehow change?

Heart pounding, she took a step closer. It stayed in the same place; she couldn't detect any sort of movement from it now.

"Perhaps we just imagined it," she said, trying to sound more confident than she felt. They continued walking until the same sound stopped them in their tracks.

Slowly she turned around, afraid of what she might see. The sculpture was gone. "Rasful," she said fearfully, reaching out for him, but he wasn't by her side.

"Rasful!" she shouted frantically searching for him around her. Both he and the plaster being were gone. Unslinging her bow, she began to run, hoping they hadn't gotten far. She would never forgive herself if something had happened to Rasful. That creature must have moved incredibly fast if it was able to snatch Rasful in the short amount of time it took her to turn around.

Here the ceiling was more intact so she was running more in shadow than in the lighted parts. Finally, up ahead she saw a small body laid out on the stone floor. She rushed forward fearing the worst but before she could get to him, something fell from the ceiling above her blocking her path. It was the plaster woman. Her head was cocked at a strange angle, almost the way a dog would when trying to figure out what you are.

Without wasting any time, Florence lifted her bow and took aim. The arrow released with a satisfying *thwap* and hit her target right where the heart would be. The creature looked down at the arrow sticking out of its chest and then slowly looked back up at Florence.

Florence had already shot another arrow by the time the creature had tried to look at her again, but it did little to stop the creature. Now that Florence was closer, she could see that the creature had strips of cloth that had been dipped in plaster wrapped around its entire body. None of its facial features were distinguishable, only the strips of cloth that wrapped around its head. It wore a dress, which was what had made it seem like a woman from a distance, but really it could have been any gender. One of the scariest things about this creature was that it hardly made any noise, besides the creaking and plunking of the plaster falling to the ground. There was no breath; no sound came from the creature itself.

Seeing that her arrows weren't making any difference, Florence put her bow back on her back and pulled out her knife. It seemed silly and small in her hand, almost as if it would be no help in this situation. The creature began to move slowly towards her, its wrapped legs creaking and dropping bits of plaster to the floor, which must have been the sound she and Rasful had heard. Florence began to step back, trying to keep the same amount of distance between herself and the creature.

Frantically she searched for anything in her surroundings that might help her fight off this being. There were no pillars or any kind of wood or rocks in the room they were now in. She could try to crush the thing by bringing the ceiling down or dropping a wall on it, but she wasn't sure how strong the foundations of the building were. She didn't want to run the risk of bringing the whole thing down while she and Rasful were trapped here.

The creature continued to move forward and Florence continued back. She was afraid to look away from the creature, knowing how fast it could move, but she also didn't want to move too far away from Rasful or stupidly walk off a cliff because the creature kept moving towards her.

Her indecision could be her undoing in this situation. She decided to do something that could be very stupid or very smart. Concentrating she began to control the wrappings on the creature, focusing on the wrappings that were around its knees and seemed to have lost most of the plaster. At first, nothing happened, but then slowly the wrappings began to unravel.

At first it didn't seem to bother the creature, who continued moving forward at the same slow pace. Then it seemed to realize what was happening all at once. It lunged at Florence with its arms outstretched. Florence, unprepared for the abrupt movement, let out a grunt as the creature wrapped its arms around her with a grip like iron.

She almost lost her concentration, but thanks to all of Eli's training, she was able to keep her magical grip on the creature's bindings. Now fighting the creature off with her small knife, she unwound the wrappings faster and faster. She lost sight of the creature in the flurry of plaster and wrappings now flying around the room. She continued to hack at the thing, trying to break free from its grasp. Finally, she realized she was just cutting the fabric that had been covering the beast, which no longer had a grip on her.

Panting, she turned to survey the room, wondering what was under the wrappings. What she saw turned her stomach. Laying in the middle of the wreckage was a woman, her limbs at strange angles. Her skin was pale and still had pieces of plaster hanging off of her. She was wearing some kind of slick material that covered the important parts, but the rest of her skin was bare.

Her head was bald and Florence moved a little closer, prepared for the woman to start moving again, but she never did. As she slowly came around to the woman's front, she saw that her mouth was open but stuffed with plaster. Her nostrils, ears and, most terrifyingly, her eyes were also stuffed with the same white plaster. Florence jumped away from it, trying not to be sick. Now was not the time to lose it; she had Rasful and Robert to save.

Rushing forward, she knelt beside Rasful, who was half covered in the same plaster covered bindings. Luckily it was only on the lower half of his body, but he wasn't moving. Florence turned him towards her, bracing for the worst. He didn't have any plaster on his face, and as she knelt closer, she could faintly hear his breathing. She sighed in relief.

Worried that there may be more of those plaster people, she had to figure out a way to carry Rasful until he woke up. After a moment she realized that she had somehow forgotten she had levitating power; she lifted his limp body as gently as she could and made her way forward.

CHAPTER NINETEEN

Florence walked into a room that was pitch black. Turning to try and get back the way she had come, she realized she didn't know where the door was. Everything was black, so to avoid tripping over something and hurting herself she decided to stand in one place. She slowly lowered Rasful to the ground next to her and knelt by him to try and revive him.

After fumbling around in the dark for a few minutes, magical light came on above, momentarily blinding her. She froze, trying to get accustomed to the blinding white light now shining in the room.

"Hello, Florence," said the Baron's disembodied voice, seeming to come from everywhere around her all at once. "I'm afraid your friend there isn't looking his best."

Ignoring the voice, she continued trying to revive Rasful. She began taking the still-wet plaster cloth off him and tried not to get stuck to them in the process.

Out of the corner of her eye she saw something moving. She looked up and spied the same bug from her nightmares, scuttling towards her. "Come now," she said, turning her back on the bug as it grew closer to her. "You didn't think I'd fall for that bug thing twice, did you?"

She heard him growl and half expected to feel the bug's pincers on her at any moment, but she didn't. Her taunting must have worked, then; she hoped she could keep him busy long enough for her to get Rasful awake. She could really use his support right now.

She saw a light turn on, off to her right this time, highlighting something that looked odd, but she was too far away to place what it was supposed to be or why it didn't look right.

"What, do you expect me to walk over there? Could you give me a little more to go off? I know you can make your voice travel, so how am I supposed to know what you want from me?"

She gasped as her body was picked up off the floor by an invisible force and brought over to the other light. No amount of struggling seemed to make any difference. She screamed when the light went out over where she had left Rasful laying on the floor. She was dropped from rather high onto the ground in the new spot of light. She would have been hurt if she hadn't used her own powers to soften her fall.

"I've had about enough of your attitude," came the Baron's voice. "Now let's move forward with the plan, shall we?"

Fuming, Florence tried to think rationally. "And what plan might that be?"

"Oh, come now, surely you aren't still confused on this matter. Perhaps I underestimated how smart you really are."

Florence said nothing and just waited for him to continue.

"No? Are you done talking to me? Well, that's too bad, I was so looking forward to another stimulating conversation with you."

"Yet you don't want my opinion, or as you say my attitude," said Florence, starting to lose her temper against her better judgement. "So, tell me what it is you want. Then perhaps we can get somewhere with negotiations."

"My dear Little Mouse, you misunderstand me. You see, there is nothing to negotiate. Either you marry me, or your friends will die."

Florence's mind raced as she tried to think of a way out. She knew the Baron liked tests. After all, that was why he had come to the farm in the first place, instead of just taking her directly to his creepy castle of doom and marrying her right then. She also knew timing was a thing that mattered here as well. Maybe if she could stall him long enough for the red moon to pass, he would lose some of his powers and she could break his magic. Well, it wasn't much of a plan, but it was really all she had at this point.

"I suppose that's right. After all," she said, choosing her words carefully. "Even if you gave me a test, I'm sure I could beat it, so that must be why there's no negotiations."

"You somehow have managed to misunderstand me again, my dear," said the Baron in a belittling tone. "I'm sure you couldn't pass any test I could create, so to save your pride I will not give you any."

Got him, Florence thought. Instead, she said, "Oh, is it to save my pride? Well, that never seemed to stop you before. In fact, I bet it's because you are afraid for your own sake that you won't test me."

"I could just kill you now," the Baron said, in an icy voice.

"But you won't," she said, her voice sounding far more confident than she felt. "If you were going to kill me, you would have by now. After all, you need me alive to get my powers. So why don't we stop this senseless chatter and get down to business?"

She felt the indecision in the air as the Baron pondered her words. After a few moments she heard him chuckle. "I must say that I may have underestimated you. What did you have in mind?"

"How about you give me a test, any kind of test you want. If I pass it, then you let me and my friends go free."

"And if you don't?"

"If I don't then I'll marry you," Florence's heart was pounding. This wasn't completely in the plan to keep him busy. She remembered what Eli said about not getting into a marriage with him, and that was definitely high on her list of worst-case scenarios, but she couldn't let this chance pass her by. "Do we have a deal?" she asked into the air, hoping she sounded braver than she felt.

"Deal," came the Baron's voice, and then she was thrown into darkness once more.

After a moment of wondering if she had made a terrible mistake, another light came on a few paces in front of her. She walked towards it cautiously, keeping her guard up.

In the light was an array of body parts. She wasn't sure if they had been cut off or if they were still attached to their owners. She tried not to think about it too hard as she approached.

"This is your first test," said the Baron from somewhere above her. "If you can pick out something of Robert's in this line up, you pass."

"What do you mean, first test? How many tests are there? This wasn't part of the deal."

"Ah, my dear, anyone can get lucky with one test. No, I'm afraid there will be a total of three tests. If you pass all of them you are free to go; if you fail even one, then you must marry me."

"Since you are changing the rules on me," she said, thinking fast. "Then here's another change to add to the rules. For every test I pass, you must answer a single question from me. Honestly," she added, thinking of any possible loopholes he might try. "And without withholding any information. You must answer it fully."

"Interesting," he sounded contemplative now. "Very well. I have little faith that you will pass this first one, so that won't be a problem for me. Now, shall we continue?"

"Yes," Florence said, heart pounding.

"Very good. Now, as you can see, in front of you are several different body parts. Your job is to pick the one that belongs to Robert. Don't worry, his body part is still attached, which is something that can't be said for the rest of them."

Florence fought down the bile rising in her throat. What kind of sick, twisted game was this?

"Two last things, my dear. Firstly, you cannot touch the body parts, or you will automatically lose. This includes your newfound gift. Second, you only have ten minutes to complete this test."

"What?!" Florence cried out in panic and outrage. There were at least twenty body parts here. How would she be able to distinguish which one was Robert's in that short amount of time?

"Time is ticking. Get to it, Florence."

Another light came up to her left, highlighting a giant hourglass counting down the time she had left. Already a small amount of sand was gathering in the bottom. Time was not on her side.

Taking a deep breath, she steadied herself and took in the body parts around her. They were mostly arms and legs with a few solitary hands and feet. She had spent quite a bit of time studying Robert so she was hoping this wouldn't be as hard as she feared.

She easily dismissed the feet by themselves because the skin was too dark. She was able to do the same with some of the arms because they weren't muscled enough. The rest she was stuck on. There were a few legs that could have been Robert's and she couldn't be sure they weren't his because she hadn't spent much time studying his legs.

"Tick, Tock Florence," came the Baron's voice. "Your time is running out."

Florence felt herself spiraling into panic. She had somewhat narrowed it down, but upon looking over at the hourglass, she saw there wasn't much sand left. There were two arms that could have been Robert's. They were the same length she remembered and had the same build. If only there was some way to tell them apart.

Moving in closer, she saw that one arm had a thin, unusual scar across it. She remembered Robert telling her about his training days, how the knife he was working with had slipped and given him a cut. With that information alone, she knew which arm was his.

"It's this one," she said pointing to it. "This is Robert."

The last grain of sand fell into the bottom of the hourglass just as she spoke her last word. The room was dead silent. The only thing Florence could hear was her own breathing and the blood rushing through her veins in time with her racing heart. After an agonizing moment, she heard, "Very well. It seems this task was too easy for you. Perhaps the next one will be more difficult."

The other body parts disappeared, leaving Robert laying on his side in the spotlight with her. She held back a sob as she rushed towards him. He turned, blinking in the bright light. "Florence!" he yelled, spotting her running towards him.

"Not so fast," came the Baron's voice as she was lifted into the air again. "I said you couldn't touch him. That rule continues until we have finished our little game." She screamed in frustration, fighting the invisible force holding her but to no avail.

"Don't fight it, Lor! I've got a plan," he grinned at her and then ran full speed into the darkness.

"No, Robert!" she screamed, kicking and wiggling, trying to get out of the Baron's invisible grasp.

"Well that made it easier for me," came the Baron's amused voice. "I thought I was going to have to dispose of him myself. I'll just let the darkness do it for me. After all, you never know what might be hiding in the dark."

Florence was trying to calm down. Stupid, idiot Robert! Why did he ever think that plan would work? Right now, the best way to help him was to find a way to break the Baron's spell.

"You owe me my prize," she growled, trying to look as dignified as she could while hanging in the air.

"Ah yes, please go ahead and ask."

"What is your story?"

After several moments of silence Florence, losing patience, said, "I'm waiting."

She heard him chuckle. "Now, now," he chided, speaking as if talking to a child. "You never set a time limit and questions like this may take some time for me to gather my thoughts."

"So, my question took you by surprise?"

"We agreed on one question," he growled. She must have hit a nerve then.

"I'm not getting any younger," she said, pushing her luck.

"Very well," he answered stiffly. She was still floating in the air, held by some invisible force, but she tried to remain as calm as possible.

"I suppose my story is not an original one. My whole life I was pushed around. I strove to become stronger, to learn magic and use it so no one else could push me around. No matter how hard I tried, it seemed like there was always someone stronger than me. This is my chance to become the most powerful person in the world. My plan, unfortunately, involves you. Not that I would mind having another plaything, but you are proving to be more and more troublesome. This is something that will have to be fixed when we are married."

Florence felt anger rise inside of her, but she knew it wouldn't help to get emotional. She took a breath in, calming herself just as she felt her feet touch the ground. Looking around, all she saw was darkness.

"Find your way out," said the Baron from somewhere above her. As soon as the words reached her ears the space was filled with a bright white light.

She fell to her knees, blinded again. When the pain in her head had subsided and she was able to open her watering eyes, she took a look around and saw she was someplace new. This wasn't the strange dark room she had been in before. As her eyes adjusted, she saw her breath coming out in a mist. It was freezing. She was kneeling on something hard and cold.

Is this ice? she wondered as she carefully began to stand up. It was slippery, but it didn't leave wet spots on her pants like regular ice typically would.

She heard a tinkling sound off to her left. It sounded like wine glasses being pushed together. *Glass*, Florence thought, looking back down at her feet. *This is glass. The floor is glass, that's for sure.*

She couldn't tell if anything else was glass, if she was surrounded by walls or if there were even walls at all. All she could see was white, which she now realized must be the glass reflecting the light source. Wherever it was.

She looked up, trying to determine if the light was coming from above her when she saw something white floating down towards her. As it got closer, she saw it was a very large snowflake. It was beautiful the way it gracefully descended, floating from side to side. It was designed with cut outs and the edges coming out into perfect triangles.

She held out her hand to it, wanting to catch it and take a closer look. As it landed in her hand, a cold then white-hot pain sliced through her hand. She cried out and dropped it. It landed on the floor, vibrating with the sound of glass on glass. It was red, a stark contrast to the reflective white. With a jolt she looked at her hand and realized it was bleeding profusely. She let out a very unladylike curse as the blood dripped off her hand onto the floor. She ripped a piece of fabric from her pants and made a bandage the best she could. Of course, it was glass too, she thought, chastising herself.

The sound she heard earlier was getting louder. As she looked over to her left shoulder, she saw what seemed to be a snowstorm coming towards her. Trying to calm her rising panic, she racked her brain for a way out of this mess. She knew she could freeze the storm if she absolutely had to, but she wasn't sure how long she would be able to hold it, especially considering it was the Baron's magic.

The storm grew closer, and she still didn't have any ideas on what to do. She began walking slowly forward, trying to put as much distance between herself and the glass storm as she could. She kept sliding on the slick glass floor, so she wasn't making much progress. The glass shards continued getting closer and Florence was all out of ideas.

Going through the supplies she brought with her, she remembered the knife that she used on the plaster person. "This could come in handy," Eli had said, winking before placing it in her hand. Maybe it was the key to this task.

She stopped moving and pulled the knife from her belt. Gripping the handle, she began to hit the tip against the glass trying to break it. Maybe if she was able to crack it, the whole thing would shatter giving her a way out. Hitting the floor with all of her strength over and over again, she slowly began seeing scratches on the glass from where her knife was cutting into it.

The glass storm was upon her, and she could feel the tiny snowflakes ripping into her skin. It propelled her to work faster and harder as her red blood began mixing with the glass. Her breath was coming out in gasps, the cold air burning her lungs along with the pain from the glass cutting into her. Just when the storm was getting too much to bear, there was a loud crack as the glass floor finally gave way. She fell, taking shards of bloodied glass with her.

CHAPTER TWENTY

Florence felt herself being pulled up and was again held by an invisible force. Her hands were bloodied, and she felt the shards of glass still digging into her scalp.

"Ah, Florence, you never cease to impress me," the Baron said, his voice once again echoing around her.

Ignoring him, she calmed herself and imagined her body rejecting the glass and slowly healing itself. Although it was nothing she had ever tried before, she had lost a lot of blood and she knew she needed healing, or she wouldn't have the strength to complete the last task. Slowly she felt her body rejecting the glass and her many cuts began to close over. Although it wasn't a perfect healing and she was still incredibly sore and tired, she felt better.

"Are you trying to kill me?" she asked into the air.

"Is that the question you would like me to answer?"

"No," she answered, quickly. "What I want to know is out of all the people in the world, why did you choose me?"

"Interesting," he said. "That was not what I thought you were going to ask. How exactly do you think this is going to help you?"

"Just answer the question," Florence growled.

"Very well. I was told that there would be a girl. A girl who would become a great sorceress. She would be the key to giving me what I most wanted: with her I could become the most powerful man in the world. So, I took you, I had my pets raise you to be compatible with me. This way I could be certain that you and I would mesh together perfectly. What I wasn't expecting was for you to form your own opinions and require me to do all this work to lure you in."

"Where did you hear all that about me?"

"Nah-ah-ah," he tsked. "Only one question."

With that she felt herself jerked to the left, then she felt herself falling. She felt her feet hit something and the rest of her body followed until something wet covered her head. She kicked with all of her strength, praying she was swimming towards the surface and not pushing herself deeper.

Finally, her face broke the surface, and she took in big lungsful of air. Gasping, she began swimming forward, trying to get her bearings. While the last task had been blinding, this one was pitch black. Her hand brushed up against something rough and solid. Tracing it with her hand, she felt that it was stone. She followed it with her hand outstretched, feeling her way all the way around in a circle. So, she was in something similar to a well then. She reached her hand up as high as it would go and felt a ceiling of sorts above her head. She began to feel claustrophobic as she swam along, her hand on the ceiling the entire time, trying to find some kind of opening. There was nothing but solid stone above her. She knew she shouldn't be surprised. The Baron wasn't going to make this easy on her.

Something brushed against her leg, making her jump. Dread filled her, knowing that somehow this task had just gotten a lot harder. The same thing, or perhaps a different thing, brushed against her leg again, this time with a little more strength. She frantically began searching the walls for something, a crack in the stone, anything that could give her a clue as to a way out.

There were many things in the water. Things that swam and slithered. What they were, she had no idea, and frankly she didn't want to spend any more time with them than was necessary.

A sharp pain started in her leg. She cried out, one of the things had bitten her. She needed to get out of this well now.

All of the Baron's other tests had been logical. Or at least somewhat straightforward. How was she supposed to get out of a well that didn't have a top?

A crazy idea had begun to form in her head. One that, if she was wrong, would end in her death. The thing in the water bit her again, and this time it broke through the skin. Once she started bleeding, she knew these things would swarm, and then she really would be a goner.

Taking a huge breath in and concentrating all of her energy on herself, she ducked underwater and began swimming down.

Down, down, down she swam for what seemed like an eternity. The slimy things swirled around her, making it difficult to be really sure if this was the correct way. She continued down, using the water around her to propel herself farther and faster than she could swim by herself. Spots began to dance in front of her eyes; she was running out of time. But if she passed out, then she would be dead for sure.

Finally, her hand broke the surface and she felt herself shooting out of the water and into the open air. Then she was falling again.

"No!" came the Baron's cry, filling the chamber with his magnified voice.

Florence felt herself hit the ground, but not as hard as she might have expected.

The light came on and there was the Baron, furiously glaring at her. She got to her feet and began walking towards him. Up until this point, she had no idea what she was going to do. Now, she knew exactly what needed to be done.

"How could you have beaten me?" he looked angry, but more than that, he seemed afraid.

Florence didn't respond, she just continued walking towards him.

"I will not let you ruin everything I have worked for!" he shouted. The wall behind him shattered, huge pieces of the wall breaking down and landing around him. He began throwing pieces of the wall at her, but she had been expecting some kind of retaliation. She blocked the pieces easily and they flew around the room, landing in various places around her.

"I won't let you do this!" he yelled and turned his attention to the floor, splitting it and making a crater, trying to prevent her from crossing.

She repaired it easily, making a bridge big enough for her to walk across. And walk she did, until she was directly in front of him.

He looked crazed and was frantically looking for a way out, like a cornered animal. She reached out her hand and touched his chest. Time seemed to freeze around them. She felt his power, power that didn't necessarily belong to him. Some of it was his, but he had stolen most of it. The bits that weren't his were easily extracted. She felt the power rushing out of him and into her.

It was an amazing feeling. She felt like she could do anything, she was powerful, and no one would ever take advantage of her again. She also knew that the temptation to keep this power was the exact reason why she couldn't. Taking a deep breath, she released the energy into the air around them. Slowly, like the sun breaking through a cloudy day, she felt the Baron's spell over this place begin to break. Once she knew she had gotten all of it, she released him, and he fell to his knees at her feet.

"For my last question," she said in a calm voice. "Will you join me?"

The Baron looked up at her with tears in his eyes. "You've taken everything I've ever wanted from me. Why would I join you? What can you gain by having someone like me?"

"You are a strong fighter and have invaluable information. I'm offering you a chance at redemption. Will you take it?" with this question, she offered him her hand.

He thought it over. He looked up at her and said, "I—" but then he broke off, looking behind her in horror. "No. No, no, no, no, please."

She turned around but there was no one there.

"Please, my lady, don't do this!" he scrambled away from Florence until his back was against the far wall. He curled in on himself, cowering. "There's no one there," said Florence, slowly walking towards him with her hands extended in a non-threatening manner.

He shook his head, his eyes wide with fear. Before Florence could get any closer, the Baron suddenly burst into flames. Florence cried out in shock and ran towards him, trying to find a way to put out the flames. The Baron's inhuman cries filled the room. Something ran into her, knocking her off of her feet. She looked up just in time to see the other grey-haired creature jumping into the swirling flames. Before Florence could even stand, the fire went out as quickly as it had started.

Florence walked over to them slowly. There was nothing remaining but unrecognizable, charred masses and the smell of burning flesh.

Florence walked out of the chamber and into a huge ballroom. The castle was slowly turning back to its normal state. The Baron's spell had been broken, leaving the castle, if you could call it that any longer, completely run down. The walls were no longer black, and the confusing passageways were no longer. Everything was as it should be. At least, it should have been, but where was everyone?

The room was filled with light, mostly from parts of the ceiling that had fallen in. Florence looked around, looking for any sign of life. She saw something blue laying in the middle of the floor, and she rushed over.

Rasful was laying on his side; Florence turned him towards her, fearing the worst, but he was still breathing. He looked peaceful, almost as though he was sleeping.

"Lor?"

Florence turned around and there was Robert. A little worse for wear, but otherwise unharmed. She stood slowly, unsure of where to begin.

He smiled at her, a smile that almost broke her heart. She walked up to him as he grinned at her and punched him.

A look of shock crossed his face as he felt his cheek where her fist had landed. "Ouch," he said.

"What was that stunt back there?" she demanded; her relief masked by anger.

A look of understanding crossed his face and he answered, "I knew he wasn't going to let us both go. He was going to use me to hurt you, so I took myself out of the equation. Also, I was making sure that creature didn't come after you. We were locked in combat for a while."

"You are thick-headed, numbskulled, pea-brained—"

"You do realize all of those words mean the same thing, right?" he asked, pleasantly.

Florence ignored him and continued, "Pig-faced, good for nothing, clod pole—"

"Wait, what is a clodpole?"

Florence felt her eyebrow twitch. "I don't know, but whatever it is, that's what you are."

"Well hold on now, what if a clodpole is something extremely foul and disgusting?"

"Well then, it would be the perfect thing to describe you."

"Or," Robert said thoughtfully. "What if it has something to do with a cod? You know, the fish. So, would a clodpole be used to catch the fish? Perhaps I'm going about this all wrong. Maybe it has nothing to do with catching the fish but is a part of the fish itself."

Florence was struggling to remain mad at him. She wanted to, but he made it incredibly difficult.

He looked at her sideways, "Well don't you want to know my theory on what part of the fish I think it's from?"

She rolled her eyes, unable to keep in the laughter that had been building up since he started this whole silly conversation. She closed the distance between them and was in his arms in an instant.

"Idiot," she mumbled into his chest.

"I missed you too, lass."

She looked up at him and he gently placed a hand on her cheek. He leaned in towards her and softly pressed his lips against hers. She sighed and for a few moments there was no talking as all the worry and stress from the past few months melted away.

She heard a cough from behind them, making her jump. She looked over Robert's shoulder to see Rasful looking suggestively at them.

"I don't mean to interrupt or anything, but I'm in some need of assistance here."

Florence and Robert laughed and regretfully broke apart. She knew there would be plenty of time for them to explore this new relationship that was just budding.

"Come on," she said as Robert picked up Rasful, resting him on his shoulders. "Let's go home."

CHAPTER TWENTY-ONE

Florence leaned against Robert as the horse walked forward. The last few days had been a whirlwind. She had taken Robert to Eli to help Rasful as well as heal any wounds they had received at the hands of the Baron. Robert had been in awe of Eli and Joshua and was extremely happy to be reunited with Lydia. He had spent a lot of time worrying about her when he had come to his senses.

"Now I know you two are probably tired, you know especially after saving the world and all that," Lydia said, getting a laugh out of both Robert and Florence. "But I have a favor to ask the two of you, if you would be willing."

"Of course!" Florence and Robert said at the same time, again making everyone laugh.

"Well, you see the thing is…" Lydia bit her lip before seeming to give herself a shake and continuing in a rush. "Joshua and I are getting married. Nothing fancy or formal but it would mean so much to me if the two of you could be our witnesses. Again, no pressure if you can't or are too tired but—"

She took a breath and Florence came up and hugged her. "It would be my honor to be part of your wedding!"

"She took the words right out of my mouth," Robert said as Florence pulled back. "We would be more than happy to."

"Oh, thank you so much!" Lydia bounced a little. "I've already made all the arrangements. We'll be ready tomorrow if you think that is alright."

"Perfect," Florence said, giving her friend's hand a squeeze.

"Oh, that reminds me," Lydia said, pointing as Joshua quietly came up to them.

"I believe there is something you need to see," Joshua said, and without another word, he led both her and Robert out of the clearing.

The first thing that she noticed was they were in the same field Joshua and her had played in. The flowers were in bloom and the rolling hills were beautiful. But there was something different. Before she fully understood what she was doing, she began racing across the meadow. When she was close enough, she knew that what she was seeing was in fact real.

"Beatrix!" she shouted as she raced across the meadow. Her beautiful horse neighed in response and raced over to her as well. "But, how—" she stammered, trying to ask a question but overcome with emotion at seeing Beatrix again. She was petting her and hugging her like crazy.

Joshua laughed at her excitement. "Most animals find their way here. Not all people do but every animal finds their way back. In fact…" he trailed off as a jet-black horse came cantering across the field and stopped directly in front of Robert.

"Duane? Is it really you?" The horse stamped his foot in answer and began nuzzling him, looking for food.

"Wait," Florence said, turning accusingly at Joshua. "Does that mean they're… you know…"

"No, they are very much alive," he smiled at her visible relief. "But they may wish to stay. Their adventuring days are finished, and they wish to be set free."

"Another ending," Florence said quietly. "I don't know how many more I can take."

"There will always be endings. That is inevitable. But, just like most things, this isn't goodbye forever. You can come back and visit them whenever you like."

Florence was filled with a huge sense of loss, and as she looked over at Robert's stricken face, she knew he felt the same. Everything from her childhood was gone, everything she had known to be true had been false or wasn't meant to be. Maybe that was part of growing up.

"Well, if that's what she wants, then I won't force her to come with me."

"Same with me," Robert interjected. "Although it pains me to let him go, Duane has never really been mine. He's always been just a little wild."

Joshua smiled at them and said, "Very well, and very well spoken. But that doesn't mean all the horses here are here for good," he gave a short sharp whistle, and a beautiful mare came galloping out of the meadow. Its pure white coat sparkled in the sunlight. It cantered to a stop right in front of them, its kind brown eyes blinking thoughtfully at them.

"This is Faux. She is willing to take you on part of your journey."

"Just part?" Florence asked, walking up to the gorgeous creature and petting her nose softly.

"Yes, she will come back to us when she's ready. Not everything can be with us forever, and Faux has other duties to attend to."

"Well, thank you, Faux," Florence said, stepping back and giving the horse a curtsy. "We look forward to traveling with you."

The horse dipped her head at Florence in semblance of a bow, making all of them laugh.

"Come, you must be tired. Rest and we will talk more tomorrow. There is much to discuss before you depart," Joshua said, and led them back through the forest.

They had called it an early night the day before so, Florence awoke to find herself well rested. Somehow, she seemed to sleep the best in her familiar four-poster bed. After a good stretch she went in search of breakfast, which she saw was already being had by both Robert and Eli.

She had finally gotten some answers from Eli, and even Robert had had some time to get to know both him and Joshua.

"I suppose you must be wondering how you were able to take the Baron's powers," said Eli once she had eaten her fill.

"The thought had crossed my mind," Florence said, playfully.

"Sometimes there are very special magic users who are able to do more than just make things float. They can use their powers for a multitude of things. They have to be born at a certain time, when the stars and planets are aligned in just the right order, so they are very rare. You happen to be one of these magic users. Because you were so pure and your intentions were for a just cause, you were able to manipulate the very magic that made up another human. While this power is great, it is something I would caution against using on a regular basis. You saw what it did to the Baron after you had finished."

"Is that why he burst into flames? That's one thing I haven't been able to figure out."

"No, that was for a different reason. One that I'm afraid I can't discuss with you right now. Don't look at me like that," he said, holding up his hand to stop her. "That is not your story, it is someone else's, so as of right now, I have nothing to say on the matter."

Although Florence wished he had just told her, she knew there was probably a reason for him keeping it from her. She didn't always understand him, but she trusted Eli and would trust him in this as well.

"Oh, very well, keep your many secrets then," she said, blowing her hair out of her face in a huff. "At least answer this, who was the plaster person?"

"Ah," Eli looked away, pain in his face. "Now remember that the Baron was a very broken man. He had experienced more pain in one day of his life than many do in their entire lives. Some of it was self-inflicted and some… well some was done to him."

"What does this have to do with the woman? And if you knew about it, why didn't you do anything to stop it?" Florence asked, not trying to keep the accusation out of her voice.

"To answer the first question: it is because of how he treated others. When you are that broken, it can go one of two ways. You can either learn and grow from the pain that you have experienced, or you can inflict that pain onto others. The Baron is the second of the two. And unfortunately, that woman was his first wife."

Florence's jaw dropped. "The Baron had already been married before?"

"Yes, and before you ask," he held up a hand to stop the questions that were already forming in her mouth, "That isn't my story to tell either. But to answer your second question, why don't I step in? It is because people have free will. They are able to make decisions in whatever way they choose. I help in my own way, and I'm always here if someone needs me. But I don't interfere."

"But why?"

"What would you have me do, Florence? Would you have me rescue every single person in the world who is hurting? Do you really think that would help?" He turned his strange eyes to her. "I'll let you know now, it wouldn't. Even if I rescue them, it wouldn't fix the main problem. People who need me, find me. And I make myself available to them."

"I see," Florence said.

"No, you don't," Eli chuckled. "But that's alright. Everyone is entitled to their own decisions and experiences. Whatever they decide to do with their lives is up to them."

"And what about me? What am I supposed to be doing?" Robert interjected, speaking for the first time and leaning forwards.

"Ah yes, the young assassin. Still so young, still trying to prove yourself," Robert flinched at the name assassin, but said nothing to defend himself. "That is entirely up to you. Young Florence could use your skill. Her story is not quite over yet. And who knows? If you accompany her, perhaps your own story will be made clear."

"And speaking of stories that aren't over yet." Eli stood, towering above them. "I believe there is a wedding to have."

In the years to come, Florence would look back on this wedding as the most beautiful thing she had ever been to. The sun filtered through the trees, creating little pockets of light. All the animals in the forest seemed to be gathered to observe, but they kept their distance. Florence could see their white fur in the spots where the sun touched them.

Lydia was stunning; her long blond hair went down almost to her waist, covered in flowers that almost looked like they were swimming in her long hair. Her dress was white but decorated with snaking green vines that had matching wildflowers to the ones in her hair. Joshua looked handsome in long button-down shirt, vest, and trousers. As soon as he saw Lydia step out from behind the trees, Florence heard him take an audible breath in and saw his eyes widen in something more like awe than surprise.

Lydia was beaming and as soon as she got within earshot, Joshua whispered so soft that Florence could barely make out the words, "You're wearing the dress from our first date."

Lydia's smile grew wider, and she nodded before whispering back, "I thought it would be a nice touch. Since our first date was ruined."

"I love it, you look stunning," he said, his eyes drinking her in.

Florence almost felt like they were intruding on the whole thing. It felt so intimate and personal. But Lydia's eyes would meet hers every once and a while and she would smile so big that Florence knew she was welcome.

After Eli pronounced them man and wife, they kissed, and Florence felt her heart swell, knowing that maybe with the right person, marriage wouldn't be the end of the world.

Robert brushed a kiss to her neck, drawing her out of her thoughts. "Where to, lass?" he asked, his breath hot on her skin.

"Is it up to me?" she asked, turning slightly in the saddle to get a better look at him.

"I would follow you anywhere," he said, kissing her firmly. When they broke apart, she smiled at him and he at her. Only two people in love could say so much to each other without words. She didn't have all the answers. She still had a lot of unanswered questions. But one thing she was certain of, if Robert was by her side, then they could conquer anything together.

Turning to face forward, she said, "Then hold on." She kicked the horse into a gallop, and they raced off into the unknown.

The End

ACKNOWLEDGMENTS

I never used to read the acknowledgment page. Not for any reason, other than it usually had a bunch of names that didn't mean anything to me. But when I started thinking about writing my own book, I started paying attention to the acknowledgements and was surprised that they were another way to get to know the author and the group of people who brought the book into the world. Here are mine.

No book goes into the world without a team of people behind it. This book is no exception even though it's an independently published one.

I would like to thank my editor Fay, for really getting my story. She gave me some interesting things to think about and gave me a new excitement for the story I was telling with Lor. I would like to thank my wonderful formatter and cover designer as well, who really brought this story to life.

I would also like to thank all of those at the Frisco Public Library for their encouragement not only to me as a new writer, but also to all of the new writers that they encourage to keep going. I would especially like to thank Lisa who was one of the first people ever to see this story, back in 2012 when I was a young fresh out of high school graduate, who didn't know where to go with my writing. She encouraged me to keep going and gave me the courage to do so. And a special thank you to Jen who always asks me in passing how my book is going, who is always cheering me on and introducing me to new writers like myself. Thank you.

I want to thank my family and friends for your encouragement and for giving me the strength to keep going. There have been many trails in trying to get this book out into the world (although mostly beginners' trial and error) and I want to thank them for their support and excitement.

I would especially like to thank my mom. Although this may come as a shock, I didn't enjoy reading as a child and my mom persevered by shamelessly bribe me to read, whether it be with toys or chocolate cake. Thank you for your encouragement, for being my biggest cheerleader and for not giving up on getting me into this thing called reading. I wouldn't be here without you.

I would like to thank my partner, Jase. Thank you for recognizing my need to create and encouraging me to do so. Thank you for always making me laugh, being my partner in crime, and for inspiring the stories I write. It is hard for me, even as a writer, to put into words what you mean to me. So, I will simply say, thank you and I love you.

Lastly, I would like to thank you dear reader. Thank you for joining me on this wild ride with Lor. She is one of my first loves and has many more adventures to come. I hope she has inspired you, the way she inspired me, to be true to yourself and to know that you are in control of your own life. To all those who create, thank you for your inspiration. We need all the light we can in this dark world, and so thank you for bringing it through your art.

Jessica Harden has been writing for the last 13 years and no, no one will ever see her first manuscript. No one deserves that kind of torture.

When she is not writing, she can be found, snuggling with her old dog named Hubble, watching her partner play video games, reading with a hot drink or doing yoga.

To keep up with her books, you can follow her on Twitter, @jjbear226 or on YouTube at Jess Go Write. This is her debut novel.

www.ingramcontent.com/pod-product-compliance
Lightning Source LLC
Chambersburg PA
CBHW032013050726
47590CB00006B/2153